BOOK FOUR

Hurricane Gold

A JAMES BOND ADVENTURE

CHARLIE HIGSON

🅳🅸🆂🅽🅴🆈 • **HYPERION BOOKS**
New York

Published by Disney • Hyperion Books, an imprint of Disney Book
Group. No part of this book may be reproduced or transmitted in any
form or by any means, electronic or mechanical, including photocopying,
recording, or by any information storage and retrieval system, without
written permission from the publisher.

For information address
Disney • Hyperion Books
114 Fifth Avenue
New York, New York 10011-5690.

First American edition, 2009.
1 3 5 7 9 10 8 6 4 2
Printed in the United States of America
This book is set in 11.5-pt. Caslon.
Reinforced binding
ISBN 978-1-4231-1412-3

Library of Congress Cataloging-in-Publication Data on file.
Visit www.youngbond.com
www.hyperionbooksforchildren.com

For Sidney

* * *

To Jim Thompson

PART 1—EL HURACÁN

CHAPTER 1—HOUSE RULES

There were thirteen men around the table. By the end of the day, one of them would be dead.

Two huge fans in the ceiling turned slowly, stirring the hot, damp air. No breeze came in through the row of open windows that looked out toward the bright blue waters of the Caribbean. A big storm was coming and there was a tense atmosphere. It was the sort of day that gave you a headache.

The men looked like they would all much rather have been somewhere else. A few of them were used to the heat, but most were sweating and uncomfortable. They tugged at their collars, fanned their faces, and pulled sticky shirts away from damp skin.

The man at the head of the table, though, seemed cool and relaxed. He sat perfectly still, staring at the others in silence, a glass of chilled fino sherry standing untouched at his elbow. He was well dressed in the style of a Mexican aristocrat, with an embroidered velvet suit and a frilly cream cravat at his throat held in place with a pearl stud.

He had a flat nose in the middle of a dark brown face that had the appearance of being carved out of old, hard wood. His thick mop of hair was pure white, as was his neat little Vandyke beard. He might have been forty, or he might have been eighty; it was impossible to tell. His eyes looked like they had lived a thousand years and seen all there was to see.

At last he spoke, in English with a strong Mexican accent.

"Gentlemen," he said, "we have a problem."

"What sort of a problem, El Huracán?" asked a lean, handsome man with a mouth that was permanently set in a mocking smile. He was Robert King, a grifter from Chicago, who had married a wealthy widow, heiress to a diamond fortune, and pushed her from their yacht in the middle of the Atlantic. He had paid off the crew to keep their mouths shut and inherited all her wealth, but the skipper was a drunk and after one too many whiskies in a bar in Nantucket had blabbed the whole story.

The next day the police went looking for King.

King fled the country, but not before he had visited his ex-skipper in his cheap lodging house and quietly slit his throat with a razor.

He had come down here to hide out, his bags stuffed with banknotes and diamonds.

"It is easily solved," said El Huracán. "But it is, nevertheless, a serious problem." He spoke quietly and sounded almost bored.

"How serious?" said King, taking a glass of cool water.

El Huracán stood up and walked to the nearest window, ignoring the question. He waited there, watching the distant waves breaking against the reef.

"Tell me," he said at last, "is it not beautiful here on this island?"

There were mumbled yeses from around the table accompanied by the weary nodding of heads.

"Is this not paradise?"

Again there were mumbled yeses.

El Huracán turned back from the window and looked around at the tough faces of the men. "So why would one of you wish to leave?"

There were a couple of grunts and mutterings, but nobody spoke up.

"Here on Lagrimas Negras we have the finest food," said El Huracán, gesturing at the table, which was, indeed, piled high with dishes: thick steaks, chicken, grilled fish and lobster, sweet potatoes, rice, salad, and tropical fruit.

"It is never cold. There is no disease. You never want for anything. Is that not true?"

"Very true, El Huracán . . ." said a fat, sunburned man with yellow piggy eyes, his white shirt stained gray with sweat. His name was Dum-Dum White. He was a holdup artist who had robbed a string of banks in the American Midwest with a tommy gun loaded with dumdum bullets. He had skipped south of the border when the rest of his gang had been killed in a shoot-out with FBI agents in Tucson.

"Here, you are all safe," said El Huracán. "You and the hundred or so other men and women who have come to my island."

"That's right," said Dum-Dum, who was melting in the heat.

"I know how you men hate authority." The brown-skinned man chuckled. "You live outside the law. But you accept that there must be a few rules."

"Yes."

"You *do* accept that?"

"Certainly. Without rules there'd be chaos," said another American, Chunks Duhaine. Chunks was a hired killer who had got his nickname from the condition in which he always left his victims.

"You are all quite new here," said El Huracán, sitting down and taking a sip of sherry. "But by now you should have learned my rules. What are they?"

"First rule—you're the boss," said a man with a wide, almost oriental face and a thin mustache. "What you say goes."

This was Abrillo Chacon, a Chilean explosives expert who specialized in blowing banks open at night. In his last job, in Concepción, twelve policemen had been waiting for him, but Chacon had used so much explosives that the entire roof of the bank had fallen in, crushing them to death.

"Correct," said El Huracán. "Every gang must have a boss."

"No problem. You're a swell boss. You run a fine setup here," said Chunks.

"Thank you," said El Huracán. "It is always so nice to know that one is appreciated." He looked at the men, taking his time, enjoying their discomfort. "What are the other rules?" he said eventually.

"All our moneys is kept in you bank," said a skinny, pockmarked man. This was Aurelio de la Uz. One night Aurelio had followed a Mafia gambler who had won a small fortune at a casino in Havana. He shot him through the back of the head, took his winnings, and slipped away from Cuba a rich man.

"*Sí,*" said El Huracán, with a slight, elegant nod of his head. "If you had not come here, you men would be dead or in jail, and your money would be scattered to the wind. Instead you are all alive and happy and your money is well looked after."

"We ain't got no choice," said Chunks Duhaine, and he laughed mirthlessly.

"If you will forgive me saying," said El Huracán, "on an island inhabited entirely by criminals, there might be a danger that one's money was not safe. There are four bank robbers in this room alone. But no one will ever rob my bank, because if they did they would have a hundred of the most heartless killers in the world on their tail."

"Damned right," said Dum-Dum. "Though I must admit that bank of yours sure is one hell of a challenge."

There was laughter from around the table, and El Huracán joined in before raising a hand for silence.

"And what is the next rule?" he said.

"No communication with the outside world." This was said by Eugene Hamilton, a small, quiet man wearing spectacles, who had stolen nearly a million dollars from an oil company. He seemed out of place here among these thugs. He looked more like an accountant than an armed robber. This was because he *was* an accountant.

"That is the most important rule of all, gentlemen," said El Huracán. "This is a unique place. An island where wanted men may hide out without fear of ever being captured. An island where their crimes do not matter. As long as you have the money to pay for it, you can live in paradise until the end of your days. But we do not want the outside world to know of our doings here. That is most important. So what is the *last* rule?"

"Once we are here we can never leave," said Luis Chavez, a Mexican gangster.

"I wonder how many of you men would have come here if you had known about this last rule?" said El Huracán.

Once again nobody spoke out. El Huracán laughed.

"This place must remain a secret, a legend, a dream," he said. "But somebody in this room has been trying to send letters. . . ."

El Huracán stood up and began slowly to circle the table, walking behind the seated men.

"Somebody here has tried to bribe one of my peons to take a message to the outside world. Somebody here wants to leave."

El Huracán walked to the door and opened it. Two men walked in. They were Mexican Indians, rumored to be from El Huracán's village deep in the rain forest of the Chiapas in southern Mexico. They were dressed in the same simple white clothing that would have been worn by their ancestors two hundred years ago, but there was nothing primitive about the weapons they were carrying, German MP 28 submachine guns.

"What is this?" said Robert King.

"We do not want any unpleasantness," said El Huracán. "It might lead to indigestion after so lovely a meal." He then said something softly to one of his men, who handed him a small glass bottle containing a clear liquid.

"What the hell's that?" said Chunks Duhaine. "What's going on here?"

"It is an antidote," said El Huracán. "You see, when I heard about how one of you was planning to betray me, I thought I would solve the problem quickly. I have poisoned his food. Soon he will begin to feel the effects. He will feel hot and dizzy. His throat will grow tight. He will sweat uncontrollably and terrible cramps and spasms will grip his stomach. Then his blood vessels will begin slowly to rupture and he will bleed inside; dark patches will appear on his skin. Within a few minutes he will be dead. Unless, of course, I give him some of this antidote. I took this precaution simply because I knew the man would not voluntarily confess. But now, if he wants to live, he must come forward."

El Huracán opened a wooden box and took out a syringe. He plunged the needle through the rubber stopper at the end of the bottle and extracted some of the liquid.

For a few moments nobody spoke. There was a terrible silence in the room. Then suddenly Robert King leaped to his feet, his handsome face distorted with fear. He was clutching his stomach, and so much sweat was pouring off him it looked like he had just climbed out of a swimming pool.

"You damned snake," he hissed. "Give me that . . ."

"This?" said El Huracán innocently, holding up the bottle and the syringe. "What for?"

"The antidote," King gasped. "Give me the antidote, you evil son of a—"

"Antidote?" said El Huracán as he stabbed the needle into a peach and pressed down on the plunger. "What antidote?"

King looked on in horror. His breath was rasping in his throat as he held out a trembling finger toward the man standing calmly at the head of the table. "You've murdered me, you swine. . . ."

"I have done nothing of the sort, Mr. King," said El Huracán, taking a bite from the fruit. "You have merely fallen for a cheap child's trick. There was no poison. It is only your own fear that makes you feel this way."

There was a harsh snort of laughter from Dum-Dum, and Luis Chavez said something quickly in Spanish.

King looked around at the other men, trying to find a friendly face. Nobody would catch his eye.

"I haven't done anything," he said.

"Then why on earth did you think you had been poisoned?" said El Huracán. "Nobody else here jumped to their feet. Though I suspected all of you. That is why I invited you all for lunch. How gratifying to see that only one of you has been foolish."

"I haven't done anything."

"You have confessed, Mr. King. That is all I required." El Huracán nodded to his guards. "Take him away," he said, "and prepare La Avenida de la Muerte so that I can show the others what happens to anyone who is disloyal."

"What's an *avenida de la muerte*?" said Eugene Hamilton.

"An avenue of death," said Luis Chavez, the Mexican gangster.

"It is my rat run," said El Huracán with a grin.

CHAPTER 2—THE AVENUE OF DEATH

Robert King was sitting on a bench inside a window-less stone cell. The walls were scarred and scratched with messages and obscenities. He was not the first man to have been held captive here. Apart from the bench there was nothing else in the cell, one wall of which was taken up by a big dented metal gate. He heard a burst of muffled laughter from somewhere above. As far as he could tell he was underground. Some time soon that gate was going to open, and he was going to walk out and face whatever challenge El Huracán had prepared for him.

He was ready.

He was a born optimist.

All his life he'd managed to get away safely. From the orphanage, from the army, from his first two wives, from the police after he'd killed his third wife, the diamond heiress . . .

All I got to do is stay alive, he thought. *All I got to do is get to the end of the rat run.*

There was a sound behind him and he turned to see three men come into his cell through a low door. They were Mexican Indians, with long noses, wide mouths, and mats of straight black hair framing their faces and hanging down to their shoulders.

Each carried a spear with a narrow blade at the end.

They said nothing. Just looked at him, unblinking. Patient. Waiting.

King swallowed. His throat was dry and his saliva felt sticky and thick in his mouth.

"Listen, guys," he said. "I'm a wealthy man. I don't know what Huracán pays you, but I can pay you more. Much more. I can make you very rich. *Mucho dollar. Sí?*" He rubbed his fingers together. "Just stand aside and let me walk out of here. It's as simple as that. Just stand aside."

The three Indians continued to stare silently at him.

Up above the cell, El Huracán was looking to the northeast where there was an angry black slash across the otherwise clear blue sky.

"Looks like a bad storm," he said. "Somebody is going to get soaked."

"We could do with some of that rain down here," said Chunks Duhaine, who was standing at his side. "This weather is making me itchy. We need to clear the air."

"I thought we *had* cleared the air," said El Huracán with a sly smile.

Indeed, the atmosphere among the men collected along the top of the rat run was markedly lighter than it had been at lunchtime. They had all known that something was up, and were relieved that it hadn't meant trouble for *them*.

They were standing on a low, wide, square structure built of white stone. It was one of a handful of ancient Mayan ceremonial buildings in a part of Lagrimas Negras that was usually out of bounds to residents.

It was the base of a pyramid. It was here, centuries before, that the Mayans had carried out their ritual sacrifices. But the pyramid had fallen into ruin, and most of its huge stone blocks had been taken away to construct new buildings.

When El Huracán had come here he had cleared the base to reveal a long series of interlinked passageways. These he had opened up and turned into La Avenida de la Muerte, his avenue of death. It started in the remains of the pyramid and snaked its way out and across the ancient site toward a large, sunken area where a second, smaller but more complete, pyramid stood.

"What's the score here?" asked Dum-Dum White, looking down into the alleyway at his feet and wiping his fat, red neck with a handkerchief.

"It is simple," said El Huracán. "When the gate is opened, Señor King will attempt to reach the other end of the run. If he is not careful, or lucky, or fast enough, one of my traps will destroy him. The different gods mark the stations of his journey."

He pointed to where images of Mayan deities had been painted on the walls at various stages of the run.

"You must place bets on how far you think he will get before he is killed. So, choose your god of death, gentlemen."

The men looked down into the rat run and at the sinister painted figures.

"There is Gucumatz," said El Huracán. "And Kinich Kakmo. Further along there is Balam-Agab, the night jaguar. Ixtab, with the rope around her neck, she is the goddess of suicides. The Mayans believed that if you committed suicide, you would go to heaven quicker. Many men, when they reach the marker of Ixtab, agree and take their own lives rather than face further pain. Señor King will be acting out a Mayan myth: the descent into Xibalba, the realm of the dead, along a road full of treacherous obstacles." He pointed toward the second pyramid. "If he's lucky enough to reach the end, he will meet the final god, Hun Came. If he gets past him, he is free to go."

"How many men have ever made it out?" said Dum-Dum.

El Huracán laughed. "Only their ghosts get past Hun Came," he said.

The men became excited, studying the dangers in the twisting alleyway below, discussing King's fitness and bravery, and noisily placing bets.

In his bleak cell beneath the pyramid, King could hear the sounds of merriment blotted out by a grinding noise as the metal gate slid up into the stonework. As it opened, it revealed the long alleyway open to the sky, with walls some fifteen feet high. He turned to the blank-faced Indian guards.

"Listen, guys—" he said, but his words were cut short as one of them jabbed him with the point of his spear. It was a practiced move. The blade hardly penetrated his skin, but it stung like hell, and a thin trickle of blood began to flow down his chest. The other two raised their own spears, and King backed away, arms raised.

"Okay, okay," he said. "I get the message."

He moved out into the sunlight. The Indians advanced and the gate slid shut behind them.

As King walked cautiously down the alleyway, he noticed evidence of animals. There were droppings and bits of bones and dried-up scraps of meat. There was a cloying ammonia smell, trapped down here by the high walls.

He came to a corner and cautiously peered around it, not knowing what he was going to find on the other side.

No signs of life. But the ground sloped downward into water, and he realized that he would have to swim under a low arch in order to proceed.

The water was scummy and dark green and smelled awful. He could barely see two or three inches into its murky depths.

He forced himself onward, wading down the slope until the water was up to his chest. There was nothing for it now. He took a deep breath and ducked under the arch.

When he came up on the other side, coughing and spluttering, the disgusting water clogging his nose and ears, King opened his eyes to find six other pairs of eyes staring back at him.

They looked like they were floating on the surface of the water. Round and black and leathery, nothing else of the animals was visible, and, as King watched, they slowly began to move in closer.

He looked around quickly. He was in a half-submerged chamber. There was light at the far end, another arch like the one he had just come through. He splashed the water to keep the things away, and in an instant they had disappeared under the water. He peered down but could see nothing in the murky gloom.

Where had they gone?

There was a sudden sharp pain in the back of his ankle as something latched on to his Achilles tendon. A second pain got him in the side, and as he put his hand down he felt a creature biting into the soft flesh at his waist.

He yelled.

"*Crocodylus moreletii*," said El Huracán. "The Mexican crocodile. They are only babies, but their teeth are sharp as needles. They don't like strangers swimming in their paddling pool."

They heard another yell from below, and seconds later King came blundering up the slope at the other end of the chamber, a small crocodile hanging from his side by its teeth. He shook it loose and it plopped into the water, gave a flick of its tail, and swam away back into the chamber.

King was a sorry sight, standing there in his ruined shirt and trousers, dripping with filthy water and with a spreading pink stain across his stomach.

"Bravo!" said El Huracán, applauding. "You have passed the sign of Chac, the god of rain. Not that I expected you to fall at the first fence. The crocs were just there to add a little bite to the proceedings!"

There was laughter from the watching men.

"Are you going to let him do this?" King shouted up at them. "You all feel the same way as me, I know it. You all want out of here. Open your eyes! Are you going to let him get away with this? We're all prisoners here. We might just as well be in Alcatraz or San Quentin. He's bleeding us dry. He takes our money and then what? Ask him. Ask him what happens when your money runs out. Go on, ask him. . . ."

"Carry on, please," said El Huracán. "There are more of my pets who are just dying to meet you."

King spat, as much to show his contempt for El Huracán as to clear the foul water from his mouth.

"What if I just stay here?" he said bitterly. "I don't reckon your three stooges are gonna want to follow me through there."

"By all means stay if you like," said El Huracán, and he laughed. "Perhaps I can make it more comfortable for you?"

King, who was still standing in about six inches of water, suddenly sensed a movement beneath his feet, and something punched upward from the stone floor. He cried out and jumped backward. A spike had stabbed the sole of his left shoe and gone right through it into his foot.

He hopped and staggered along the alleyway as more rusty steel spikes began to shoot up all over the floor. He saw that it was studded with small holes, and there was no way of knowing where the next spike would emerge.

The crowd of men following his progress found this hugely entertaining. They whistled and roared and screamed with laughter, forgetting that less than an hour ago King had been one of them.

King had to keep moving now or risk being stabbed again. As he stumbled along he left a trail of blood and water behind him.

Muttering curses under his breath, he tried to outrun the spikes, ignoring the pain that jolted up through his leg every time he put his injured foot down.

One spike grazed his ankle and another snagged his

trousers; a third one went through the front of his right shoe. Miraculously, though, it somehow slid between his toes and caused no damage.

"Go on, King, you can do it," someone shouted. "You're nearly there."

There were more cheers of encouragement from above. King knew that they didn't care about him at all; they just cared about their bets. Not one of them would have bet on him going down this early, but it was plain that if he fell over now, one of the spikes could kill him.

He made it to the end of that stretch of the run and was now faced by what appeared to be a solid wall. He looked wildly around, hearing more spikes slicing up through the stones with the sound of knives being sharpened.

At last he spotted a narrow gap along the bottom of the wall, just wide enough to squeeze under. He threw himself on his belly, at any moment expecting to feel one of the spikes drive into him.

He wriggled forward, unable to see what was ahead of him. His hand touched something. It felt like dry twigs, but as he brushed them aside, he felt a nasty sting in his wrist.

From above, the watching men could see that King now had to get through a chamber filled with scorpions. He would have to crawl all the way, as horizontal steel bars prevented him from standing up.

The watchers followed King as he wriggled along, every now and then his body jerking as one of the scorpions got him with its tail. He would twist away each time, only to put himself within range of another one. Then he would squirm and writhe in the opposite direction.

"Ek Chuah," said El Huracán, "the Mayan scorpion god."

King screamed. One of the creatures had got him in the cheek. He could feel his whole face swelling up. He moved more quickly. The nasty little bugs skittered and rattled around as he roared at them and vainly tried to protect himself from their stings.

The exit was only a few feet away. He concentrated on it, trying not to think about the terrible pain he was in.

He had been bitten in the heel and the belly, stabbed in the foot, and now stung all over.

What next?

He soon found out. At the end of the scorpion chamber, he was faced with a drop. He didn't hesitate. He just wanted to get out of there fast. He flung himself over the edge and fell six feet. He was relieved to land on something soft.

His sense of relief was rather short-lived, however.

It was hard to decide which of the two was the more surprised: King, or the massive, sleeping anaconda.

As soon as King realized what he had landed on, he forgot all about his injuries and began scrabbling for a way out. For its part, the huge snake wrapped a length of its fat body around King's leg. It sensed that something was attacking it, and it was fighting back the only way it knew how.

"He has reached the sign of Gucumatz, the snake god," said El Huracán as King grabbed hold of the top of the wall and tried to haul himself out. The great weight of the anaconda, which must have been a good twenty-five feet long, was pulling him back, though. He kicked out as it began to crush his leg. The coils slid further and further, up his shin, past his knee, and along his thigh toward his groin.

"Get off me, you filthy brute," King snarled and he pounded the animal against the stonework. He managed to hoist himself up on to the top of the wall, his lower half still dangling in the snake pit.

He shook his trapped leg and felt a slight lessening of the grip, and then, with an almost inhuman effort, he wrenched it free.

The snake had to be satisfied with his shoe, which it proceeded to mangle in its coils. The shoe had been handmade in Italy and cost more than the average Mexican peasant would earn in a month.

King didn't stay around to watch, though. He struggled to his feet and then winced from a fresh pain as he tried to walk.

He had twisted his ankle trying to get it away from the snake, which now meant that neither of his legs was much use to him.

He yelled every foul insult he could think of up at El Huracán, who was busy taking money off those men who had lost bets so far.

"You'd better hotfoot it to the other end, Señor King," El Huracán called down to him. "Because when you see what I have cooked up for you next, you are not going to want to stay for dinner."

"What are you talking about, you reptile?"

King looked around him, trying to work out where the next threat would come from.

The floor of this section of the rat run was made entirely

of riveted iron plates. The sun was burning down and had heated up the metalwork. King could feel it through his sock.

Well, at least there wouldn't be any animals around. It would be too uncomfortable for them here.

King hobbled forward, the floor seeming to get hotter with every step.

He spotted a series of vents along one side of the alley. Smoke was seeping out.

And then he understood.

The floor wasn't just getting hotter from the heat of the sun.

There was a fire down below.

El Huracán's men were deliberately heating the iron plates. If he didn't get out of there fast, he was going to be fried like a shrimp on a griddle pan.

But moving quickly wasn't possible with a badly cut foot and a twisted ankle; he could only shuffle along like one of the walking wounded from a battle.

Soon the heat had burned through his sock, and there was nothing to protect the skin of his foot. He tried to run, but only managed five steps before he stumbled. He put out his hands to break his fall, and as they pressed against the red-hot metal, he screamed in agony. When he tried to pull them away they were stuck fast. He gritted his teeth and pulled hard, leaving two gray handprints of flayed skin behind.

Somehow he got to his feet again and staggered on, the smell of cooking meat filling the air.

He wondered what sort of twisted mind could dream up such a place. What sort of mind could take pleasure in the pain and suffering of others? But he knew the answer. A

21

mind like his own. A mind like all the men on this island possessed.

A heartless, criminal mind.

He was delirious with pain now, his vision blurring, his heart racing, his breath scalding his lungs. The heat was so intense it burned the sole off his remaining shoe and through the sock. Both of his feet were now naked and each step was a fresh agony.

He just made it to the end of the hot plates before he passed out, and flung himself into the water-filled trench that divided this section of the rat run from the next.

The water felt deliciously cooling, and for a moment he didn't care what creatures might be lurking in it.

"Congratulations, Señor King, you have made it as far as Kinich Kakmo, the sun god. You are nearly halfway. But I wouldn't stay too long in your bath, that water is teeming with leeches."

King floundered across the trench and flopped onto the other side. He saw an ugly black leech attached to the back of one hand, but he ignored it. Compared to what he had been through, a leech was nothing to worry about.

"Who has bet that he would get no further than Balam-Agab, the night jaguar?" asked El Huracán, and several men nodded.

"Few men get farther than this," said El Huracán, his black eyes shining.

Even as he said it a door slid open in one wall, and a deep animal growl came out from the chamber behind it.

King added a long, sad moan of his own and managed somehow to stand up. His legs were like lead weights, but he forced one aching foot in front of the other, plodding along like a ninety-year-old man.

He heard a movement and glanced back to see exactly what he had been expecting to see: a big black cat, sleek and hungry-looking, its yellow eyes fixed on him. It was creeping forward in a low hunter's crouch.

King glanced ahead, his senses sharpened by fear. The door at the other end of the alley didn't look too far away.

But what was the point? What was the damned point? On the other side of the door would be something else, something worse.

The will to live is powerful, though. No matter what terror awaits, no matter what fresh torture, if there is a slim chance of life, of escape, most men will reach for it.

"You can do it," King mumbled through cracked lips. "All you got to do is get to the end, you can do it . . . Go on . . . Run!"

Miraculously he was running, his legs pounding on the hard stone. Maybe the jaguar was behind him, maybe even now it was getting ready to jump on his back and sink its teeth into his neck. . . .

Then suddenly he was no longer running. He couldn't move. He couldn't feel any part of his body. The pain had all gone. He could hear the steady drip of blood.

Strung taut across the alleyway were thin strands of narrow flattened wire, their edges razor sharp. Distracted by the jaguar, King had run straight into them.

One wire was at the height of his neck, another at his stomach, one more at his thighs. He stood there, held up by the wires buried deep in his body; twitching, growing cold, as the life drained out of him.

The men above watched in silence as King slowly stopped moving. They held their breath as the jaguar crept up to him and delicately pulled him off the wires with its claws. Then it began to drag him back to its lair.

It was all over. In the end death had come fast, and King had got less than halfway through the rat run.

These were tough men; they had all seen some terrible things in their time. Most had tasted their fill of blood and smelled its rusty stench. Most were killers.

None of them had ever seen a show like this before, though, and they were left stunned and awed and just a little unsettled.

What had they become? What were they turning into on this beautiful island in the Caribbean?

"Gentlemen," said El Huracán, cheerfully clapping his hands together, "let us settle our bets, and then I would like to invite you all for cocktails on my terrace, where we can watch the sun set."

My dear James,

The weather here is as grim as usual. Just look at me! I have been in England too long. I have become English. Unable to talk about anything except the weather. But, dammit all, an English winter is a terrible thing and I do not think that I shall ever get used to it. I am more jealous of you being in Mexico than you can imagine. I went home to India at Christmas after our adventures, and it was lovely to see blue skies and sunshine and bright colors again, and to eat some decent sock.

After the excitements of the last half, it is all back to normal here at Codrose's. The food is as awful as ever and Codrose is as bad-tempered as ever. Actually, if anything, he is even worse (if that is possible) since the fire and the break-in. The building still smells of smoke. Katey the maid never really recovered from the shock of bumping into the intruder, and she has left. Joy of joys, she has been replaced, not with another old crocodile but with a young Irish girl called Roan. She is rumoured to be only seventeen, and everyone is in love with her. Even me.

And I have never really seen the point of girls before. The thing is, you can talk to her as a friend. I am sure you will like her.

Actually, I say things are back to normal, but they are not. The new Library are a bunch of pirates. There was too much going on last half for us to really notice, but now that you are not around and things have quieted down, it has become clear that the boys in charge of Codrose's are the most bloodthirsty, uncaring gang that the House has ever had to put up with. They lord it about the place like a bunch of little Mussolinis. The worst of them all is Theo Bentinck. He has beaten so many of us, often for no reason at all, that he has been nicknamed Bloody Bentinck (although some boys call him worse). He seems determined to make our lives a thorough misery. I feel if you were here to stick up for us lower boys, things might be a little different. As it is we are all timid and scared of our own shadows. We stay in our rooms and keep the noise down and try not to be noticed. Hurry back, please. We need our James.

Our sporting achievements have been pretty dismal this half. Despite Theo Bentinck threatening to beat everyone if they don't win, the lower boys in the House have been lost without you. Everyone has been lost without you. I saw your friend Perry Mandeville the other day, and he said that

26

even the Danger Society has been quiet. He said they have started work on restoring your Bentley, though. I think they had some foolish idea that they might have it ready for your return, but I do not think this will happen. Perry seems to like talking about things more than actually doing them. By the way, he has been going about the place showing off and bragging about his involvement in the Fairburn incident and your part in it has almost been forgotten. (Knowing you, though, I think that is how you would want it. You always hate getting too much attention.)

In short, we all miss you and look forward to your return. I fear that you are the only one who can sort out the gang of mobsters who have taken over Codrose Library. So please try not to get involved in any more adventures while you are away. Get plenty of rest as you will need to be fit and well when you return. We want you back in one piece, not missing any arms or legs, or wearing an eye patch like Lord Nelson!

I will write soon with more news.

Yours,
Pritpal S. Wandra

CHAPTER 3—ANGEL CORONA

James stuffed the letter into his pocket and smiled, leaning back against the cabin of the fishing boat and feeling the throb of its diesel engine. Eton felt like it was on the other side of the world. Part of another life. He pictured it as cold and wet and gray. Mind you, it was turning gray here now. The day had started warm and bright and sunny, promising so much, but it had broken its promise and turned sullen.

He squinted toward the horizon. Heavy clouds were building to the east, where they hung low over the dark water, so that it was impossible to tell where sky ended and sea began. There was a yellow flash and he heard the distant grumble of thunder.

Somewhere far out in the Gulf of Mexico a storm was raging.

Here, though, the sea was calm and flat.

"Too calm, and too flat," Diego Garcia, the skipper, had said. Indeed, the day felt dead, as if time had stopped. James watched as Garcia squatted down, leaned over the side of the boat, and dipped his hand into the water.

He frowned.

"The water is too warm for the time of year," he said, and licked the salt from his fingers. "Currents from the south."

Garcia was a big, strong man who always had a broad grin on his handsome features. They had been traveling slowly down the coast from Tampico, and when he had time, Garcia had shown James the secrets of sea fishing. They had caught nothing today, however.

"Is why the fishes are not here," said Garcia, who for the first time since James had met him was not smiling. "Usually they are here. But today, no. The water is too warm. We must hurry, there is going to be a big storm."

The shriek of a seagull broke the eerie silence, and they looked up to see a large flock circling the boat.

"Is wrong," said Garcia, shaking his head. "The birds should not be here. They confused."

He narrowed his eyes and peered toward the mainland, which was a distant, hazy strip of gray to the west.

"We are at least an hour out," he said. "It will be difficult to outrun the storm completely. But I think I can do it."

James felt the boat rise up on a swell, as if the sea had suddenly woken from a deep sleep, and a blast of cold wind whipped across the deck, followed by a spray of icy rain. He shivered and got to his feet as Garcia shouted an order to his crewmen in Spanish.

The ominous band of black to the east was spreading, like a dark blanket being drawn across the heavens.

The boat lurched as a second big wave caught it.

"Better get below," Garcia shouted to James. "She is coming fast."

James clambered below deck to where his Aunt Charmian sat studying a map in the tiny cabin with her guide, Mendoza.

"I think it might get rough," said James.

"Garcia's a good sailor," said Charmian.

"I don't fancy getting caught up in a storm," said James.

Mendoza shrugged. "It is in the hand of God," he said.

James smiled. He had been traveling in Mexico with his aunt since January, and he was getting used to the fatalistic ways of its people. Everything that happened was down to God, or Jesus, or the Virgin of Guadalupe, or any one of the lesser gods, demons, saints, sinners, and weird magical figures the locals believed in.

The amazing sights and sounds and smells of this new country had put all thoughts of England out of his mind, but Pritpal's letter had reminded him of home and all that he had left behind.

Christmas had been a quiet affair. James had been allowed out of the hospital three days before but had still been weak and in need of sleep. He had hurried around Canterbury on Christmas Eve and found some presents for Charmian: a pair of leather gloves, a book on birds, and a pretty brooch he spotted in a secondhand shop.

They had eaten a fine fat goose together on Christmas Day and unwrapped their presents after lunch. Charmian had given James a Fu Manchu novel and a telescope, and he was very pleased with her presents.

James had slept for most of Boxing Day and was awoken on the following day by a ring of the doorbell. There stood Mr. Merriot from Eton. He was James's classical tutor and was responsible for his schooling.

Merriot and Charmian had talked for hours in the sitting room while James went for a long walk in the fields. His arm was in a sling while his broken collarbone knitted itself back together, and the wound in his shoulder caused by a large splinter of wood was very sore. He knew that it would all heal in time, but the emotional scars might take longer. He had seen some awful things. He needed mental as well as physical rest.

At teatime James returned home and was met by the adults.

"We don't think you should go back to school just yet," said Charmian. "Not until you are fully well. People will have questions to ask about what happened with Mr. Fairburn, and we think it's best to let things die down a little."

"When school life has returned to normal and you are strong again, we'll have you back," Merriot added.

"I'll make sure you keep up with your schoolwork," said Charmian. "After all, I taught you at home before you went to Eton; it won't be so very different."

"What about when you go away?" James asked. "To Mexico."

"We'll see how you are at the time," said Charmian. "Then you can either go back to Eton or come with me. The sea air on the voyage out would do you good, and Mexico would be an education in itself."

"What say you?" asked Merriot with a friendly smile.

"I shall miss my friends," said James. "But I think a few weeks' rest would do me good. I do feel pretty feeble still."

"'Pretty feeble,' he says!" barked Merriot. "Do him good! Let's hope so, eh? We don't want you getting into any more scrapes, do we, lad? I seem to remember the last time I was down here with the Head Master he said very much the same thing—keep your head down and your nose clean—and just look what happened." He grinned at James. "I shall expect Eton to return to its peaceful old ways with you out of the picture."

Now, five weeks later, there was just a dull ache and a slight stiffness in his shoulder, and for the most part he felt fit and well. He had filled out on solid Mexican food, full of beans and corn flour and fiery hot chilli peppers, and had adjusted to the slow pace of life.

They had docked in Veracruz and taken a train to Mexico City, where Charmian had spent several days talking to some professors at the university. She was an anthropologist and was hoping to make contact with an ancient Mayan tribe in the southern rainforest that was apparently unchanged since the time of the conquistadores. From Mexico City they had flown to Tampico, where many Indians lived. They had left their homes and villages and traveled here to find employment in the oil fields. Charmian spent several evenings in the bars and cantinas talking to them and finding out all she could about the people and places she would be visiting. It was in a bar that she found Mendoza. He had been working as a scout for an oil company, and he knew Mexico well. She chose him to lead her expedition.

The Tampico stores and suppliers had all the equipment and provisions she needed for the trip. She had chartered Garcia's boat, loaded it with all her things, and they had headed south. James was not going all the way, though. She had arranged for him to stay with an American family in Tres Hermanas while she went into the jungle.

James sat down next to his aunt and looked at the map. "Here's where we're going today—Tres Hermanas," she said, pointing with a pencil to a small town on the Gulf coast. "Then I'll continue on to Carmen." She drew a line down the coast. "From there I'll get another boat to take me upriver toward Palenque." She extended the line inland, following the twisting shape of a river into the heart of the rain forest. "That's where I'll pick up the rest of the expedition."

James focused on the tiny dot on the map that represented Tres Hermanas. It looked like the middle of nowhere. He had enjoyed traveling around with Charmian, helping her to get everything ready for her adventure. What would there be to do in that sleepy fishing village?

Garcia was true to his word. He managed to just keep ahead of the storm. But the sky was darkening as they pulled into the busy harbor and tied up for the night.

Tres Hermanas was larger and livelier than James had expected, and the locals were getting ready for a carnival the next day. The town was busy with tourists and Mexicans from outlying villages. The locals were busy decorating floats. A huge effigy of a grumpy-looking man had been built in the main square, ready to be burned. A stage had been built opposite, and a ragged brass band was rehearsing. There were flags and banners and colorful papier-mâché figures strung up across the streets, and noisy, excited men scurried across the rooftops preparing fireworks.

James and Charmian took a coffee in a small cantina in the square, looking out at the activity and occasionally glancing up at the darkening sky.

There was a gloomy, tense feeling; the familiar sense of doom that you get before a thunderstorm. The air was charged and heavy. A group of locals at the bar were arguing about whether to take down all their carefully hung decorations or risk them getting ruined. What had been intended to be an explosion of music and color and dancing now looked like it was going to be an explosion of thunder and lightning and rain instead. Some men just shrugged and put it down to fate. If God wanted to rain on their parade then that was his choice, there was little they could do about it.

Charmian, who spoke Spanish well, listened in on their conversation. "We'd better shake a leg," she said, finishing her coffee. "If God does decide to empty his bathwater on us, I'd rather be safely indoors when it happens."

As they stepped out into the square, though, it started to rain. Big cold drops of water pattered down all around them.

"Ah, well," said Charmian, unfurling an elegant umbrella. "Perhaps the storm will pass over quickly and tomorrow will be bright and clear. I must say I'm sorry I shall be missing out on all the fun, but I will need to set off first thing."

A passing Mexican in a sharp suit winked at her and said something approving. Charmian smiled politely, though coldly, back at him, and said good afternoon.

James had become used to men staring at Charmian and making comments. As an unaccompanied, single woman, she was considered fair game, and as an attractive, single woman she excited the macho passions of the Mexicans.

The comments were mostly harmless, and the men, in their way, were only being gallant. Charmian was a seasoned traveler, who had spent time in some of the remotest parts of the world. She had known from the start how to deal with Mexicans.

They left the main square and squeezed into a narrow street that was crammed with people. James had to fall back behind his aunt as they forced their way through the crowds.

Charmian was carrying a large leather saddlebag, her traveling bag, which she always took with her when she went away. It had originally been made for an Argentinian gaucho and was scratched and worn from years of use. It was large enough to carry everything she needed: her purse, a first-aid kit, maps, a compass, field glasses, bottled water, toilet paper, and countless other essential items.

As they struggled down the street, James saw a boy of about his own age slip in behind Charmian and keep pace with her. He thought nothing of it until he noticed a small, quick movement. It happened so fast and was so unexpected that at first he wasn't sure exactly what he'd seen. Had it even happened?

Yes.

The boy had pulled out a knife and cut through the shoulder straps of Charmian's bag. Before she had even realized what was happening, the boy had snatched the bag, turned and run, brushing past James as he went.

For a moment James was too surprised to do anything. He was left standing there like an idiot and marveling at the boy's neat handiwork. But then he snapped out of it. All of Charmian's life was in that bag: her money, her passport, and all her documents. If she didn't get it back, she would have to cancel her trip.

"Hey!" he yelled, and without thinking, set off in a sprint

after the boy, who was dodging through the crowds twenty feet ahead.

James shoved a couple of people out of his way. He knew that if he lost sight of the boy he would never see either him or the bag again. But he was a fast runner, and, as the thief ran, he cleared a path through the milling people, making it easier for James to keep up.

James shouted again and watched as the boy ducked into a side alley.

James barged in after him.

The boy pounded down the alley, a silhouette in the darkness. The other end opened out into a small, dingy courtyard overlooked by tall buildings. There was a well in the center surrounded by flies. Washing hung down on all sides and the stuffy air smelled of food.

James put on a burst of speed and grabbed the boy's shoulder. He wheeled around, slashing his knife in a wide arc. James just managed to jump back out of the way.

The boy smirked, holding the knife out in front of him.

James glanced around the courtyard. There was no other way out.

He'd fallen for a trap. The boy hadn't come in here to try to escape. He'd come in here to get rid of James.

For the first time, James got a proper look at him.

He was wearing a short-sleeved shirt and loose, wide trousers. His hair was black and oiled, and he had a faint fuzz of hair on his top lip. He was almost exactly the same height as James, and but for the fact that he had brown eyes instead of blue, the two of them could have been brothers.

The boy raised his knife higher, taunting James.

James was unarmed, and he knew never to get into a fight with someone who had a knife. The damage that even a short blade could do was appalling.

"Give me back the bag," he said calmly.

The boy said something defiant in Spanish and cocked his chin at James.

"The bag," said James, nodding at it.

The boy held it in his free hand. Without its straps it was heavy and awkward.

"*Americano?*" said the boy.

"English," said James.

"You like I should cut you, Ingleesh?" said the boy. "So you always remember the name of Angel Corona?"

James said nothing, but held Angel's gaze and tried to appear neither scared nor angry. He wanted to do nothing to provoke the boy.

It made no difference, Angel lashed out at him anyway, and once more James had to jump back.

Angel advanced on him.

"I slit you belly and spill you guts, yeah?" he said, and smiled widely, showing his perfect white teeth.

James held his palms up toward the boy and kept on slowly walking backward. He knew that in a few paces he would have his back against the wall, and there would be nowhere for him to go.

"You are stupid," said Angel. "You should never have chased me, Ingleesh."

James had to agree. He had acted without thinking.

He sensed something above him. It was a bedsheet, hanging from a line. He thought quickly. It might be his only chance. He raised his arms higher in a gesture of surrender, and as his fingertips brushed against the cotton sheet, he grabbed hold and tugged hard. The sheet flapped down onto Angel. It was just enough to distract him. James kicked hard at his wrist.

He was wearing a pair of stout English-made shoes with hard leather soles and toe caps. He connected with the underside of Angel's wrist, and the force of his kick knocked the knife flying.

Angel was furious. He tossed the sheet to one side and hurled himself at James.

But James had the advantage now; without the knife and weighed down by the bag, Angel was no threat to him.

James brought up his forearm and smashed it into Angel's throat as he ran at him. Angel croaked and fell back, dropping the bag and clutching himself. He spat out a curse and came back at James in a roaring scramble. James stepped to one side and raised his knee at the same time, driving it into the boy's stomach. As Angel doubled over, James grabbed him around the neck, and holding him tight in the crook of his elbow, marched him over to the well and shoved his face under the water.

Angel struggled and flailed about, and when James reckoned he'd had enough, he let him go and dropped him to the cobbled ground. He sat there, coughing and spluttering and looking at James with a mixture of fear and hatred.

"Maybe *you'll* always remember the name of James Bond." James retrieved Charmian's bag, then picked up the knife and dropped it into the well. "*Adios,*" he said finally, and walked back down the alley toward the main street.

He found Charmian at the other end, standing in the middle of the road, calling out his name. James waved and called back.

"James, that was very reckless," said Charmian when she saw him. "That boy could have killed you."

"I know," said James. "I didn't think. I got your bag back, though. Everything's still in it, but you'll need new straps."

"I should have been more careful," said Charmian. "I shall have to replace them with thin chains, then they'll be harder to cut."

James saw Charmian's eyes go suddenly wide and fearful. She had seen something behind him. He spun around to see Angel tearing out of the mouth of the alley, the knife once more in his hand.

Hell. He should have checked. The well obviously wasn't as deep as he had imagined.

But the next moment there was a commotion as two burly men in suits grabbed hold of the boy. They both had mustaches, and one was holding a pistol.

Angel struggled, but the man pressed the pistol into his face and he calmed down. They said something quickly to him in Spanish; the only words James could understand were the boy's name.

The second man took the knife and snapped a pair of handcuffs on Angel.

As the two men dragged him away, they stopped briefly by Charmian, and the one with the gun bowed.

"Good afternoon, *señora*," he said. "I am sorry about this unfortunate incident. The boy is known to us. We have been trying to catch him at his games for many weeks now. We lock him up, *señora*. You come in the morning to the police station and make a statement, yes?"

"Yes, of course." Charmian smiled politely and watched as the men dragged the struggling boy away down the street.

As they went, they had to push past a group of tourists, four Americans and a Japanese. They pointed at Angel.

"Give 'em hell, kid," one of them shouted, a short slab of a man who was almost as wide as he was tall, with no neck and a big square head.

"Whatzat?" said one of the others, who was as bony as his friend was solid.

"I said, 'Give 'em hell,'" the squat man repeated loudly.

"That's right," said his friend, and they all laughed.

All except the one woman who was with them, a beautiful blonde wearing a wide-brimmed hat.

"Come along," said Charmian, taking James by the elbow. "I have no intention of going to make a statement in the morning. For one, I fully intend to be a hundred miles away by then, and for two, the less we have to do with the local police the better. I know that boy *did* try to rob me and probably tried to kill you, but I'm afraid I do feel rather sorry for him. The police do not have a good reputation."

Just then there was a rumble of thunder and the heavens fully opened, pouring down a torrent of rain onto the dusty street.

"We should hurry," Charmian yelled. "Or we shall be drowned."

In his haste to escape the rain James quickly forgot about Angel Corona and the five tourists.

He could have had no idea what part they were all going to play in his life.

CHAPTER 4—A BROKEN DOLL

The Stones' house stood alone on the west side of Tres Hermanas, on a high rise of land, looking out over the other houses and the pink-tiled rooftop of the church of Santa Maria toward the sea. It had been built as a palace for a local aristocrat, and designed by an imported French architect in neoclassical style, with pillars and balconies and ornate carved stonework decorating every surface.

"I met Jack Stone in Texas about ten years ago," Charmian shouted over the noise of the pounding rain. "At an air show. He was quite famous then. A war hero. Fighter pilot. Very dashing. I think you'll like him."

A servant met James and Charmian at the wide, wrought-iron gate and led them up the gravel driveway. There was a huge avocado tree and a clump of palms standing on a well-kept lawn among rows of hedges that had been clipped into stylish geometrical shapes.

But it was raining too hard for James and Charmian to stop and admire the grounds.

"I'll stay tonight and make sure you're settled in," said Charmian as they approached the house. "But I shall have to leave before you are up. I have no way of knowing how long I will be in the rain forest, but if I am not back in time, Mr. Stone will take you to Veracruz and put you on the boat."

There were two crouching stone lions on the terrace guarding the front door, water streaming down their carved manes. A row of roses in heavy lead urns and two big red-leaved poinsettias in tubs were drooping under the downpour.

Another servant—an elderly Mexican with white hair and a simple black uniform—opened the front door. He welcomed them inside and took Charmian's bag and umbrella.

The entrance hall was dark with a polished marble floor. Bronze statues stood in the corners, and a huge crystal chandelier gave off only a dim, flickering light. One wall was covered in portraits of forgotten Mexican generals. On the wall opposite hung a gigantic painting of an aerial dogfight. Two biplanes, one American and one German, were shooting at each other. The artist had painted the machine guns in some detail. Bright orange flashes sprouted from their barrels, and spent cartridges flew off into the air. Fire and white smoke were streaming from the German's tail. In the background was a battlefield, with men charging from a trench into no-man's-land.

James wondered if the American airman was meant to be Jack Stone.

"Charmian, welcome."

James looked up to see Mr. Stone coming down the stairs. He was wearing a leather flying jacket and high boots. With his thin mustache and swept-back hair he looked every inch the air ace from the Great War.

"Jack," said Charmian, "you don't look a day older. May I introduce my nephew, James."

"Pleased to meet you, James," said Stone in a Southern drawl, pumping James's hand. "Welcome to Tres Hermanas. And welcome to my home."

Before James could say anything Stone turned to Charmian and suddenly became brisk and businesslike, setting his jaw firm and fixing her with a steely look.

"Don't get too settled," he said. "I'm afraid there's been a change of plan."

"Oh," said Charmian, taken aback.

"Don't worry." Stone smiled, showing a row of perfect white teeth. "It's none too serious. As you've probably noticed, there's a big storm moving in off the gulf."

"We could hardly not have noticed," said Charmian, who, despite her umbrella, had managed to get rather wet.

"They reckon it might settle in for a spell, which means there'll be no boats in or out of the harbor. If you don't get out of town tonight you might well be stuck here for days."

"Oh, but that would be a disaster," said Charmian. "I absolutely *have* to get to Palenque before next Saturday."

"Well, you won't make it by sea. And you sure as shooting won't make it by land. The roads are bad enough at the best of times, but any heavy rain and they all get washed out."

"So what am I to do?" asked Charmian.

"I'm going to fly you down there," said Stone, offering Charmian a big, heroic grin. "There's an airstrip in the jungle one of the mining companies built. We can land there, so you'll be ahead of schedule."

"But, Jack, I can't impose on you. . . ."

"Think nothing of it, ma'am," said Stone, and he saluted and winked. "I love to fly and I rarely get the chance these days. This'll be a good excuse. But I'm afraid we're going to have to hurry. If we don't get in the air in the next half hour or so we'll be grounded."

"This is very gallant of you," said Charmian. "But what about my luggage? My equipment?"

"I took the liberty of sending some of my servants down to the harbor," said Stone. "They're already loading everything on board my plane. Your man Mendoza's been supervising. Trust me, there really isn't any other way."

Charmian sighed and turned to James. "It seems I am going to have to desert you, James," she said. "There is no arguing with the man."

"My staff'll look after you well until I get back," said Stone, giving James a reassuring look.

"Don't worry about me," said James, and he smiled at his aunt. "The important thing is that you don't mess up your expedition."

Stone put an arm across James's shoulders.

"Good man. Well, what do you reckon?" he said, showing off his hallway with a sweep of his free arm. "Not a bad little shack to spend the next month in, eh?"

"It's very nice," said James, who secretly felt that the place was overstuffed and ugly. He had no idea why someone would want so many bits and pieces. He preferred things to be simple.

"Now," said Stone, who still had his arm around James, "I'll bet you'll be wanting to go up and play with the kids."

"Yes," said James bravely, although he had no desire just then to play with anyone.

"Me and your aunt will get ourselves fixed," said Stone.

"Then we'll come up and see you before we leave. Alonzo will show you to the playroom."

Stone nodded to the elderly servant who had been hovering nearby.

Alonzo led James up the staircase, along a landing, and up another staircase to a second, smaller landing. At last they arrived at a large, heavily carved oak door and went through it into a vast playroom, filled with every toy imaginable. There was too much to take in at first, but James noticed a doll's house and a playhouse, two rocking horses, a pile of stuffed animals, a piano, some skittles, toy soldiers, a pedal car, a castle, and a train set. This was a children's paradise, but not a thing was out of place. He was wondering if the children kept it like this when he spotted another servant on all fours, tidying something away. She was a young Mexican girl with a tired, scared-looking face.

A girl's voice came from somewhere.

"You are not to touch anything. Boys are clumsy and they break things."

Presently, James spotted the owner of the voice. Sitting at a large makeup mirror, painting her nails.

She was wearing a long, elegant dress made of shiny gold material, and her dark hair was set in a short, fashionable style with tight waves that someone must have spent ages setting in place.

"You must be James," she said without looking around.

"That's right," said James.

"I am Precious," said the girl, who had the manner and accent of a haughty Southern belle. "And that is Jack Junior. You may call him JJ, everyone does."

A boy of about seven, wearing a smart suit, appeared from behind the doll's house, carrying a doll.

"Pleased to meet you," said James.

"Will you play with me?" said JJ. "I never get to play with other boys."

"You might as well know we don't want you here," said Precious before James could reply. "It was not my choice. I don't want another boy about the place."

"Yes, I know," said James. "We're clumsy and we break things."

He went over to the window. "It's a little stuffy in here," he said, pushing it open and looking out.

The playroom was two floors up and overlooked a small terrace at the side of the house. The rain was drumming down and making large puddles in the garden.

"Come away from the window," said Precious. "You are blocking my light."

"You're a friendly creature, aren't you?" said James.

"You're English," said Precious, peering at his reflection in the mirror. "The English don't know how to dress. Your clothes are horrible. My clothes are the height of fashion."

James laughed at this formal phrase, and Precious finally turned to look at him.

"You don't have a lot to say for yourself, do you?" she said. "You're boring, like all boys. Boys are dull and igno-rant. They're not interested in fashion and books and movie stars. Go away and play with JJ. I don't play anymore. I'm too old for all this. My dolls bore me. You bore me."

She said this in such a snooty manner that James was

momentarily lost for words. This girl was acting like his superior, even though she was the same age as him, probably a little younger. She was wearing so much makeup it was impossible to tell. She looked like she might have been quite pretty without it all, with her big dark eyes and her wide mouth.

"Listen," said James, keeping his cool. "I'm going to be here for a while. So we need to find some way to get along with each other."

Precious ignored him. As if he had suddenly ceased to exist. She looked right through him at JJ.

"What are you doing with that doll?" she said. "Bring it here."

"Leg's broken," said JJ, holding it up and shaking it.

Precious took the doll off him and inspected it. It had a painted china face, real hair in yellow ringlets, and an expensive-looking silk dress.

"I used to love this doll," she said. "I'm too grown-up for it now, of course."

She jumped up and took it over to the window, where she made it dance along the ledge.

"Oh, look at me," she sang in a mocking, lisping, put-on childish voice. "I am the prettiest doll in all the world. See my pretty dress and see how well I dance. Oh, but my poor leg is broken . . . Oh no . . . I have slipped."

So saying, Precious tossed the doll out of the window and, laughing, watched it fall to the paving stones below.

"Oh, the poor thing. I think she is killed." She suddenly stopped laughing and turned from the window to the Mexican girl, who was still tidying the room.

"Dolores, my doll has fallen out of the window. Go and fetch her for me."

Dolores nodded quickly and left the room, her face worried and pinched.

"They do everything I say," said Precious, walking past James and returning to her place at the mirror. JJ, meanwhile, was running noisily around the room messing up everything that Dolores had tidied.

"Is that necessary?" said James.

"You are a guest here," said Precious. "You don't tell us what to do."

"I'm going," said James, and he headed for the door.

"Wait," said Precious, a note of softness in her voice.

James stopped.

"I'm sorry."

James turned to the girl. She had a sad, slightly anxious expression on her face. She looked different, younger.

"I am not used to having other children here," she said quietly. "There's only JJ and me. It's sometimes very lonely. I guess we can get a little crazy. Mother is never here."

"It's okay," said James. "There's no reason why we can't be friends."

"Yes," said Precious, and her whole face lit up with a sweet smile. She walked over holding out her arms, and clasped James's hand briefly.

"Come on. I'll make it up to you," she said. "Let's play with JJ."

James shrugged. He couldn't remember the last time he had played with anyone.

"What do you want to play, JJ?" said Precious excitedly.

"Blindman's bluff," said JJ.

"Good choice," said Precious, running to a dressing-up box. "First we'll make you blind, James." She whipped out a scarf and tied it around James's head. Then the two children spun him around, singing a childish rhyme. Finally they stopped.

"Now what?" said James, wobbling giddily on his feet.

"Now this," said Precious and she pushed him hard. He stumbled backward and tripped over something, landing painfully on his backside. He tore the blindfold off and saw JJ kneeling on the floor, helpless with laughter.

At last James lost his cool. He was flushed with anger. It was not that the trick had hurt him. It was the pettiness of it. It was such a silly, pathetic thing to do, and yet these two children thought it the funniest thing in the world.

James got up. "You're a spoiled little—" He stopped himself from saying something he might regret.

"What?" said Precious. "I'm a spoiled little what?"

At that moment Dolores returned, carrying the broken doll. She looked utterly worn down, and when she saw the state of the room she put her hands to her face and burst into tears.

"It's all right," said James. "I'll help you."

He started to put things away, and Precious stared at him with scorn.

"You look just like a servant," she sneered.

"Go to hell," said James.

Luckily, before anything else could happen, Jack Stone arrived. He was wearing a long leather coat over his flying gear and carrying a crocodile-skin attaché case. He took one look around the untidy room and said something harsh to Dolores in Spanish. Dolores nodded and worked harder, her tears falling onto the expensive carpet. Then Stone beamed at Precious and JJ, and they assumed the stiff-backed pose of dutiful children.

"I hope you kids have been playing nicely," he said.

"No, Daddy," said Precious petulantly, her voice that of a five-year-old. And when James looked at her he saw that she was crying tears as real as her maid's.

"James has been nasty and horrible," she sobbed. "He threw my doll out of the window and she broke. She was my favorite, too."

"Don't worry, angel," said Stone. "I'll buy you a new one." He turned on James with raised eyebrows. "I'm disappointed in you, James," he said. "If you're going to stay here, you're going to have to make more of an effort to get along with Precious and JJ."

James bit his lip and said nothing.

Stone kissed his children on their foreheads.

"I'll be back as soon as I can," he said. "And I'll bring you a whole planeload of presents."

"And new dresses?" said Precious.

"And new dresses for my best girl," he said, and kissed her again.

"Now, James," he said, straightening up, "do you want to come down and say good-bye to your aunt?"

"Please," said James, wishing with all his heart that he were going with Charmian instead of being stuck here with these two monsters.

CHAPTER 5—FOUR MEN WITH GUNS

The three powerful engines of the Ford Trimotor "Tin Goose" struggled to pull the aircraft through the turbulent sky. The propellers thrashed and whined, and when they hit pockets of dead air, they seemed to cut out altogether. The whole plane was shaking and rattling, and it bumped up and down like a fairground ride. Heavy rain smashed into the windscreen, and the wipers were struggling to clear it.

Strapped into the navigator's seat behind Jack Stone and Beto, his Mexican copilot, Charmian could feel her teeth clattering. She looked over at her guide, Mendoza: he was white with fear and looked like he was about to be sick. The poor man had never been up in an aeroplane before. This was not a good introduction to the pleasures of flying.

Stone shouted something into his microphone, and even with her headphones clamped to her ears Charmian had trouble understanding what he was saying over the roar of the engines and the wind and rain.

She just made out the word "house" and looked down to where Stone was pointing through the side window.

A wisp of low cloud momentarily obscured her view, and then she could clearly make out the Stones' house on top of the hill overlooking Tres Hermanas.

"I sure hope they get the storm shutters up in time," said Stone. "Otherwise I'm going to lose some windows."

"Don't worry about them," Charmian shouted. "You just get us safely away from here."

The house looked so secure and solid down there, while she felt totally at the mercy of the growing storm. The plane seemed tiny and fragile, as if the wind could tear its wings off and bat it clean out of the sky.

She had to admit to being rather nervous herself.

Stone pointed again, this time out to sea, and she gasped as she saw a bank of black cloud towering up into the heavens.

"Looks like we just made it in time," he yelled.

The black mass was swirling and boiling in a fast circular motion, and it was bearing down on the town like a huge angry beast.

"It's not the hurricane season," said Stone, his voice made thin and harsh by the headphones. "But that sure is some storm."

In the storm's dark heart there were flashes of lightning. Charmian wiped her window, which had steamed up. As she tried to look, however, a gust of wind knocked the plane sideways and they banked steeply.

"I'm gonna head inland," shouted Stone. "Try and outrun it. Once we get enough height we'll be fine, but it's pretty choppy out there just now."

The engines complained as Stone pulled back on the controls and eased some more power out of the throttles. Charmian was forced back into her seat as the plane climbed higher into the sky.

She heard Mendoza being sick into a paper bag.

How she envied James, snug and warm inside the house.

James was in the middle of supper, but he wasn't enjoying it at all.

It was Precious. She was quite the rudest and most self-centered person he had ever met, and she treated the Mexican servants horribly. He supposed that since her father had gone she was relishing the opportunity of being the mistress of the house, and he feared that she was also putting on a show for his benefit.

"Oh, don't be so clumsy, Rita," she said to the plump middle-aged woman who was trying to serve some boiled potatoes. "You are too careless. You nearly dropped them in my lap."

Rita muttered an apology while Precious poked at the potatoes with a fork.

"These won't do," she said. "Take them away. They are not cooked properly. I won't have any potatoes, bring me rice."

As Rita waddled out with the serving dish Precious shook her head.

"The problem is that they don't really understand about good food," she said. "They eat such slop themselves, it's foolish to think they could serve anything halfway decent for civilized people like us. I have told Daddy that we should get a chef from Europe, preferably France, and definitely not from England. The English do not know how to cook. Rita is just a peasant. All they know about is beans and rice. But they will eat anything, you know. I hear they even eat lizard.

Ugh. Can you imagine that? Even if I was starving to death I would never eat a lizard, but they do not know any better."

The three of them—James, Precious, and JJ—were sitting around a large antique mahogany table. There was silver cutlery and silver candelabra and silver serving dishes, all laid out neatly on a gleaming white lace tablecloth.

On the wall behind Precious was a large painting of her and her brother, posing formally in stiff expensive clothes. It looked like it had been done by the same artist who had painted the dogfight in the entrance hall. James thought he was better at painting aeroplanes than he was at painting people. On the wall opposite was the portrait of a woman. She was thin and beautiful and cold. James thought it must be Mrs. Stone, Precious's mother.

He took a sip of water from a crystal glass. He was sweating badly. The air in there was damp and thick. The humidity was terrible, and the rain, which hammered down in a steady monotonous torrent, hadn't helped to clear the atmosphere. Maybe when the heart of the storm hit it would help. There was a rumble of thunder, some way off in the distance still, but growing nearer.

A big ornate grandfather clock in the corner chimed five. It was going to be a long evening.

Outside, Alonzo was struggling with a storm shutter, trying to fix it over a window, but the wind was already strong and the shutter was heavy. Luis was supposed to be helping him, but he'd been sent off to fetch a hammer and nails ten minutes ago and still hadn't returned. Luis was fifteen and the youngest of Mr. Stone's servants. As far as Alonzo was concerned, the boy was more trouble than he was worth, though. He was lazy and slow and cheeky. That was the problem with young people nowadays: they had no respect for their elders.

Alonzo cursed. He was too old for this. His arms were aching, and he was cold and already soaked to the skin. If Luis didn't come back soon he was going to give up. The house had stood for two hundred years; it wasn't about to be blown over by a little wind.

Just then Luis appeared with a stupid grin on his face.

"I am sorry, Alonzo," he said. "I couldn't get the storeroom open. The door is warped."

"I don't want to hear your excuses," Alonzo snapped. "Help me with this damned shutter!"

"What do you call this?" Precious was once again scolding Rita, who was standing patiently with a bowl of steamed vegetables. "They are mush. Will I have to come into the kitchen and cook something myself? This is a joke, Rita. I can't eat this. Take it away."

"I'll have some," said James. He wasn't really hungry, but he felt sorry for the servants who had gone to so much trouble to prepare the food, none of which Precious would eat. JJ was tucking in. He was slightly pudgy and had a permanent smirk on his round face. He worshipped his sister and laughed at her every petulant outburst.

Rita smiled at James, but Precious held her by the wrist.

"You will not," she said, staring at James. "They will make you ill."

"They look all right to me," said James.

Precious spat into the dish.

"It is not fit for pigs," she said.

Rita looked very tired. She sighed and waddled slowly out with the dish of vegetables.

"I sometimes think they do it on purpose," said Precious. "Because if I won't eat it they can scoff it all themselves in the kitchen. Well, they won't be scoffing those vegetables in a hurry."

JJ laughed and spat into his own plate.

"Stop that, JJ," said Precious. "It's not funny. You have been spending too long with these peasants. You are becoming one of them."

JJ laughed again and spat again. This time Precious couldn't stop herself from sniggering.

"I'm sure they spit on our food," she said. "When we are not looking."

I wouldn't blame them, thought James.

Precious pushed her plate away. She had not touched a thing. The food sat cold and dry on the white porcelain.

"Oh, this is too much," she said. "I can't eat anything tonight. It is too hot. Come along, JJ, let's go upstairs. We'll get Rita to bring us up some cake later." She looked at James. "You may come with us."

"I'm tired," James lied. "I think I'll go to my room."

"As you wish," said Precious, and she got up. On her way out, past her brother, she whispered something in his ear that made him look guiltily at James and snort with laughter.

When they had gone James pushed his chair back, stretched out his legs, and finished his water. He then refilled his glass and drank some more. He had had some nasty stomach upsets since he had been in Mexico, but he assumed that the Stones' water would be clean and pure.

He wiped the sweat off his neck with his napkin. He knew it wasn't good manners, but there was nobody around to see him. He was just standing up to leave when Rita came back in with a bowl of rice. She saw that the other two children had gone and put the bowl down wearily on the table.

"They went upstairs," said James.

Rita looked at the rice, muttered something in Spanish, sighed theatrically, and returned to the kitchen.

James wiped his neck once more. In the few seconds since he had last wiped it, it had already become soaked again.

He walked out into the hallway. He looked at the painting of the dogfight. He looked at the ugly bronze statues. He hated this house already. He knew that if he wasn't careful he was going to get very bored in the days ahead.

He trudged up the stairs toward his room. When he got there he found that he had left the window open, the shutters were flapping and banging in the wind, and rain was pouring in onto the expensive-looking carpet.

"Hell," he said. He could get into trouble for this.

He hurried over to the window and grabbed a shutter, but the wind pulled it out of his grasp. He got hold of it again, but no matter how hard he tried, the wind seemed insistent that it stay open.

Alonzo was once more waiting for Luis. What would his excuse be this time? Surely it didn't take twenty minutes to fetch a simple stepladder. They had only got four storm shutters up; there were still many windows left to secure.

He dropped his tools and headed around to the front of the house. His wide hat kept the water off his head, but the rest of him was drenched. When he had finished he would have to go into the kitchen and sit by the stove to dry off. Maybe he would have a nice glass of wine. Or some of the rum he kept hidden in a drawer. That would restore his spirits. He was just picturing the cozy scene when he saw a shape on the grass.

"Luis? Luis, is that you?" He trotted over. It was Luis all right. He was lying with his eyes closed. Blood was trickling from his hair just behind his ear.

"Oh, Santo Dio!" said Alonzo and he knelt down. There was a faint pulse. The boy was not dead. But what had happened?

He looked up to see two men striding across the grass toward him. One was Japanese, the other was short and wide and looked like an American.

"Don't bother to get up," said the American, and before Alonzo could say anything, the man flicked a blackjack toward his head.

It was a small movement, but the blackjack hit Alonzo with the force of a train.

There was a flash of bright light, a sudden burning pain, and Alonzo blacked out.

James had seen everything from his bedroom as he wrestled with the shutters. When he saw Alonzo fall lifeless to the wet grass he forgot all about the window.

He ran from his room and looked over the banisters just as two more men and a woman came into the hallway. He recognized them as the group of tourists he had seen in Tres Hermanas.

But he had the feeling that they weren't tourists at all.

The guns the men were carrying were the biggest give-away.

As Alonzo's attackers joined them, James ducked back and bolted up the next flight of stairs toward the playroom.

He pushed the door open, breathless and panting.

JJ looked up at him. He was on the floor playing with some toy soldiers.

"Where's your sister?" James said.

"You should always knock," said Precious snootily. She was back at her mirror, trying on some earrings.

"Oh, shut up," said James. "There's trouble. You need to hide."

"Ha, ha, very funny," said Precious. "I suppose you think we're going to fall for that, do you?"

"I'm deadly serious," said James. "I just saw someone attack your servant Alonzo. He's lying outside on the lawn with another servant. Unconscious."

Precious opened her mouth wide and let out a high shrieking laugh. JJ looked at her and joined in.

"Who was it attacked him?" said Precious. "Frankenstein's monster? King Kong?"

"There are four men downstairs with guns," said James.

"Oh," said Precious. "It must be public enemy number one, public enemy number two, and public enemies three and four."

JJ thought this was just about the funniest thing he had ever heard, and he rolled on the floor kicking his legs in the air, wheezing and snorting with laughter.

James heard shouts and footsteps from outside the room.

"Hide!" he yelled, and made a dive for the playhouse. He just had time to get into a position where he could see out through the curtains when the playroom door burst open and a young man came in. He was nattily dressed and holding a large pistol. Precious screamed and JJ burst into tears.

"Believe me now?" James whispered, but he could take no satisfaction from what was happening. Much as he didn't like the two children, he realized that he was going to have to try to help them.

That was just assuming he didn't get caught himself.

CHAPTER 6—IN THE BELLY OF THE STORM

James watched as the young man waved his gun at Precious and JJ.

"Where's your father?" he yelled. "Tell me or I'll hurt you."

"He's not here," wailed Precious. "He's flown down south. He won't be back until after the storm."

As Precious said the word "storm" three things happened at once. There was a terrific crack of thunder, the whole house shook, and the lights went out.

The storm had finally arrived.

Precious screamed. The young man snarled at her to shut up. There was just enough light coming through the window for James to see him grab the two children and drag them out of the room.

James stayed put, breathing heavily. The intruders seemed to have come prepared, but with luck they wouldn't know that he was here at all.

James waited in the playhouse for a full five minutes. Once he was sure that the man wasn't coming back he crept out of his hiding place and tiptoed over to the playroom door.

He hardly needed to be quiet. The storm was making a fearsome racket as it buffeted the house. There was a cacophony of different sounds: crashing, hissing, roaring, squealing, rumbling.

As he moved out into the corridor James felt the full force of the wind slam into the house like a physical object. He could actually feel the floor moving beneath his feet, and the walls seemed to sway and shudder. He glanced out of the window, but all he could see was a swirling maelstrom of cloud and rain. There was a startling flash and another blast of thunder, then a gust of wind so powerful it blew the windows in. The rain followed, hosing down the corridor in horizontal bars. The walls were instantly soaked, and a picture flew off the wall.

The noise from outside was like nothing that James had ever heard before, like boulders crashing down a mountainside. The wind was whipping around in the corridor, and the house was vibrating as if at any moment it might crack up and be blown away.

James dropped to his knees and crawled along the sodden carpet as bits of debris were hurled past his head.

He reached the stairs and slid down them on his backside in the darkness. He made it safely to the lower landing and peered out between the banisters into the hallway below.

The servants were being rounded up and herded into the dining room by two of the men. The raid had been planned like a military operation.

James was the only person who might be able to get out and go for help.

He backed away from the banisters, ducked into his bedroom, and pulled the door shut.

He stood there for a moment, with his back to the door, breathing deeply. Rain was pouring in through the open window, and the carpet was soaked. There was already a large pool of water forming in the middle of the floor. James was sweating again. But it was a cold sweat, caused by fear, not heat. The temperature had dropped dramatically.

He considered his options and found that he had only one: to climb out and make a run for it.

He remembered seeing a little ornamental balcony outside and some thick jungly creeper up the side of the house.

He stepped toward the window, then suddenly threw himself to the floor as a piece of wood the size of a tabletop exploded through the window, spraying the room with jagged splinters. It was a broken door. The wind must have ripped it off another house and tossed it up here.

Over the sound of the storm James heard shouts and someone running up the stairs.

He quickly pulled the bedclothes off the bed and covered himself with them, leaving just enough space to see out.

He saw the door open and a pair of legs come in.

"It's just the storm," the person shouted. "Window's smashed. It's getting pretty hairy out there."

The legs departed and the door slammed shut.

James crawled out from under the bedclothes. The room was strewn with bits of wood and shredded leaves. He battled his way to the window and looked out into the belly of the storm.

It was hopeless. He wouldn't last five minutes out there. Even if he made it out of the garden, which was unlikely, he doubted that there would be anybody who would be able to help him. No one would risk leaving the safety of their home to brave this storm.

The wind was throwing stuff in every direction. The palm trees were bent over, and as he watched, a large shrub was uprooted and sent spinning across the lawn. It ended up tangled in the iron gates. Another, even stronger gust tore the gates loose from their hinges. They tumbled into the road and bounced off out of view.

Occasionally the wind would change direction, the clouds would break, and he would get a glimpse of Tres Hermanas. No lights were showing. The buildings were a black tumble. The electricity must be out everywhere.

James couldn't tear his eyes away. He was mesmerized by the awesome power of the storm. A set of garden furniture rolled across the lawn and knocked over a statue. A large tree near the road, unable to bend, snapped in half and collapsed onto the perimeter wall, flattening it. All the tiles from the roof of a nearby outbuilding were plucked off and James only just managed to duck down out of the way before they came clattering against the side of the house, as if thrown by some bad-tempered giant.

His face was wet and his eyes stung. He couldn't tell whether it was him or the house that was shaking.

Probably both.

He had never known a storm like this before.

There was no point in staying here. He picked himself up and ran in a crouch to the door, teased it open, checked that the coast was clear, and squeezed out of the room.

He crept along to the top of the stairs and once more looked down. The hallway was deserted now and in almost complete darkness. He moved stealthily down the stairs. As he reached the bottom he could make out voices from a room off to the right. The door hadn't been closed properly. He crossed the marble floor and peered in through the narrow crack.

He could see into what must be Stone's study, lit by hurricane lamps. The smell of burning oil filled the air.

The blond woman was standing next to an unopened wall safe. With her were the Japanese man and the flashily dressed young man who had taken the children from the playroom.

James couldn't see Precious and JJ from where he was, but he could hear them, sobbing.

"I'll ask you again," said the woman. "What's the combination of the safe?"

"I don't know," came Precious's voice. "I really don't know. Daddy would never tell us that."

"So where does he keep the combination?"

"In his head."

"I think they are telling the truth, Mrs. Glass," said the Japanese man. He was big, with small hands and feet, and dressed in Western style in a suit that was slightly too tight for him. "They are very scared. I think they would tell us if they knew."

Mrs. Glass took out a cigarette and lit it, the smoke curling around her face. She was still dressed for the weather in a waterproof coat and wide-brimmed hat that shadowed her face.

"I guess you're right, Sakata. You reckon you can crack it?"

"I can try, but it is a very new design. Very clever."

"What do you want me to do with the brats?" said the young man, pinching his lower lip between thumb and finger.

"Lock 'em up somewhere out of the way," said Mrs. Glass. "We'll take 'em with us. It might be useful to have a coupla hostages. This storm is going to make everything difficult. If we don't need 'em, we'll bury them in the jungle someplace."

"Sure, boss," said the young man, with a grin.

"Oh, and Manny," Mrs. Glass went on, "see if you can't find some tools. We may need to dig this damned thing out of the wall."

"Sure," said Manny, and he turned toward the part of the room that James couldn't see. "Come on, little lady," he said, slicking back his hair with his free hand. "And you, squirt, you're coming with me."

James shrank back into the darkness and held his breath.

In a few seconds the two children came out of the study. They looked very young and very scared. Manny came out after them, holding his pistol casually in front of him and a hurricane lamp in his other hand.

James didn't move and Manny never looked in his direction; instead he studied himself in a large mirror and used the back of his pistol hand to once more straighten his hair. He was a handsome young man, and he knew it. Satisfied, he turned back to the children.

"Up the stairs," he grunted, and the children obediently did as they were told.

James followed, keeping to the shadows, the raging storm again muffling any sounds he made.

When they came to the landing at the top of the stairs Manny halted.

"Hold it right there," he said, and looked around. There was a tall window here, and a bright flash of lightning suddenly threw the young man into silhouette. He was a sinister shape with his gun and lamp. James flattened himself on the stairs, but again Manny didn't look in his direction. Instead, as a clap of thunder boomed outside he prodded the children toward a bedroom door.

"Okay," he said. "Get in there."

"What are you going to do?" asked Precious.

"Just whatever the hell I want to do," jeered Manny, and he rattled the sights of his pistol across his teeth.

"We're not going in there," said Precious.

So the girl had some fight in her.

"Wanna bet?" said Manny.

"We're not," said Precious. "And you can't make us. You won't kill us. She told you not to."

"You think?" said Manny. "I'll tell you what: if you don't get in there right now, I'll shoot you where you stand."

Manny smiled and raised his gun with slow and deadly menace.

The next moment all hell broke loose as a palm tree crashed through the window, flattening Manny. Its great ragged leaves, black and glistening, tangled with splintered wood and shards of broken glass, filled the landing.

After a moment's shock Precious grabbed her brother.

"Run, JJ," she said, and they bolted along the landing.

Manny was bleeding from a cut in the side of his head, and he was soaked through, but he wasn't badly hurt. He got to his feet and fired his gun at the ceiling. Even with the sound of the storm howling through the broken window, the noise was loud and startling.

The two children ran screaming into a bedroom at the other end of the landing, and locked the door.

Manny swore and limped after them. When he got to the door he rattled the handle and roared at the top of his voice, "Open up, you stupid brats. You're only making it worse."

He waited a moment, then stood back and fired three shots into the lock.

There was another window in the end wall and James saw his chance. He had seen how easily the one by the stairs had broken. The wooden frames were old and rotten from the damp sea air.

While Manny was distracted, James darted to the top of the stairs and pelted along the corridor toward him. Manny turned at the last moment, but it was too late. James barged into him and sent him sprawling into the window.

The effect was spectacular. The frame gave way, the glass shattered, and Manny fell through. For a second he appeared to hang in space, an amazed look on his face. Some trick of the churning air was holding him up, then he was struck in the head by some flying debris, and he was whipped quickly away out of sight.

The corridor was turned into a wind tunnel now as the storm howled through the broken windows. It was all James could do to stay on his feet.

He pushed the bedroom door open and the crippled lock fell away.

He could see nothing in the darkness on the other side; Manny had taken the hurricane lamp out into the night with him.

James stood there, waiting for a flash of lightning to illuminate the room. He was just about to whisper Precious's name when something rushed at him, thudded heavily into his chest, and knocked him over backward.

He was badly winded. It was like being attacked by a wild cat, but a lightning burst showed him that it wasn't an animal—it was Precious, her face white with fear.

"Stop it," he gasped. "It's me, James."

"Where's that man?" said Precious.

"He stepped outside for a breath of air," said James.

"What?"

"He's gone. I pushed him out of the window."

Precious helped him up and they moved into the room to shelter from the rain that was driving along the landing.

James saw that Precious was shivering in her thin gold dress.

"We'll be all right," he said. "Where's JJ?"

"Here," said a small voice, and there was JJ, his eyes very wide.

"Is there anywhere we can hide?" said James. "Anywhere they wouldn't think of looking?"

"What about the attic?" said Precious.

"No, that'd be the first place they look."

"There's the icehouse," said JJ. "In the yard. We sometimes hide there from Dad."

"What's an icehouse?"

"It's like an underground room," said the boy. "It's not

69

used anymore. Dad bricked it up, said it was dangerous. But we found a way in last summer."

"How do we get there from here?" said James. "Do we have to go outside?"

"Yes." JJ nodded his head sadly.

"We can't go out there," said Precious.

"We have to," said James. "Even if it wasn't for the gangsters it'll be a lot safer than staying in the house. The storm is tearing the place apart."

"I am *not* going out there," said Precious tetchily, back to her old self.

"We don't have any choice," said James. "Any minute now they're going to come looking for Manny." He turned to JJ. "Once we're outside, how far is it to the icehouse?"

"Not far. You could get there in less than a minute."

"You feeling brave?"

"Yes," he said quietly, though James could tell that he was lying.

James looked at Precious. "And you?"

"It's not bravery," she said. "It's stupidity."

"Sometimes," said James, pulling her out onto the landing, "there's very little difference."

The three of them struggled along to the stairs, which had been turned into a waterfall. The rain was coming in and pouring down them, creating a shallow lake in the hallway.

"We can't risk going to the front door," said James. "If anyone came out of the study we'd be done for."

"Then what?" said Precious.

"We'll climb down the tree," said James.

Before she could stop him, James went over to where the

top of the tree jutted in through the broken window. It was pitch dark outside now, so he couldn't see how bad the storm was, but the noise of it was worse than ever.

Don't stop to think. Don't talk about it. Just do it.

"Be careful," he said, pushing his way past the fronds. "They've got sharp spines, and—" The rest of his sentence was plucked away by the wind.

James could not have prepared himself for just how awful it was outside. The trunk of the tree, which was resting at a forty-five-degree angle, was sharp and slippery at the same time, and the wind thrashed him, like a team of men with broom handles. He clung on with all his strength and slid slowly down.

A lightning strike hit a chimney, which crumbled, spilling bricks down the side of the house. In the brief instant of brightness James saw JJ scrambling to get a hold on the trunk above him.

James shouted some words of support, but they were lost. He had to concentrate on not falling off himself as he inched his way downward, and the next time he looked up there was no sign of JJ, but Precious was out of the window.

James dropped the last few feet and found JJ huddled behind a low wall. He had evidently fallen off, but the ground was so soft and sodden from the rain that he didn't seem to be injured.

At last Precious joined them, fighting for breath, her pretty dress ruined. The three of them had to cling on to each other so as not to be blown away. The air was loaded with flying rubbish and something gave James a nasty, stinging slap in the face.

He put his mouth right next to JJ's ear and shouted as loudly as he could.

"Which way?"

JJ pointed. They were going to have to move across an open stretch of lawn.

This was suicidal madness. James knew it. He closed his eyes. The noise was terrible. The rain forced its way into his nose, his mouth, his ears. He felt like he was drowning.

He held on to one of JJ's hands and Precious took the other.

"Let's go," said James, and they stood up.

CHAPTER 7—YOU HAVE TO LAUGH

Half-crouching, half-crawling, leaning into the wind, they fought the storm inch by inch across the lawn. James and Precious had hold of JJ and they dragged him between them, the rain drilling into their faces, blinding them.

James thought that if they could only just ignore the wind and rain and keep putting one foot in front of the other, keep moving slowly forward, they would eventually make it to safety. They had gone no distance at all, however, before they were blown off their feet and sent spinning and tumbling over the lawn like fallen leaves. They ended up tangled in a hedge that was somehow standing up to all that the elements could throw at it. They wriggled through to the other side and saw that if they slithered on their bellies and kept their heads down, they could use the hedge as a windbreak. The bottom of the hedge was in a small dip where the rain was collecting. The ground had been churned into mud, and the three of them splashed along on their elbows and knees.

But the hedge soon ran out, and when they reached the end James tried to see where they were. The rain was pouring down his face. There was so much of it, it was like being underwater. His body was bruised all over. JJ managed to crawl up next to him. The little boy was coming off the worst of the three of them. He looked like he'd been put through a mangle.

"Where do we go?" yelled James, and JJ tried to get his bearings.

A lightning strike lit the garden bright as daylight for an instant.

"There!" JJ screamed, pointing across the lawn. "That dark patch. There are bushes."

The mound of shrubbery was less than thirty feet away, but it might as well have been three hundred. With no cover, they would be exposed all the way. James looked to see if there was any other available shelter and spotted a white-painted gazebo that until recently had been covered in rambling roses. All that was left were a few tattered stems. The framework was set into a semicircular stone wall that looked just tall enough to offer some protection.

The gazebo wasn't directly on the way; it would mean zigzagging. They would first have to cut diagonally across to the left, into the wind all the way, and then come back to the right. But it was a better bet than striking straight out across the lawn.

James gestured to the others.

"Wait for a lull in the storm," he shouted. "Then we'll make a run for it."

The wind was mainly blowing one way, but it kept swirling and switching direction. In these brief lulls, when it was making its mind up which way to go, there were moments of calm, lasting a few seconds at the most.

James waited, listening for a dip in the deafening roar, feeling the hedge as it strained and flapped next to him.

There.

The noise dropped. The hedge fell still.

"Go!" he shouted, jumping to his feet and grabbing JJ's arm.

He ran for it, hoping that Precious was with them.

Halfway there the wind came back with renewed fury, and to his horror, James saw the gazebo tear loose from its foundations. The whole structure came rolling and bouncing toward them. James threw himself to the ground, hurling JJ into the mud, and the gazebo flew over their heads.

He looked around. Precious was by his side.

"That was close," he yelled, and she nodded. "Think you can try again?" Once more she nodded.

They struggled to their feet, both holding tight on to JJ, but he lost his footing and was plucked up into the air like a kite.

"Don't let go," James shouted, and they managed to pull the poor, bedraggled boy back down to earth.

"We'll have to crawl!"

And crawl they did.

It took them ten minutes. Ten long, hard, painful minutes—rain and mud slicing into their faces, bits of tree, stones, broken wood, and roof tiles whizzing past and occasionally crashing into them. At last they reached what was left of the gazebo and huddled below its broken wall.

The next leg would be easier. This time they would have the wind behind them, but they would still have to be careful not to get blown over or pushed too far along.

James couldn't look at the other two. He didn't want to see the hopelessness and fear in their eyes. Instead he just took hold of JJ's hand again. It felt tiny and cold and fragile.

"Let's move," he said and set off, letting the wind carry them along. It was almost like sailing a boat, or crossing a river with the current. They were nearly flying; they bounded across the lawn with giant strides and hurtled into the shrubbery. Precious crashed in next to them in a mad rush.

They had made it this far.

James went after JJ as he scrabbled across the earth beneath the bushes to a small brick construction like a chimney top. There was a hinged wooden board covering the opening. James pulled it up and JJ wriggled inside. James made sure Precious got in safely then followed her down, pulling the board shut over his head. There were metal rungs set into the wall, and James groped his way down until he felt a solid floor beneath his feet.

It was dark down here and quiet and unexpectedly dry.

After a few seconds there was the scraping of a match, and then an oil lamp's glow illuminated the room.

They were about twenty feet below ground in a round, windowless chamber with a domed ceiling. The walls were built of tightly packed stone blocks.

"What is this place?" said James.

"Before electricity they used to store ice down here," said JJ proudly. "It'd stay cold all year."

"Where did they get the ice from?" said James.

"They'd bring it down from the mountains," said JJ, "cut from frozen lakes and ponds."

James smiled at JJ. "Well done," he said. "They'll never find us down here, and we can sit out the storm in safety."

"We built a den," said JJ, and he showed James a pile of old mattresses, blankets, and cushions.

"Perfect," said James, and JJ gave a great, happy grin.

"We could have been killed," said Precious.

"Yes," said James, "but we weren't. Isn't that a good feeling? The gods are smiling on us today."

"Smiling on us?" Precious gave a bitter snort of laughter. "Well, I would hate to see what happens when they're angry."

"We've been lucky," said James. "Isn't that enough?"

Precious shook her head. "This is terrible," she wailed. "Just terrible. Look at my dress; it's ruined. I just got it a week ago. It's by Jean Patou of Paris."

James couldn't help laughing. The dress looked like a bundle of wet rags.

"Maybe you should have worn a swimsuit," he said. JJ laughed.

Precious gave them both a filthy look. "Why did nobody try to help us?" she said. "The servants? Why didn't they help?"

"What could they do?" said James. "Those gangsters had guns. Maybe they *did* try to help. You don't know. What was in your father's safe anyway?"

"All his money," said Precious. "Everything. He doesn't trust Mexican banks."

James laughed again, but he stopped abruptly when Precious slapped him hard on the face. "How dare you laugh at us," she said, and the next moment she burst into tears. "I'm sorry," she said. "But I'm so scared. I don't know what's happening."

"Don't worry about it," said James. "I'm scared too."

He wiped his face, and his hand came away bloody, but it wasn't his own blood. He realized that Precious's hand was bleeding.

"Are you all right?" he asked, nodding toward the wound. She hadn't even noticed the cut before, but now that she did she let out a sob and went very white. James looked at himself and saw that he was also covered in small nicks and cuts, probably from climbing down the palm. He had scratches all down his front, and he felt truly battered.

"I think I'm hurt too," said JJ in a small, quiet voice. Sure enough, there was a nasty gash in the little boy's thigh.

"Have you got anything in here we can clean that with?" James asked.

"Like what?" said Precious.

"I don't know," said James. "Antiseptic, alcohol, clean water . . ."

"There's nothing," said JJ, sadly shaking his head.

"Never mind," said James. "The rain should be clean enough. Once the storm passes we'll sort you out, but we should bandage it at least. We don't want to get any dirt in the cut. Precious, tear a strip off your dress."

"I will do no such thing," she protested.

"You said yourself it was ruined," said James. "He's your brother, help him."

"Turn away."

"Oh don't be so silly," said James, and he stepped forward, snatched up the hem of her dress, and tore off a long strip where it was already frayed.

Precious said nothing, but James felt that if he hadn't been attending to her brother, she might have hit him again.

He soon had JJ bandaged, and Precious tore off another strip to put around her own hand.

JJ sat quietly on a pile of cushions with his back to the wall, looking very young and very small. He was obviously terrified, and the shock was just starting to show. James felt sorry for him, and knew how lonely he must be right now. He put a blanket around him and the boy looked pathetically grateful.

It was cold in here, but the lamp gave off a feeble heat, and the three of them huddled around it, lost in their own thoughts. Outside, muffled by several feet of earth, the storm was a distant rumble and clatter.

James eventually fell into a fitful, feverish sleep. When he awoke some time later he was coughing and his whole body ached. He got up and stamped about the place to try to force some life into his muscles. It was only after a while that he noticed that he couldn't hear anything.

There was a tiny glimmer of light coming down the ventilation shaft. He hobbled over, his stiff joints creaking.

He looked up. Sunlight.

He climbed the rungs and gingerly pushed the door open.

Bright sunlight.

Warm sunlight.

He crawled out.

The storm had passed. He had never been more pleased to see a clear blue sky. He fought his way through the wreckage of the shrubbery and stumbled out onto the lawn.

He turned his face up to the sun and let its energy fill him as he breathed in fresh, clean air.

It was good to be alive.

He went back to the shaft and called down to the others. Soon they emerged, blinking, into the daylight, and Precious even managed a smile.

Her smile soon died, however, when she saw what the storm had done. There was hardly a tree left standing, the garden looked like a battlefield, and the house was badly damaged.

Inside it was worse; water and debris had got in everywhere, and there was a fetid, damp smell.

Apart from three frogs and a lizard in the hallway, there were no signs of life. The staff seemed to have all left, as had the intruders, leaving a large, ragged hole in the study wall where the safe had been.

Precious sat down on the stairs and wept.

"What are we going to do?" she said.

"We're not going to sit around here feeling sorry for ourselves," said James. "That's for sure. We're going to go down into the town. Somebody there will be able to help us."

"Will Dad come for us?" said JJ.

"If he can," said James. "If he can find somewhere to land. If he didn't get caught up in the storm."

"If, if, if . . ." said Precious. "You don't know anything."

James sighed but said nothing. Instead he turned on his heel and went back outside into the sunlight.

Presently, the other two joined him. Precious looked sullen and grumpy, JJ looked anxious.

"What's that on the lawn?" he said.

James looked where he was pointing.

"Maybe all the servants didn't leave after all," he said.

"What do you mean?" said Precious.

"I think that's Alonzo," said James.

They walked over.

Sure enough, it was the elderly servant. He was lying on the lawn, half-hidden by a mess of leaves and branches.

He had either died from the blow to the head or he had drowned. James didn't have the stomach to try to find out how. Mercifully the old man's face was hidden from them.

JJ stared with fascinated horror at the body. He had never seen a dead person before.

It wasn't the only body they saw that morning.

On their way down into town they passed several collapsed buildings where weeping families were digging in the rubble. It was like the aftermath of a war. Everything was flattened and smashed. People were wandering around in a daze, not knowing what to do. Here and there were awful reminders of what might have been: flags and bunting from the carnival, wrecked floats.

The town center was worse; most of it was under about a foot of water. The drains had not been able to cope, and the sea had surged inland, bringing wrecked boats with it. It was as if someone had simply picked up the town and shaken it.

To make matters worse, fires had broken out. The locals were working together to try to deal with them, but there seemed to be no one in charge.

James and the two children wandered the drowned streets aimlessly.

"Somehow we need to get in contact with your father," James said eventually. "Maybe if we could find a radio set somewhere?"

"We could try the police station," said Precious.

"Good idea," said James.

Their hopes of getting help at the police station were short-lived, however, because when they arrived they were met by a bizarre sight.

A large fishing boat was jutting out of the front of the building, which had been reduced to little more than a pile of rubble. A group of policemen were standing around arguing and waving their hands.

It was a few moments before James realized that it was the very boat he had come down from Tampico on. And there was the skipper, Garcia, standing a little way off, talking quietly with one of the plainclothes detectives who had arrested the pickpocket.

James and the others hurried over.

"Garcia," said James, "what's happened?"

"Is very bad," said Garcia, nodding sadly at his boat.

"Is all very bad," said the policeman, looking the children up and down.

"We need help," said Precious, and the policeman laughed.

"Join the line," he said. "Everybody in Tres Hermanas needs help. What makes you so special?"

"I am Precious Stone, my father is—"

"Go home," said the policeman flatly.

"It's not that simple," said James.

"Yes it is," said the policeman. "There is nothing I can do for you. Maybe in a couple of weeks we will be back to normal, maybe a couple of months, maybe a couple of years. Come back then."

"Please," said Precious, and the policeman rounded on her angrily.

"Go away. Leave me alone," he snapped. "I have a whole jail of escaped prisoners to catch."

The policeman walked off, fuming.

James turned to Garcia, who shrugged.

"I don't know what to do," he said. "My boat was my whole life. My only income, and now . . . look at her."

James looked. "I'm sorry," he said, but despite everything, he found himself wanting to laugh. The boat looked so funny sticking out of the building. He put a hand over his mouth but couldn't stop a snort from escaping. The next thing he knew, Garcia was grinning too.

"She does look funny," he said, and in a moment the two of them were both helpless with laughter.

Precious made a face. "I'm glad you've found something to laugh about," she said, which only made the two of them laugh even more.

"Sometimes," said Garcia, when he had calmed down, "when God makes a big joke like this, you have to laugh."

James introduced Garcia to JJ and Precious, and then told the Mexican everything that had happened last night.

"So you can see the trouble we're in," said Precious when he had finished. "Is there nothing anyone can do for us?"

"All the lines are down," Garcia explained. "There is no power in the whole of the town. No way of communicating with the outside world. It could be the same as this all the way along the coast. I am going to try and see if I can get my radio from the boat. If it is undamaged, it has a battery. It may be useful. If I were you I would try to get inland."

"We can't leave town," said Precious. "What if Daddy comes looking for us?"

"How will he get here?" said Garcia. "The roads are blocked, boats sunk, harbor in ruins, water everywhere. There will be nowhere he can land his plane."

"We're not leaving," said Precious.

"You must," said Garcia. "There is no electricity, no food, no drinking water. The sewers have all burst. Soon there will be sickness and disease. The boy is bleeding. You must get him to a doctor. There is nobody here who can help. You will find nurses in Puente Nuevo, in the mission house on the other side of river. They will look after you. Take what you can and get up there. There is still one road open. If the river breaks its banks, then even this will close. If I can get my radio fixed I will try and contact your father, tell him you have moved to safety. He has a radio on his plane. But, please, go from here while you still can."

"I don't believe this is happening," said Precious.

James looked at her.

"Does your father have a motorcar?" he asked.

"He has three," said Precious. "But what good will they be to us?"

CHAPTER 8—"IT'S A DOOZY"

The garage doors were hanging half off their hinges. James forced them open. The roof had been blown off and it was full of leaves and water, but, miraculously, the three cars were largely undamaged.

In pride of place was a big silver Duesenberg Model J. It was long and low and powerful-looking, with a great square bonnet ending in a gleaming radiator grille and huge twin headlamps. James ran his hand admiringly along its sleek flank.

"Do you like it?" asked JJ proudly.

"It's beautiful," said James.

"It's a Doozy," said JJ.

"I know," said James. "I've seen pictures of it in magazines, but I've never seen one in real life before."

Four creased exhaust tubes snaked out of the bonnet from just in front of a side-mounted spare wheel and disappeared down through the wide running board that swept back from the front wheel arch.

James whistled. This was the very latest model, an SJ, with a supercharger fitted next to the engine. It put out 320 horsepower and had a top speed of an incredible 135 mph. There were only a very few of these in existence, and they were all owned by film stars and royalty and wealthy gangsters.

The soft roof had been damaged by the storm, so James folded it back.

"Just what do you propose we do?" said Precious. "Drive it ourselves?"

"Right first time," said James.

"No," said Precious. "Oh no. Daddy would never allow that."

"I think you are probably more valuable to him than his damned car," said James. "Although if it was down to me, I'd pick the car."

JJ made a face and James smiled at him.

"It's all right," he said. "I was only joking."

JJ brightened. "Do you know how to drive?" he said.

"I do," said James.

"But you're not old enough," Precious protested. "I won't let you."

"Okay then," said James, "we'll stay here and rot."

Precious narrowed her eyes and thought about their situation. She looked at JJ. He was very pale and his trousers were stained with blood. At last she nodded.

"Good," said James. "Get together anything you might need for the journey."

James went to his wrecked room and found the sodden suitcase that he had never got around to unpacking the night before. All his things inside were soaked through. He needed to change, though—the clothes he was wearing were filthy and ripped. He searched the house until he came to the servants' quarters at the top. Miraculously there was an undamaged wardrobe in one of the rooms whose contents were dry. He changed into a loose short-sleeved shirt and a pair of baggy trousers. He looked at himself in the mirror.

His skin had darkened in the weeks he had been out here. He could easily pass as Mexican.

He collected some dry blankets and a coat, then went down to the kitchen to salvage any food that wasn't spoiled. He also found two large canisters of drinking water.

He was loading the Duesenberg when the two children arrived, lugging a heavy suitcase each. Precious had changed into another impractical dress and brought all her best clothes. JJ had brought his toys.

James was too tired to argue. He had already filled the luggage box at the back and one of the small rear seats. He found some rope and tied the children's cases to the side of the car.

They climbed aboard: Precious in the front next to James, and JJ squeezed into the back next to the luggage.

James familiarized himself with the controls and then gingerly drove out of the garage. In five minutes they were nosing down the hill away from Tres Hermanas toward the wide, flat plain that lay inland behind the town.

The car was a beast, frighteningly powerful. James had to struggle to keep it under control. If he lost concentration the four-foot-long engine would leap into action, and the car would tear away like a wild bull.

At the bottom of the hill the road was blocked by a group of men with scarves and handkerchiefs tied around their faces. For a moment James feared that they were bandits, but then he saw that they were clearing something out of a storm drain by the side of the road. The handkerchiefs were to protect them and keep out the awful smell.

James slowed down carefully and stopped.

Lying in the dirt were the bloated bodies of several dogs and a goat. And laid out under stained sheets were the shapes of three people.

The men were hauling out another body, and as it came up out of the drain, James realized with a shock who it was.

It was Angel Corona. He must have escaped from the jail when Garcia's boat smashed it open, only to end up drowned and stuck in a drain.

James got out of the car and walked over.

The men put Angel down. He lay there as if asleep. There were no signs of any injuries. James was once more struck by how similar the two of them looked. How easily it could have been *him* lying there. The hand of death had passed over Tres Hermanas last night, and it hadn't cared who it touched.

The last of the bodies was up now, and the men cleared the road. James got back into the car.

"Let's get out of here," said Precious, a hand over her nose.

James shifted the car into gear and eased ahead. He longed to get on to the open road and let the car loose a little, but it soon became obvious that there *was* no open road. When they reached the main route out of town they found it clogged with traffic.

A silent, bedraggled stream of humanity was pouring out of Tres Hermanas. Men and women, old people, children, some in carts and wagons, many riding donkeys or horses, but most on foot, carrying bundles on their back or pushing handcarts laden with clothes, valuables, chickens, and babies. A handful of cars pushed their way slowly through, the drivers leaning on their horns. An old bus crawled along, belching out black fumes. It was packed with people, and more passengers were clinging to the luggage rack on the roof.

The road, which was slightly raised, stretched away across submerged fields toward the distant mountains of the Sierra Madre Oriental. The devastation caused by the storm seemed to go on forever. The wind and rain had scoured the countryside, drowning the land, stripping the crops, and flattening trees. There were dead cows floating everywhere, their bodies swelling in the heat.

James joined the procession and they crept forward, the sun burning down onto their heads. It was stop–start all the way, and James had to keep turning the engine off to prevent it from overheating. By midafternoon they had traveled only a few miles, and the three of them were hot and grumpy and frustrated. Precious had done nothing but complain all day. She complained about leaving Tres Hermanas; she complained about James's driving; she complained about the other people on the road; she complained that her cut hand was hurting; she complained when JJ complained that *his* cut leg was hurting. She complained about her servants.

"They probably planned the whole thing with that woman," she said. "I bet they planned to rob us all along. You can't trust a Mexican. That policeman, he was the same. He didn't care one jot that we are in trouble. They hate us. They hate us because we are American, because we are rich . . ."

At first James tried to forgive her. She was tired and scared and missing her father. She had shown some courage during the storm, but she wore him down, and no matter how hard he tried to shut her voice out of his head, it whined on like a fly trapped in a jar.

By the time the sun was setting and the light fading from the land they could just make out the town of Puente Nuevo up ahead, but they had come to a virtual standstill. Nothing seemed to be moving, and the people were getting even more packed together on the road.

In the end, James found a relatively dry spot and pulled over to the side so that they could sleep.

The night was crystal clear and cold. The great black dome of the sky was studded with thousands of shining stars. A full moon shone down, turning the standing water silver. James marveled at how the deadly, stinging rain of last night had created this magical scene.

He sat there watching the endless procession of people passing slowly along the road in silence.

As the night became colder they wrapped themselves in the blankets that James had brought from the house and tried to get some sleep.

By sunrise most of the refugees from Tres Hermanas had passed by. There were a few stragglers, but the road was much clearer.

"We should make better progress today," James told Precious when she woke up.

"I hope so," she said, and checked her appearance in a small vanity mirror she had brought along.

She was not pleased.

"I look a fright," she moaned. "My hair is a mess. My face is sunburned. This is a disaster."

James ignored her and prepared a breakfast of stale bread and cheese. They drank some of their precious water, and then, with a cool breeze blowing, James gunned the Duesenberg toward Puente Nuevo.

They overtook a couple of broken-down vehicles: an ancient truck with twenty or so patient Mexicans squatting in the shade it cast as the driver tried to repair the engine, and a dusty Ford with a flat tire. Then they came to a party of nuns on mules going the other way. James presumed they wanted to see if there was anything they could do to help out in Tres Hermanas.

As they went past, the nuns pointed back toward Puente Nuevo, and all talked at once in high, anxious voices.

"What are they saying?" said Precious.

"I don't know," said James. "My Spanish isn't that good."

"Something about a river," said JJ.

James noticed another broken-down truck farther along the road. As he was idly looking at it, he saw, with a shock, that there was a safe loaded onto the back of it. He made slits of his eyes and squinted into the glare of the sun.

There were three men standing next to the truck. Unmistakably members of the gang who had come to the Stones' house the night before.

"Squash down on the floor and cover yourselves with the blankets," he hissed to his passengers.

"Why?" said Precious.

"Just do it," said James. "And do it quickly. There are some people up ahead you don't want to meet. This car's pretty conspicuous and they're bound to give it a look over."

Precious and JJ did as they were told, and as soon as they

were clear of the dawdling nuns, James put his foot down and shifted gear.

The engine gave a great crackling roar, and James was forced back into his seat as they leaped forward. By the time they came to the truck, they were traveling at speed and the three men were a faceless blur. James kept his foot down, gripping the wheel tightly as he steered along the uneven, pitted road. For a moment all his worries were forgotten, and he felt a wild exhilaration. He wanted to whoop and howl and drive on recklessly, but the next thing he knew they had arrived at Puente Nuevo, a jumble of buildings tightly packed together on either side of a wide river.

The town was busy with refugees, and James had to slow down and drive carefully through the narrow, winding streets, scared that he might run someone down.

Puente Nuevo had been built long before cars had been invented, and the length of the Duesenberg made it difficult to get around some bends. At one point they came to a crumbling covered archway, and James scraped the side of the car trying to fit through it.

"Be careful, you clumsy idiot," said Precious, wincing.

"Perhaps you'd rather drive," said James.

Precious said nothing in response to this, and they drove on in angry silence until they came to the tail end of a traffic jam. A bus and several cars were stuck, and there was no room to turn around. The buildings on either side cut out all the light and kept the street in inky shade.

"You said it would be better today," said Precious, grumpily.

"I was wrong," said James.

"Can't you do anything right?"

"It seems not."

"We'd be better off by ourselves. You're only making matters worse, dragging us across the countryside."

James turned off the engine.

"All right," he said. "That's it. You're on your own." He got out of the car and slammed the door.

"Don't leave us," whined JJ.

"It's all right," said Precious, "he doesn't mean it. He's calling our bluff."

"Am I?"

JJ began to cry.

"Oh, don't be such a baby," said Precious. "If this rude English boy wants to abandon us, then let him. I've had enough of him."

"I like him," said JJ. "He saved us."

"You do *not* like him," said Precious. "I forbid it. You are my brother and you will do as I say."

James leaned on the side of the car and glared at the girl.

"Listen to me," he said. "I'm going to go and see what the holdup is. You can be here or not when I get back, I don't much care either way. The choice is yours. If you want to go and find someone else to help you, that's fine with me. But if you *are* here, you're going to put up with me. All right? You're going to stop complaining and you're going to do as you're told."

"Well," said Precious. "I think you have shown us your true colors, James Bond. You go off, if you like, but I can tell you now, we will *not* be here when you get back."

"Good," said James, and he strode off angrily and squeezed past the bus.

The street opened out into a small, busy square. On the far side was a bridge that was choked with traffic. James realized that it must be the only way across the river, which was why everything had slowed down last night as people approached the town.

Garcia had said that they'd find the nurses in the mission house on the other side of the river. It looked like it would be some time before they could make it over. He wondered if there was anywhere he could buy some fresh food while they were waiting, but could see no shops or stalls.

There was a gaggle of excited villagers along the riverbank, and he now saw that some of them were carrying sandbags and rocks and bits of masonry. He went over to see what they were doing, and his heart sank.

The level of the river was dangerously high, and the locals were trying to shore up the bank.

He looked back toward the bridge. The people making their way over looked nervous. The people waiting to cross looked even more nervous.

If the river burst its banks there would be chaos.

A thin trickle of water had already started to snake across the flagstones near the water's edge. Four men rushed over with shovels and a wheelbarrow. They frantically started shoveling sand and grit into the breach.

It was hopeless—just as they stopped up one gap, another one would open up until soon there were three or four small streams flowing into the square.

James had spent many happy hours on the beach when he was younger, building dams across streams. Half the fun of it was watching the dams give way when the pressure of water behind got too great. He remembered just how quickly a tiny dribble coming over the top could soon turn into a raging torrent and wash away everything in its path.

He turned and ran back toward the street where the Duesenberg was parked, then dodged in and out of the line of cars until he saw Precious and JJ waiting for him.

"I wanted to leave, but JJ insisted we stay," said Precious.

"We're not out of danger yet," said James, vaulting over the side into the driver's seat.

"What do you mean?" asked Precious.

"We've got to get out of here, fast," said James, putting the car into reverse. Luckily there was no one behind them. "The river's about to flood," he explained. "That must be what those nuns were trying to tell us."

He twisted around in his seat and started to move the car slowly backward.

"Look," said JJ.

James faced the front. Water was beginning to stream down the road. A young girl and a woman carrying a baby squeezed past them, shouting.

"Hell," said James. "It's coming faster than I feared."

He stepped on the accelerator and reversed as quickly as he dared, bumping and scraping the car on both sides as he went. Precious shouted at him to be careful, but in a moment there was a great roaring, rushing sound, and her shouts turned to screams of terror.

James risked looking back the way they had come.

A wall of water was surging down the street, pushing everything in front of it.

He was going to have to try to outrun it.

CHAPTER 9—THE RETURN OF ANGEL CORONA

Swollen by the abnormal amount of rain that had been dumped on the countryside, the river was carrying twice as much water as it would normally hold. There were breaks all along its length that were harmlessly spilling water onto the land, but here in Puente Nuevo, where it squeezed through the town, its pent-up force was potentially lethal.

And now that force had been released and it rushed free, like a genie from a lamp. Water surged through the narrow streets, searching for a way out. Anything in its path was picked up and bowled along.

There was nowhere to turn the car around, and James could do nothing except drive backward down the street, the Duesenberg's meaty engine howling in complaint.

He was just managing to keep ahead of the racing flood, but a car can only go so fast in reverse, and the water was gaining on them.

"Faster," Precious shouted.

"I can't go any faster," James protested.

They came to the archway the car had clipped earlier. James swore. It had been hard enough getting through forward, going through backward at speed was going to be nigh on impossible.

Just as he feared, they hit the opening at the wrong angle

and the car crunched to a halt, throwing the children back against their seats.

They were wedged in the arch, unable to go either forward or backward. They had lost the race. Before they had a chance to recover from the crash, the water hit them, smashing into the front of the car and foaming up over the bonnet.

Unable to flow through the archway, the water rose steadily. Soon it was pouring over the top of the doors.

"We can't stay here," said James. "We'll have to get out."

"My things," wailed Precious.

"Leave them," said James. "You'll be drowned."

It was a mad scramble, but the three of them just made it out of the rear of the car, which was acting like a giant cork stuck in the archway. Some of the water was getting past, but the bulk of it was being held back.

James, Precious, and JJ hurried down the street, ankle deep in filthy water. JJ was limping badly.

"The car should stop it for a while," said James. "We might be in luck."

Even as he said it, though, there was a groan and a crack behind them, and James looked around to see part of the arch give way and fall into the street. He took hold of JJ's hand and pulled him faster.

The next moment the rest of the arch collapsed and the car sailed out, like a great steel gondola.

It barreled down the street toward them, carried along by the sheer force of water behind it.

Precious screamed.

James tried to speed up, but it was difficult running

through the rising water, which tugged at his legs. It was clear they would never make it as far as the next side street. James desperately looked for an open window or door, but the houses were all still closed up after the storm. Then he spotted, about fifteen feet ahead, a stairway leading up on to the roof of a building.

"If we can just make it to those steps, we'll be all right," he said, picking up JJ. With nothing to weigh her down, Precious overtook him, running surprisingly fast in her dress.

Behind them they could hear the rushing, roaring sound of the water and the car grinding nearer and nearer, banging and crunching into the walls on either side.

"Hold on," James gasped to JJ. His legs were giving out and he hoped he would have the strength to reach the steps.

Precious got there safely and raced up to the roof. James was right behind her, but so was the car. It knocked into him and he lost his footing; then something else bashed into him and JJ was torn from his arms.

James was thrown forward onto the steps; the water washed over him like a wave. Then, coughing and spluttering, he got to his feet and dragged himself to the roof.

"Where's JJ?" he gasped, sick that he had lost the boy when he had been so close to safety. "Can you see him?"

Precious pointed into the street, too terrified to speak.

There was JJ, being carried off by the water, clinging to the bonnet of the car.

"We've got to help him," Precious yelled, and James quickly looked out across the flat roofs to get his bearings. There was a clear view of the town from here, and he could see water flowing down all the streets on this side of the river.

He saw the route that the car would take, and he plotted his own route across the rooftops.

"What can we do?" Precious shouted.

James sprinted along the roof and jumped across to the next house, and then the next, keeping pace with JJ. He thought that he could take a shortcut and maybe get ahead of the car, and as he raced along, he checked the way ahead. Luckily the buildings were tightly packed, but there were still a couple of hair-raising gaps that he had to get across.

He didn't stop to think twice. He was used to this sort of thing, and he ran as fast as he could, timing his jumps perfectly. The first wide gap he took in one clean jump, and on the second one he landed on his belly on the edge of the next building, and despite being badly winded, he scrabbled up and carried on.

His calculations were right. Soon he had overtaken the flood. He ran on until he found the perfect spot and threw himself off the roof just as the car passed beneath him.

He landed in the front seat. The car rocked from side to side. He held on. The Duesenberg was half full of water, but it was still afloat. And JJ was still clamped to the bonnet and holding on for dear life.

James stretched a hand out over the windscreen toward the little boy.

"Don't panic," he said. "You'll be all right. Just stay calm."

JJ looked at him and nodded.

"Can you reach me?" said James.

JJ said nothing. He steeled himself, then let go with one hand and held it, shaking, in the air. James grabbed hold and hauled him into the car.

"That was kind of fun," said JJ, but James could feel his whole body trembling.

"It's not over yet," said James.

"You'll look after me, won't you?" said JJ.

"Of course."

"You won't leave us, will you? Whatever Precious says."

"No. Everything's going to be all right now."

But what James hadn't seen was that just ahead of them three streets came together. Water was pouring down all of them and meeting in a great churning, foaming, turbulent mess of scummy, yellow floodwater at the junction.

The car steamed into the middle of it, and its nose went under, throwing James and JJ out. James was spun over and over, around and around, with no idea which way was up and which was down.

He was smashed into the wall of a building, then dragged along the ground, then somehow he was thrown clear and found himself washed up on someone's window ledge.

He vomited up a bellyful of water and looked for any sign of JJ.

Two dead bodies washed past, but neither of them was JJ, thank God. And then he saw a tiny dark shape bobbing in the waves. It was JJ's head. There was no way James could get to him, though. To go back into the water would be suicide.

Maybe the boy would stay afloat. The escaping floodwater couldn't go on like this forever. Sooner or later it would peter out.

But the boy was only seven, and James didn't even know if he could swim.

"Don't give up, JJ," he said bitterly, choking back hot tears. "Don't give up. . . ."

James felt utterly useless. Twice he had lost the boy now. He had let him down badly. He made a promise that if JJ lived he wouldn't sleep or eat or think about himself for one moment until he and his sister were safe and well.

But would JJ live? He watched the little boy's head being carried away down the street. Every so often it would sink from view, and James would hold his breath until it appeared again; each time, though, it stayed under longer.

Then he saw someone step out into the raging flood, which was almost up to his chest.

It was Garcia.

He stood there, battling the water that was trying to push him away, and snatched JJ from the torrent. James saw that he had a rope tied around his waist, and he used it to get them back to safety.

James wept with relief.

James stayed on the window ledge for half an hour while the flow of water gradually died down. Then he heard someone sloshing along the alleyway, and there was a very miserable-looking Precious.

He jumped down from his perch. There was still a sizable stream flowing, but he could stand up safely without fear of being washed away.

"Where is he?" said Precious, fear cracking her voice.

"He's all right," said James.

"Oh, thank God." Precious collapsed into tears, and James took hold of her.

"He's all right," James repeated. "We'll find him."

Precious seemed numb. James told her what had happened and took her to the spot where he had seen Garcia pull JJ from the water.

They found the two of them on a balcony. Garcia was wiping the boy's forehead and drying him in the sun. JJ was awake but very feeble. Precious hugged him and kissed him, and babbled about how worried she had been. JJ responded well to this mothering. He sat up and smiled and started talking feverishly about his adventures "on the boat."

The strip of dress he had been wearing as a bandage had been torn off in the water, and his cut leg was exposed.

The wound looked red, raw, and ugly. The two sides were not healing. Garcia inspected it, a frown on his dark, handsome features.

"Be brave," he said. "You must hold on. Everything is going to be all right. I fixed up my radio. I was coming here to find you and tell you the good news."

"What good news?" said Precious.

"Your father is all right," said Garcia with a reassuring smile. "He landed safely in the jungle near Palenque, but his plane is damaged. He is stuck there."

"Did you speak to him?" said Precious.

Garcia shook his head. "He made contact with the port authority in Veracruz. I spoke to them and passed on a message telling him that you had come to Puente Nuevo." Garcia stood up. "Now," he said, "we will need to find something to clean the wound. James, you come with me; we will see what we can find."

James followed Garcia down a flight of steps to the street.

Garcia put a hand on his arm. He looked serious.

"The boy is not well," he said. "His leg is becoming infected, and he swallowed a lot of dirty water. We cannot get to the mission now. The flood will have taken the bridge. We must find medicine and clean water on this side."

"I'll go and see if I can find what happened to the car," said James. "I might be able to salvage something."

"Good," said Garcia. "I will meet you back here."

James found the car about a hundred yards down the street on the outskirts of town, lying on its side, wrecked. He felt sorry that such a beautiful thing had been spoiled. There was no sign of the suitcases. They had been ripped from the sides. The food was ruined, but one of the water canisters was still in the luggage box on the back. He unscrewed the cap and took a drink. It was warm and tasted horrible, but he knew that it would do some good.

He looked in the glove compartment and found a pair of sunglasses and a soggy map. He stuffed the map into his pocket and put the sunglasses on. The sun was harsh and bright this morning, and he had the beginnings of a headache.

He lugged the water back up the road to the house, but when he got to the balcony, Precious and JJ had disappeared. He called out their names and looked around, but there was no sign of them. He wondered whether Garcia had got back before him and taken them to safety, but when, a few moments later, the Mexican showed up, carrying a bottle of neat alcohol and a roll of clean bandages, he said that he had no idea where they were.

Then Garcia spotted a cigarette butt, still smoldering on the floor of the balcony.

"That was not here before," he said. "Someone has come."

"Maybe someone's helping them," said James, hopefully, though there was a cold feeling of unease in his gut.

"Would the girl go without saying anything?" said Garcia.

"I wouldn't put it past her," said James. "I'm not her favorite person in the world."

"We must find them," said Garcia.

"They can't be long gone," said James. "Maybe if we split up. They didn't go down the main road away from town, because I would have seen them."

"And they did not come up toward the main square either," said Garcia. "They must have gone down one of the other streets."

They walked back up to where the two side streets joined, and James and Garcia took one each.

James hurried along, glancing into alleyways as he went. A few people were beginning to emerge from their houses and survey the damage. James stopped and asked a couple in a mixture of pidgin Spanish and dumb show if they had seen an American girl and boy. On the third time of asking, an old peasant pointed James in the direction he was already headed.

He ran on, and as he rounded a bend, he came to a small square. There was an arcade around the edge, and a few tatty trees stood in the middle. He saw Precious and JJ sitting in the shade of a tree and was just about to call out to them when some sixth sense told him to hold his tongue.

He looked again.

There was a familiar truck parked nearby, with its bonnet

up. On its back was Mr. Stone's safe, and standing around it, peering at the engine, were the American gangsters.

James backed into the shadows and jumped as someone clapped a hand on his shoulder.

He spun around, ready to fight, but it was only Garcia.

"It's them," said James, putting a finger to his lips and shrinking deeper into the shade. "The people who came to the house."

"Do they know you?" asked Garcia.

James shook his head.

"None of them saw me last night," he said. "Except maybe the one I pushed out of the window. Manny, I think he was called. He may have got a look at me, I don't know. But there's no sign of him."

"Good."

"What will we do?" James asked.

Garcia looked him up and down and pushed his hair back from his face.

"Pretend you are with me," he said. "We will call their bluff. We cannot leave the children with them."

So saying, Garcia strode into the square with James tagging along behind. As they got nearer, Garcia plastered a big stupid grin on his face.

"*Hola*," he said, exaggerating his accent. "You have a problem? Your engine, he not work, eh?"

The three men and the woman straightened and turned warily.

"You know about engines?" said the short, square one, his voice harsh and grating. There was a battered look about him. Like he had been in one too many fistfights.

"*Sí*," said Garcia, cheerfully. "I know about engines. You like I fix him for you?"

"Maybe," said the short man. He had a slight squint so that it was hard to tell exactly where he was looking. But now he seemed to be looking at James for the first time. James smiled back at him, and he frowned, flicking his focus from one eye to the other.

"Don't I know you?" he said after a while.

"I no think so," said Garcia. "He is my cousin."

One of the other men looked over. It was the skinny one with the big ears.

"Whatzat?" he said, his large Adam's apple bobbing in his stringy neck. "What you sayin', Strabo?"

"I recognize the kid from somewhere," said the short one, loudly, almost shouting.

"Sure you do," said his skinny friend. "He's the kid we saw the local coppers nabbing in Tres Hermanas."

"Yeah. That's right," said Strabo.

"My name is Angel Corona," said James, with an attempt at a Mexican accent. It didn't sound at all convincing to him, but he prayed that it would fool the Americans.

"What happened to you?" said Strabo, who had evidently bought it. "They let you go?"

"I escaped in the storm," said James, growing more confident. "The jail was broken."

"I heard that," said Strabo, and he laughed. "Good on you, kid, you put one over on them beaner flatfoots."

James laughed now and Garcia joined in.

Precious and JJ were looking at them in complete bemusement. James took off his sunglasses for a second and winked. To the gangsters it would have appeared to be just a show of macho cockiness, but he hoped that Precious would take the hint and keep her mouth shut for once.

"So what is wrong with your engine?" said Garcia.

"Damn thing keeps cutting out on us," said Strabo. "You fix her up, we'll pay you well. And if you can get us out of this stinking place we'll pay you even better."

"I like the sound of that," said Garcia, grinning more widely than ever. "Angel will help me."

"That's fine with me," said Strabo. "He's one of us, after all."

"Where you wanna go?" said Garcia.

"Back to civilization."

"No problem," said Garcia.

Strabo glanced over at the safe on the back of the truck.

"We've got us a rather precious cargo, though," he said.

"No problem," said Garcia again, and he walked over to inspect the engine.

Throughout all this, the blond woman, Mrs. Glass, had been smoking a cigarette and watching. Her face showed nothing beneath the wide brim of her hat.

"Can we trust them?" she said finally.

"All Mexicans care about are greenbacks," rasped Strabo. "So long as we pay him, he's one happy greaser."

"We don't want any trouble with the law," said Mrs. Glass.

"Who does?" said Garcia, looking up from the engine.

Mrs. Glass sniffed.

"You cause us any trouble," she said to Garcia and James,

"and I will personally shoot your eyes out and use your heads as bowling balls. *Comprende?*"

"Sure," said James, imitating Garcia's stupid grin. "You tough guys, huh? Bang bang, you dead."

"The toughest," said Strabo, and he put an arm around James's shoulders.

"I like your style, kid," he said. "You and me are going to get along just fine. Welcome to the gang."

PART 2—ONE OF THE GANG

Regent's Park
London
England

Dear James,

Greetings from the Danger Society. Sadly, as you will soon learn, this will be the last-ever letter from the Soc. We are no more! And you will see from my address that I have left Eton and am back home at Mandeville Mansion in Regent's Park. But I am getting ahead of myself, as usual. As you know, I am not a big one for letter writing, but the tale must be told. At least with a letter you don't have to put up with any of my blasted stammering.

Actually, I have no idea if you will ever get this letter. I don't suppose the Mexican postal service is up to much. I cannot imagine what it is like out there. I picture you in a big sombrero, riding a donkey and strumming a guitar. If I remember, you are not very musical, so I am glad I am not there to hear your efforts.

There has been much excitement at Eton, and you will kick yourself that you were not here to be a part of it. Actually, to be brutally honest, I think you are better off out of it, old thing. So, come along, Perry, spill the beans!

By the way, I saw your messmate Pritpal before I left (it was he that gave me your forwarding address). He was limping about the place and clutching his backside. A beastly boy named Bentinck seems to have instigated a reign of terror at your House. He has beaten Pritpal twice, if you can believe it. Once so hard with a piece of rubber tubing that he was bleeding for two days afterwards by all accounts. And what heinous crimes had he committed? Being too noisy at breakfast and eating in the High Street, the second of which was a wholly trumped-up charge. Pritpal is the most law-abiding boy I have ever come across. I am sure in all your travels in Mexico you will not meet anyone as thoroughly nasty and brutish as Theo Bentinck.

But back to the meat of the letter. As I say, the Danger Society is no more. It all started when I allowed a new member to join, Alistair Seaton. He had been begging me all half. Fool that I am, I finally gave in. Well, the sap boasted to his older brother all about it on long leave, and his brother blabbed to his parents. They were horrified to find out that their darling son, in whose mouth butter wouldn't melt and all that rot, was the member of a secret society dedicated to danger, risk-taking, and generally breaking the law of the land. They went to the Head, who stamped about the place huffing and puffing and kicking up a mighty stink. He hauled me and the rest of the chaps up before him and grilled us. I, of course, kept mum. He couldn't crack me.

The upshot of it was, however, that I decided to shut things down for risk of being found out, but not before we had carried out one last daring exploit. An act of defiant revenge!

I really am a born fool, James. If only you had been here I am sure you would have talked me out of it and made me see sense.

It went off like this. First of all we kidnapped a flock of sheep from a field near Eton Wick. Do you kidnap a sheep? Or do I mean we rustled some sheep? Well, anyway, we borrowed some sheep. And it wasn't really a flock, if truth be told, unless you count five sheep as a flock. I'm no farmer, so don't ask me. Well, we shepherded them back to school and got them up into the Head's room under cover of darkness while he was in chapel. (Gordon Latimer had magicked up a key from somewhere.)

So we installed the flock in his room, unscrewed all the light bulbs, and made good our escape.

Picture the scene as the Head returned, tired and cold, from chapel. He enters the room. No light . . . but what's that noise? Egads! There's some kind of fearsome beast in here! No. There's hundreds of them.

I imagine he must have been pretty terrified. And then, of course, pretty angry, particularly as the sheep had eaten some rather valuable furniture.

I hadn't thought through the consequences, though. "Who," thinks the Head, "would be rash enough to try a stunt like this?"

Answer—Perry Mandeville.

The beaks caught me red-handed trying to brush wool off my coat back in my room. They threatened to expel every member of the Danger Society if I didn't make some sort of confession. So I fell on my sword to protect the others. I took all the blame in return for nobody else being punished.

That, then, was the end of my illustrious career at Eton. My father is sending me as far away as he can manage, to some godforsaken place called Fettes in Scotland.

So long then. Spare a thought for your old pal Perry, but don't shed any tears. I will endure.

Adios, amigo!
Perry

CHAPTER 10—THE WHIPPING POST

El Huracán stood on his balcony overlooking the main square of Lagrimas Negras and lit a cigar. A Cuban brand, El Rey Del Mundo—The King of the World. He drew in the warm smoke, filling his mouth with the taste of spices and chocolate, wood and nuts. He smiled. It tasted of success.

The King of the World? Well, he was certainly king of this world.

From below rose a gentle hum of voices as men strolled in the evening air and chatted to friends. They all wore expensive handmade suits and some had a woman on their arm. The women were all the same: young and beautiful— their dresses shimmering in the soft glow of candlelight coming from the colored-glass globes that were placed around the square. More twinkled from the trees and among the bougainvillea or were hung from the grape vines and jasmine that clothed the mellow stone walls.

People sat at tables outside the three bars taking a drink before dinner under the stars. Soon the others would settle down to eat at one of the restaurants. Already, waiters in crisp white shirts were setting places, polishing glasses, arranging silverware, and putting champagne on ice.

A mariachi band was playing "La Adelita," one of El Huracán's favorite songs. He hummed along to it, letting out a cloud of cigar smoke and stroking his short white beard.

He sat down in a big wicker armchair and took a sip from the chilled glass of fino sherry that had been left out for him on a marble-topped side table. He looked at the tray of *antojitos*, tasty appetizers, which had been prepared for him: *tostadas, sopes, empanaditas,* and *guacamole con totopos.* He picked at the *guacamole.* He wasn't really hungry. He rarely was these days and had only a small appetite. There had been parts of his life, though, when he had been so hungry he had eaten rats and bugs to survive.

There came the sound of a cork popping and a little burst of laughter from one of the bars.

The square was a place for fun and relaxation. The men enjoying themselves down there were bank robbers, extortionists, kidnappers . . . Here they could feel safe and enjoy themselves to their hearts' content. They had nothing to fear from policemen, governments, or honest citizens. There *were* no honest citizens here. This was the ultimate hideout, the original den of thieves.

In the lazy, carefree atmosphere of Lagrimas Negras the men soon forgot their violent ways, and they all looked forward to the evenings when they could show off their expensive clothes and enjoy the fine food and drink that El Huracán laid on.

In the center of the square on a raised terrace stood a short stone column with two iron rings set halfway up its sides. It looked slightly out of place here, in these elegant, romantic surroundings. El Huracán had no doubt that every so often a man would stop and notice it and wonder what it was and why El Huracán hadn't replaced it with something more attractive—a statue or a fountain, maybe.

But El Huracán would never get rid of it. It was a reminder of dark times, a reminder of the penal colony this place had once been.

The column was a whipping post. In days gone by, prisoners had been shackled to it and flogged with a bull-whip or a cane. Sometimes they would be shot and left to rot there in the sun as a warning to others. The flagstones around the base of the column were worn down from being scrubbed. So much blood had been washed down into the drains around it.

So much blood.

The imposing house where El Huracán now lived, at the head of the square, had once been the administrative block. The prison governor had lived and worked here. The buildings around the square that were now shops and restaurants had once been guardrooms and punishment cells.

Lagrimas Negras lay between Mexico's Yucatán Peninsula and the Caymans, part of the chain of Caribbean islands that sweep down from Cuba, through Jamaica, Haiti, Puerto Rico, and scores of smaller islands, to Trinidad off the coast of Venezuela.

The first settlers here had been Mayans. Nobody knew for sure when they first arrived, but some time in the tenth century they had built several monumental structures, including temples, tombs, the two pyramids, a ball court, and an observatory. Not much of these original buildings remained. Later settlers, with no regard for history, had dismantled them to use the stone for new structures, and in some cases had simply built on top of the old Mayan ruins.

In the seventeenth century Lagrimas Negras had become an important staging post for the slave trade, sitting as it did between the other Caribbean islands, Central America, and the southern United States. A slave market was established, which was later turned into a penal colony for captured runaways, troublemakers, and slaves who refused to do as they were told on the plantations.

For the Mayans the island had been sacred to the god Hurakan, who had drowned the world in a great flood after the first humans·had angered the gods. He had then made the world again, calling it up out of the floodwaters. The Mayan name for the island had been forgotten and it had come to be known as Lagrimas Negras—Black Tears.

Lagrimas Negras became feared throughout the slave communities. If there was one thing worse than being a slave, it was being sent there.

In 1830, though, the prisoners rose up, overthrew their jailers, and declared Lagrimas Negras an independent free state. There were already many Maroon settlements along the mainland coast: villages and even towns that had been created by runaway slaves. Lagrimas Negras was just one more.

They might have been left in peace if President Santa Anna hadn't declared war on the United States in 1846. The Americans needed a naval base in the area, and realizing the strategic importance of the island, they sent in gunships. There was a brief and bloody battle. The ex-prisoners, poorly armed and badly outnumbered, didn't stand a chance.

Only one man escaped—El Huracán's father, Gaspar.

He stole a boat and sailed southwest to British Honduras. He moved quickly inland, deep into the heart of the rain forest, eventually settling with a family of Lacandon Indians. By the time he died at the age of ninety-seven he had ten children and thirty-eight grandchildren.

His youngest child was named Hurakan, after the god who had protected Gaspar. He grew up rarely seeing sunlight, and by the time he was twelve he had learned how to survive alone in the unforgiving jungle environment. He was restless, though, and knew from his father's tales that there was a world outside the forest. He wanted to see the ocean and the big cities. He wanted to see fields and horses and sheep, and he wanted to see an open sky.

He left home.

That was fifty-five years ago.

Since then he had seen a lot more than he could ever have imagined.

He had worked as a guide for loggers in the jungle. He had been a sailor. He had worked on a sugar plantation in Cuba. He had fought for the Cubans against the Americans in the Spanish–American War. He had returned to Mexico and fought in the revolution, riding with Pancho Villa's elite cavalry, *Los Dorados*, the Golden Ones. There he acquired his new name, his Spanish name, El Huracán, the Hurricane. He would come down out of the hills with his horsemen like a sudden fierce storm and destroy everything in his way.

Along the way he had been a train robber, an encyclopedia salesman, a banker, a gunrunner, a bootlegger, a farmer, and a shopkeeper. He had drilled for oil and dug for gold. For a while, he had been a politician, but had decided he preferred honest crooks to the ones he found in government. He knew the most important people in Mexico, from the aristocrats and ruling classes to the peasant leaders, from the crime bosses to officers in the police and army, and he had become a very wealthy man.

He had been married four times and outlived each of his wives. His first wife had died in childbirth, his second had died of smallpox, the third was shot by one of Carranza's soldiers, and the fourth had died in a riding accident.

In 1918, at the age of fifty-two, he had finally visited the island of Lagrimas Negras to see where his father had come from. It had been abandoned. The fortified harbor was silted up. The buildings were empty and quiet, home to bats and snakes and scorpions.

He had had a vision of what he could do with this lonely place.

The Americans still claimed ownership of the island, but they had left long ago to build a larger and more useful naval base in Cuba. They were pleased to get Lagrimas Negras off their hands and sold it to El Huracán for thirty-five-thousand dollars.

He brought a loyal gang of followers out here, Mexican Indians, mostly, from the Chiapas, but also a few Maroons and some ex-revolutionaries who had fought alongside him.

He rebuilt the houses, he dredged the harbor. He installed electricity, sewers, and running water. He made elegant streets and built new villas. He converted an ammunition dump into a bank. By the time he had finished, Lagrimas Negras had been turned into a luxury resort, but the guests were not going to be ordinary holidaymakers.

He started to put the word around: if you were on the run, if you were in trouble, if you needed somewhere to hide, you could come to Lagrimas Negras, and you could stay there, free from harm—at a price.

Gradually criminals arrived. If they had enough money they were allowed to stay. If not, El Huracán would capture them and send them back to the Mexican police, or to the Americans, or Brazilians, or wherever they had come from.

His plan worked. His island was full of desperadoes. His bank was full of money.

He was King of the World.

CHAPTER 11—AN ANCIENT JAPANESE ART

"**G**o on, Corona, stab him," yelled Strabo, his voice rasping and husky, as if he needed to clear his throat. "Stick him in his fat Jap gut."

"Whatzat?" said his skinny friend, who was half-deaf. In fact he said "Whatzat?" so often that the others all called him Whatzat.

Whether he knew it or not, James wasn't sure.

"I told the kid to stab him good," said Strabo, shouting right into Whatzat's ear.

James was holding a hunting knife. A big, mean brute with an eight-inch blade, serrated along one edge. Sakata, the Japanese member of the gang, was unarmed. He was standing there in the firelight, at ease, a faint smile tickling his lips. He was a huge man, overweight and bloated, but at the same time he was very light on his small feet. He moved with a graceful daintiness, like a dancer. He said very little and kept himself apart from the others.

James didn't know what to do. He was still pretending to be a tough Mexican street kid. A pickpocket. Handy with a knife. The men were only playing, but they played hard. James knew that to save face he would have to show that he was one of the boys. He had to at least look like he was trying to stab the big Japanese.

Sakata's absolute calm was impressive. For all he knew, James might try to kill him.

They were in a wide clearing in a forest. It was late at night and a fire was blazing. The two American men were drunk. Mrs. Glass was sitting off to one side, ignoring them. Quietly smoking a cigarette and staring into the darkness.

Garcia was sitting with Precious and JJ, who both looked pale and dirty and tired. JJ was huddled in a blanket, shivering and sweating. Garcia had done his best, but the wound in the little boy's leg was infected.

Mrs. Glass and the others didn't care, and James had to also pretend not to be bothered. But JJ was clearly sick. Even if they could get him to a hospital in the next few days, James was worried that his chances of pulling through were not looking good. He was young and weak; his small body could only take so much. If the infection spread there was no medicine in the world that could cure him. He might lose his leg. He might lose his life.

The last few days had been frustrating for Mrs. Glass and her gang, as they had tried to get away from the storm-ravaged stretch of land along the coast. Many areas were still under several feet of water, and the river had grown too wide and too fast to cross. They had had to travel farther and farther inland on roads that were little more than dirt tracks.

James had sworn to help JJ and Precious, and he wished he had more of a plan for getting away from the gang when the time came. For now it seemed sensible to stay with them until they got nearer to a large town where they could get help. At least they had food and transport. The truck became slower each day, however. Garcia was using all his ingenuity to keep it going, but there wasn't much life left in it. There was hardly a part of the engine that he hadn't repaired.

He drove, sitting up front with Mrs. Glass and Sakata. James and the children sat out on the back with the other two men, where they felt every bump and dip in the road. Strabo needled Whatzat constantly about the truck, blaming him for not boosting something more reliable. Whatzat grumbled that it wasn't his fault; the two of them had chosen the truck together.

James had plenty of time to study his traveling companions, and the more he saw of them the less he liked them. Strabo, as well as being short and wide and meaty, was also the hairiest man James had ever seen. His neck was hairy. The backs of his hands were hairy. Hair curled out of the top of his shirt and from between the buttons. He would shave first thing in the morning, but five minutes later his chin would be shaded blue and covered in bristles. You could almost see his beard growing as the day went on.

In contrast, Whatzat was bony and raw-looking. With his fuzz of close-cropped hair, he looked like a soldier or a farmer. He seemed uncomfortable in his own skin. The heat brought him out in a rash, and he was forever scratching himself. He was fidgety and irritable and on a very short fuse. His inability to hear properly made him mad at the world, and he would fly off the handle and yell at the children with little warning.

James didn't want to get on the wrong side of either of these two. He humored them. He laughed at their coarse jokes. He listened to their stories, which, more often than not, were about starting a fight or beating someone to a bloody pulp. In the evenings he drank with them and played cards while they argued and complained to each other. All the time he was slyly probing them, asking them questions. One of the things he found out was that they had lost Manny in the storm, and, in their haste to get away with the safe, they hadn't looked for him.

He hardly touched the bottles of weak Mexican beer they gave him, hoisted from a ruined bar in Tres Hermanas. He drank a little but poured most of it away when they weren't looking. He needed to keep a clear head, because every moment of every day he spent looking for ways to escape.

Tonight had been no different. Strabo and Whatzat's raucous laughter filled the night. Growing bored with arm wrestling and ever-more inventive name-calling, they had egged James on to start a fight with Sakata. James had held back, but in the end Strabo had handed him his knife and nodded toward the Japanese man.

"This should even the odds," he had rasped as Whatzat dragged James up and shoved him toward Sakata.

Sakata had sprung lightly to his feet and stood waiting for him.

And now here they were, facing each other in the firelight.

"Go on, kid, let's see the color of his blood," Whatzat screeched. "He's just a no-good, lousy Jap."

James locked eyes with Sakata, trying to read him. It was impossible. The Japanese man was giving nothing away. He stood as still and impassive as a rock.

"I will kill him," said James, who no longer had to think

before using his Mexican accent. The men had fully accepted him as a local.

"Whatzat?" said Whatzat. "What'd he say?"

"I said I will kill him," James shouted.

"You won't kill him, kid," said Strabo, and he burped. "You won't get near him."

Sakata smiled fully now. "Don't worry," he said quietly. "I am ready for you. Come as hard and as fast as you like."

"Okay." James laughed and shook his head, then, with a yell, he ran at Sakata, holding the knife in front of him. He wouldn't try to kill Sakata, but if he could draw blood the men might be satisfied.

He wasn't entirely sure what happened next. Sakata barely seemed to move, but somehow he grabbed hold of James by the arm and the shirt front, dropped neatly onto his back, raised a leg, and launched James into the air. One moment James was running forward, and the next he was flying face-first into the fire. He landed on the edge, scattering sticks and hot embers, and quickly rolled clear before he was burned.

Strabo and Whatzat were helpless with laughter. James coughed and dusted himself down. His clothes were singed and spotted with blackened holes. His face was covered with soot and ash, but he wasn't hurt. He turned to Sakata, who was back on his feet and looking as calm and composed as before.

"You want to try again?" Sakata said.

James picked up the knife, weighed it in his hand, grinned, and nodded. He would be more careful this time. He moved forward cautiously, on the balls of his feet, swaying from side to side, swinging the knife through the air. Sakata stayed still, in a low crouch, his arms slightly extended in front of him, his hands open.

His eyes never left James's.

James lunged, and again Sakata was ready for him. Quick as a cat, he grabbed James's wrist and turned him. There was an excruciating pain in his elbow. He dropped the knife and the next thing he knew he was flat on his back with Sakata standing over him, still holding his arm in a lock.

This time Sakata helped him up.

"Had enough?"

James shook his head. Sakata handed him the knife.

"Don't hold back," he said.

"I wasn't," said James.

Sakata smiled and James spun quickly, hoping to get him before he was ready. He lashed at him with the edge of the blade in a powerful sweep, but Sakata simply skipped out of the way. James tried to get him on the return sweep, but Sakata was too quick for him, and in a flurry of confusing moves he soon had James pressed facedown in the dirt, his knife arm pinned behind his back.

"You had enough this time?" said Sakata.

James couldn't move, every joint from his shoulder to his fingertips was on fire, but he managed to mumble "yes," and Sakata let him go.

James sat up painfully.

"How do you do that?" he said.

"It is called jujitsu," said Sakata. "It is an ancient Japanese art of fighting. It was part of the training for all samurai warriors."

"Could you teach it to me?" asked James.

"Maybe," said Sakata, and James noticed that there was blood trickling out of his sleeve, which was ripped. Sakata noticed it too, and raised an eyebrow.

"Looks like you scratched me after all," he said approvingly. "Yes. I think you would make a fine samurai. You are brave and you are not scared to fight. I will show you."

James quite liked the big Japanese man. There was a dignity about him that was lacking in the other two men. But he had to keep reminding himself that Sakata was still a gangster. He had gone to the Stones' house to rob it. In the process a man had been killed, and nobody seemed the least bit bothered about it.

James had too many unanswered questions. The gang was after something, but he didn't know what or why. Why had they come all the way down to Mexico to carry out a robbery? What was in Stone's safe that was so valuable? Why were they holding Precious and JJ hostage? What was Mrs. Glass's story?

He needed to find answers to these questions. The more he knew about the gang the better position he would be in when it came time to act.

Sakata showed James some simple moves. James was a fast learner and Sakata was impressed.

"You must either throw your enemy or hold him in such a way that he cannot move," he explained. "You use the joints against themselves. You must understand all the weaknesses of the human body."

James nodded. He already knew quite a lot about the weaknesses of the human body.

"You must be light and soft, you must bend easily, like a

young bamboo, but you must lock your opponent so that he cannot use his muscles against you. That way you can defeat an enemy who is much bigger than you."

After an hour James was exhausted, covered in bruises, and soaked with sweat. Sakata was as cool and relaxed as when they had started. Finally, James limped over to Precious and Garcia.

He took a drink of water from a canteen and sat down on a log.

JJ was sleeping, his head in his sister's lap.

"You seem to be getting on very well with them," said Precious.

"Don't be a fool," said James, dropping his Mexican accent. "You know our only chance is if they think I'm on their side. I'm going to find a way out of this. We're going to get away."

"We must wait," said Garcia. "When the time comes we will know it."

James was glad they had Garcia with them. It was four against four.

He turned to Precious. "The biggest thing in our favor is the safe," James said. "They were relying on your father to open it for them, so they didn't bring any heavy cutting tools or dynamite with them. The fact of the matter is that they'll have to find a better truck soon or abandon it altogether."

"They will not do that," said Garcia. "They came all this way to get what's in it. They won't leave it behind."

James waved away a mosquito and scratched his neck.

"If the truck were to completely break down, we'd have a chance," he said. "They couldn't all come after us;

they might not even bother to give chase at all."

"And how would we travel?" said Precious, her eyes glinting in the firelight.

"However we can," said James. "On foot if necessary. Or are you too high-and-mighty to walk anywhere?"

"I'll walk to the South Pole and back if necessary," snapped Precious. "But how far do you think JJ would get?" There was a harshness in her tone, but James knew that she was scared for her brother.

"I'm sorry," he said.

"I'm tougher than you know," said Precious.

"I said I was sorry."

"I know you hate me," said the girl quietly, looking away, "and maybe I was mean to you, but we've got to work together now. And I'm not leaving JJ behind."

"Neither am I," said James.

"I could carry him," said Garcia. "I am strong."

Precious turned away so that they wouldn't see the tears that had come into her eyes.

"It's hopeless," she said. "Just hopeless."

James wanted to hug her, to reassure her, but he knew he mustn't show her any affection in front of the gangsters who were chatting noisily on the other side of the fire.

"Don't worry," he whispered. "I said I would get you out of this, and I will."

"Why can't they just let us go?" said Precious. "If it's the safe they want, why do they need us?"

"Good question."

James and Precious looked up to see Mrs. Glass. How long had she been there? How much had she heard?

She stood over them for a moment, then dropped her cigarette to the ground and treaded on it. It was past eleven and she was still wearing her hat. She only took it off to sleep, and even then she kept a scarf wrapped around her head. The wide brim meant that her eyes were often shaded and hidden. But now the light was from below, from the flames, and James could clearly see her face.

Her perfect, creamy white skin, her pale blue eyes, and the glossy, blond curls that spilled out from under her hat gave her the looks of a movie star. But there was an iciness in those eyes that made her both beautiful and frightening.

"You're our insurance, sweetheart," she said. "Until we've got what we came for, we're keeping hold of you."

"But you've got it," said Precious. "You've got the safe."

"But what if we get it open and find it's empty. Hmm? What then?"

"Then you've wasted your time, haven't you?" said Precious acidly.

Mrs. Glass smiled. "It's just possible," she said, "that your father took what we're after with him. Or hid it somewhere else. And I'm betting he'll swap you two for it."

"What are you talking about?" said Precious. "He keeps all his money in the safe."

"We ain't really after his money, sweetheart," said Mrs. Glass, and she lit another cigarette.

"What do you want?" asked James, adopting his Mexican accent again.

Mrs. Glass blew smoke at him. "You interest me, Corona," she said. "You're the only blue-eyed Mexican I ever met."

"My mother was not from here," said James. "She was Swiss."

"Swiss, huh?"

"Yes," said James, who so far wasn't lying.

But now he lied.

"She was a nurse. She was working here. My father, he fell in love."

"All his brothers and sisters have blue eyes," said Garcia.

"Is that so?"

"*Sure*. They are famous in Tres Hermanas."

Mrs. Glass squatted down on her haunches and stared into James's face for a long time, without saying anything. James kept his expression dull and bland.

In the end it was Precious who broke the silence.

"When this is over my daddy will hunt you down," she said. "He will hunt you down and catch you and make sure you hang."

"I don't think you should be too sure of just what your daddy might do, honey," said Mrs. Glass.

"You don't know him."

"Don't I now?"

"He's a hero."

"He *was* a hero," said Mrs. Glass. "Shot down a lot of Germans in that plane of his during the war. Just how many men did he kill?"

"Don't speak about him."

"The thing about heroes, honey, is that when the war was over they all found out that their country didn't have a lot of use for them. If you only knew your daddy better, you'd understand that he and I, we're playing in the same band."

"Shut up, just shut up," said Precious angrily.

Mrs. Glass blew another mouthful of smoke toward James.

"So, what happened to your mother, blue eyes?" she said.

"She died," said James, once more telling the truth.

Garcia put an arm around his shoulders and shook him roughly.

"He went a little crazy when she died," he said. "He fell in with the wrong crowd, as you say."

"The wrong crowd, huh?"

"And you?" said James. "How did you end up here?"

Mrs. Glass raised an eyebrow. "Maybe I'll tell you someday."

"I'd like that," said James.

"It's not a very nice story," said Mrs. Glass, standing up.

"Does it have a happy ending?" James called out to her as she walked away.

"We'll see," she called back.

"I hate her," hissed Precious when she was out of earshot. "I want to kill her."

"I wouldn't try it if I were you," said James. "She'd eat you alive."

But as he said it, James saw a light come into Precious's eyes, and she seemed to change. He had never seen her like this before. She suddenly looked very old and very fierce. He felt a shiver of fear.

"I swear," she said, "I will kill that woman. I will kill all of them for what they have done to us."

CHAPTER 12—FANFARE OF DEATH

They made better progress the next day, climbing steadily out of the forest and into the foothills of the Sierra Madre Oriental. Gradually the lush vegetation thinned, and the air became cooler and drier. From the back of the truck James could see the mountains rising against a clear blue sky.

At one point they heard the sound of an aeroplane and scanned the heavens.

"Maybe it's Dad," said JJ feebly, shielding his eyes from the glare. "Maybe he's fixed his plane and come to look for us." He struggled to sit up and Precious helped him, glad to see the boy still had a spark of liveliness.

But when they eventually spotted it, it was only a heavy-looking cargo plane. It crawled slowly across the sky, heading northwest.

"He's never going to find us," said JJ quietly, and he began to cry.

Precious put an arm around him, murmuring soothing words until he fell asleep.

On this steeper track, the truck struggled and its failing engine whined. Twice James had to jump down and help the others push. Eventually, though, the track leveled out and joined a proper road that appeared to be the main north–south highway. The way north, however, toward the

United States border, was blocked. The rain had brought rocks down onto the road. A gang of local men were trying to clear it, but it would take them days.

"We will need to go south. We have no choice," said Garcia after talking to the men. "This is the only way that is open. Is okay. We will be able to cut across toward Mexico City. From there you might take a plane, or head north by road."

"What about Veracruz?" said Mrs. Glass. "Could we get a boat from there?"

"It depends how bad the storm hit," said Garcia.

"You think you can get us there?"

"I can try."

"Good," said Mrs. Glass. "We got to get as far as we can before the truck gives up the ghost."

They rattled on, passing no other traffic in either direction. The sky darkened and night fell. James could see no sign of human life at all, no lights anywhere, no towns or villages. He felt like they were alone in the world. He tried to sleep, but it was too uncomfortable. Parts of the road were unmade and pitted with ruts and holes, and the truck had no suspension. He lay on the floor, his head knocking against the safe, looking up at the stars. He thought how far away they were, and how small this planet seemed.

Finally, just before midnight, there was an almighty bang and a hiss, and the engine fell quiet. The truck coasted to a halt by the side of the road. Strabo cursed.

"That didn't sound good," he said, standing up. "Looks like we'll be walking from here."

Garcia got out of the cab and opened the bonnet. A cloud of steam billowed out.

James climbed stiffly down and stretched his legs, breathing in the scented night air and relishing the silence after the ceaseless pained complaints of the engine. He wandered over to Garcia, who was using a match to see what damage had been done.

"She is dead," he said, running his fingers through his hair. "I can do no more with her."

Strabo joined them.

"Lousy Mexican truck," he said.

"Actually, Señor Strabo," said Garcia, straightening up, "she is an American truck. If I had the parts I could fix her and make her go. But . . ." He shrugged.

Strabo kicked a wheel and went over to give Mrs. Glass the bad news.

"We'll sleep here and decide what to do in the morning," she said, opening her door and jumping down.

They made camp, and while they waited for Whatzat to cook some food, Sakata taught James some more jujitsu. It was very late by the time they all settled down to sleep.

They were awakened by the sound of an engine, and James felt like he had only just dozed off. His body felt bruised and heavy from sleeping on the stony ground. Still half-asleep, he wondered whether, despite everything, Garcia had managed to coax some life back into the poor old truck.

He forced his eyes open and blinked in the harsh early-morning sunlight. He soon discovered that it wasn't their engine he could hear. Another vehicle was approaching. A Mexican army truck with an open back.

Mrs. Glass, Sakata, and Strabo were already awake and

standing up, watching the road. Whatzat was snoring loudly. Presumably he hadn't heard the engine. Strabo kicked him with the side of his foot, and he grumbled, shivered, and sat up.

There were six soldiers in the back of the army truck, wearing scruffy uniforms. They looked tired and bored. An officer sat up front with the driver. As soon as the truck ground to a halt, he put on his cap and got out, grinning. He had a pistol strapped to his side in a highly polished brown leather holster.

"*Buenos días,*" he said, looking them over. He was a scrawny, skinny little man with big teeth and a thin mustache.

Two of the soldiers joined him. They had rifles slung across their backs. They looked scarcely older than James, and one of them had bare feet.

"*Buenos días,*" said Mrs. Glass, and the officer grinned even wider.

"*Americanos?*" he asked, and Mrs. Glass nodded.

"Good morning to you, *señora,*" he said with a heavy, rough accent. "Is this your truck?"

"Yes," said Mrs. Glass. "Is there a problem?"

"No problem," said the Mexican. "Where are you going?"

"South. To Veracruz."

"To Veracruz?"

"Maybe. Is it far?"

"Not far," said the officer. "About one day, maybe two. But is a big shame you are going to Veracruz."

"Why?"

"We need trucks like yours. We are going to the coast.

The storm has done much damage. We are going to help. A truck like this would be very useful."

"I'm not sure it would," said Mrs. Glass. "It's broken-down. Beyond repair, I'm afraid."

"Broke down, huh?" The officer walked slowly over to the truck. He whistled when he saw the safe in the back. "What have you got here?" he said.

"What's it look like?"

"It looks like a safe. You taking it to Veracruz, huh?"

"That's right. Did the storm hit there?"

"*Sí.* But not so bad as in the north. There was some damage. Some small boats sunk."

Two more of the soldiers had got down from their truck. They squatted in the shade, their rifles resting across their knees, staring openly at the Americans. The insistent ticking of the engine droned on.

The officer now came over to look at Precious and JJ, who were still on the ground wrapped in blankets. He smiled at Whatzat.

"These your kids?" he said.

"Whatzat?" said Whatzat.

"I said are these your kids?"

"What? Whaddid you say?"

"You deaf or something?"

"You asking if I'm deaf?"

"*Sí.*"

"Maybe I am. You got a problem with that?"

"No problem." The officer smiled at him.

"You think it's funny?" said Whatzat. "You think it's funny I don't hear so good?" He stood up, pulling on his suit jacket. "I get ringing in my ears, okay? I can't hear nothing else. All day and all night. Like an alarm going off in my head. Drrrrrrrrrrrrr. You think that's funny? You laughing at me?"

"I never said it was *fonny*, *señor*."

"You're grinning like an ass."

"You calling me an ass?"

"Leave it, Whatzat," said Strabo, coming over and putting a hand on his friend's arm.

Whatzat shook him off.

"This beaner thinks I'm funny."

"He was just being friendly," said Strabo. "He was just asking about the kids."

"Whatzat? Whatzat? I don't like his attitude."

Strabo sighed and approached the Mexican officer, shaking his head.

"Yeah, these are our kids," he said. "We're one big happy family on the way to Veracruz to deliver a safe."

The Mexican officer stood there for a moment, sucking his big buck teeth and thinking.

For the first time, James took in his surroundings. They were on the side of a hill, the road following its contour, winding between clumps of prickly pear, agaves, and low, scrubby bushes. To the right were steep rocks, and beyond them, mountains; to the left the ground fell away down a boulder-strewn slope to a pine forest about fifty feet below them.

The little Mexican officer came to a decision. His expression turned serious.

"Can I see your papers?" he said.

"Whatzat? What did he say?" said Whatzat, frowning.

"Your papers. Show me your papers."

"What papers?"

"All of your papers," the Mexican officer shouted. "For this safe. For the kids. You got passports? Huh? You understand? You hear what I am saying?"

"I hear you," mumbled Whatzat, and he went over to the truck. "I'll show you the papers."

Whatzat reached up into the cab, still muttering to himself.

The Mexican officer stood there in the sun, his head cocked to one side, smiling at Mrs. Glass. Suddenly there was a shout from Whatzat.

"You want to see my papers? Read this!"

Whatzat was walking quickly forward with an automatic pistol in each hand.

James threw himself to the ground as four shots rang out in quick succession.

The officer wasn't so quick to get out of the way. He wasted time fumbling to release his pistol from its holster, and by the time he brought it up, four bullets had punched into his chest, and he fell backward into the dirt with a little cry.

At the same time Strabo was coming up from the other side of the truck with his own gun, firing at the two soldiers who were still up on the army vehicle.

Mrs. Glass had also produced a gun from somewhere, too fast for James to see, and was firing on the four men who had dismounted.

The doomed soldiers were thrown into a panic and had

no time to react. Their rifles were too big and clumsy to be much use up close, and the Americans moved quickly and methodically among them.

For a few seconds there was a hideous, chaotic racket of shooting and yelling. A brief fanfare of death. And then there was silence. Absolute, dead silence. Even the insects were still. It lasted a second or two before James heard flies, already homing in on the scent of blood.

He stood up. He couldn't bear to look at the dead bodies of the soldiers.

Then Whatzat shouted, "They're getting away."

The driver and two of the soldiers were running off down the slope, scattering rocks and stones as they went.

Strabo snatched up a rifle from the hands of a dead soldier, quickly checked it over, then slid the bolt back and forward to shunt a bullet into the chamber.

"They're too far away," said Whatzat.

"Shut up," said Strabo, closing one eye and resting the butt into his shoulder. He pulled back the hammer, took aim, and squeezed the trigger.

A sharp bang echoed, but the bullet missed. James saw a prickly pear splatter. Strabo swore, reloaded the rifle, and fired again. This time, the driver, a heavyset, older man who couldn't run very fast, threw out his arms and fell headlong down the slope.

"Good shot," said Whatzat appreciatively, and Strabo laughed.

"Could hardly miss the fat idiot."

"Betcha can't hit the other two."

"Oh, yeah?"

There was another bang and one of the soldiers was hit. He stumbled, but carried on running. Strabo's next shot stopped him for good.

"Where's the other guy?" said Whatzat. "There was three of them."

"Damn," said Strabo, lowering the rifle and peering down the slope. "Musta made it to the trees."

"Get down there and find him," said Mrs. Glass. "We don't want any witnesses."

Strabo and Whatzat ran off awkwardly down the hill.

Garcia came over to Mrs. Glass. He was shaking with anger. "Are you crazy?" he said.

"You got a problem, Garcia?" she replied, lighting a cigarette.

"Sure I got a problem. You just killed seven men in cold blood."

"They were only Mexicans."

"I am a Mexican."

"It was a typical Mexican shakedown," said Mrs. Glass dismissively. "What was I supposed to do, Garcia? Let them rob us, or arrest us, or shoot us, or whatever the hell they were going to do to us? Besides, we need their truck. Now help me get these bodies out of the road."

Garcia picked up a dead soldier and gently laid him down next to the safe. He said a few words, then crossed himself and closed the man's eyes.

James spotted the skinny officer's revolver, lying half under his body, and while Mrs. Glass was distracted, he picked it up and stuffed it inside the waistband of his trousers, under his shirt. Then he went over to comfort

Precious and JJ, who were crying. Sakata was with them and it struck James that he hadn't joined in the firefight.

"They are all right," Sakata said without emotion, and went over to help Garcia.

Precious stopped crying, wiped her face, and shouted at Mrs. Glass.

"Is that what you're going to do to us? When we're no longer any use to you? Will you shoot us in the road like dogs?"

"I never killed anyone I didn't have to," said Mrs. Glass flatly.

"What about JJ?" said Precious. "You're killing him. He needs medicine."

"It's in the hands of God," said Mrs. Glass.

"God?" scoffed Precious. "What do you know about God?"

"Good question," said Mrs. Glass, and she walked off laughing.

Twenty minutes later Strabo and Whatzat returned, having found no sign of the last soldier.

"That's not good," said Mrs. Glass.

"What can he do?" rasped Strabo. "We're miles from the nearest town. He's on foot. We'll be in Veracruz before he can tell anyone what's happened."

"It makes me uneasy," said Mrs. Glass. "There could be other patrols around. He could be picked up. We take their truck, it's going to stick out like a sore thumb. And that damned safe." She threw her cigarette down and crushed it under her boot.

"How about we—" Strabo started to say something but was cut off by Mrs. Glass.

"Shut up, I'm trying to think."

Strabo immediately stopped talking. James was impressed by how much authority the woman had. These tough men were happy to have her order them about, and they never seemed to question that she was in charge. He had seen her in action against the soldiers and saw what a ruthless and expert killer she was. The more he saw of the woman, the more she scared him.

"We need to open the safe and get rid of it," she said. "Then we need to get rid of the truck and find some other transport." She turned to Garcia. "You know this area?"

"A little."

"Is there any place around here we might find something we can use to get this safe open?"

Garcia rubbed his mouth. "Somewhere off this road, I think there is an old oil field. My brother was working there. It is closed down, but there could still be some tools there, drills maybe. Perhaps even some dynamite."

"How far?"

"I'm not so sure." Garcia looked around and then pointed toward a distant, snowcapped peak that soared above the brown hills. "That is Pico de Orizaba," he said. "We keep heading toward it, I think we maybe find the track to the oil field."

"Okay," said Mrs. Glass. "Now, let's get to work."

They shifted the safe onto the army truck. Then Whatzat climbed into the cab of their old truck and released the hand brake. The truck rolled slowly down the hill and he steered it to the edge of the road. At the last moment, as it bumped over the lip, he jumped clear and watched it trundle down the slope, gaining momentum as it went. The men cheered as it careered into the trees and disappeared, leaving a trail of dust.

"Good riddance to bad rubbish," said Strabo, and he spat.

"Saddle up," said Mrs. Glass. "We're out of here."

Precious looked at James. "I can't take much more of this," she said miserably.

"Don't worry," said James. "When we get to the oil well, we'll make our move. JJ's going to be all right."

He only wished that he were more confident than he was trying to sound.

CHAPTER 13—THE DEVIL'S SWEAT

The metal sign was rusted and it looked like someone had used it for target practice—it was peppered with holes and dents. The writing was still just about legible, though:

MEXICOIL
Servicios de la exploración y el perforar
Pozo número 23. Localización Verde De Las Colinas.
CARACTERÍSTICA PRIVADA

Underneath was a newer sign, crudely hand-painted with an added skull and crossbones warning of danger:

MANTIENE DEL PELIGRO HACIA FUERA.
INSEGURO. CERRADO.

The truck pulled off the main road and lumbered up a crude dirt track, winding between high rocky crags. The recent rain had created deep puddles that were unable to drain away into the heavy clay soil. The truck frequently got stuck and struggled to free itself, the spinning wheels sending up a spray of filthy water behind them.

The track seemed to go on forever, and because of the hard going and the tight bends they made very slow progress.

The air was cooler and less humid than it had been down by the coast. It was too early in the year for it to get really hot, but in the middle of the day the sun could still get very strong, and James and Precious did their best to keep JJ shaded. His lips were dry and cracked, and his eyes were red as if he had been crying.

At last the land opened out and they found themselves on the edge of a large saucer-shaped area that looked like it had been gouged out of the hill. It must once have been a lush, green area full of trees and shrubs and flowers, but the oil-drilling activities had stripped the fertile land away and left a brown, barren scar on the landscape. Tough, wiry weeds were growing here and there, but it was mostly a dreary expanse of mud and rock. A small stream meandered its way across the wasteland between great multicolored pools of stagnant water. Some were green with algae, others orange from pollution and rust; still more were a horrible purple-brown color from spilled oil that left a rainbow sheen on the surface. In the far distance they could just make out a tall wooden derrick surrounded by a few abandoned buildings.

This was an ugly monument to Mexico's scramble for oil and wealth. But the oil had run dry and the well had been left to rot.

It didn't appear to be utterly deserted, though. There was a chain across the road with a warning sign hanging from it, and to the right was a hut with a battered dark green Chevrolet sedan parked next to it. As the truck pulled to a halt two men came out of the hut. They looked surprised to see the new arrivals. One was a heavyset man wearing a suit and hat, the other was wearing a uniform jacket with baggy white trousers and no shoes. As he stepped into the sun he pulled on a security-guard's cap and said something in Spanish.

A third man, also wearing a guard's cap, peered out of a window. He looked ancient and toothless.

Strabo and Whatzat got off the back of the truck and walked over to the hut. They soon established that they were Americans and that the man in the suit spoke English.

"You are lost?" he said.

"We've come to view the oil field," said Strabo.

"The well, she is closed," said the man in the suit. "It is unsafe. There is nothing here." He tried to wave them away, but Strabo and Whatzat stayed put.

"We're from a big American drilling concern in Texas," said Strabo. "We may be interested in buying the place."

"She is not for sale. She is closed. There is no more oil here."

"We believe that might not be the case."

"No, *señor*, I can assure you, there is nothing."

"Can't we at least have a look around?" said Strabo. "We've come a long way."

"Sorry, *señor*. You have had a wasted trip, I am afraid."

"What's in those buildings down there?"

"There are still some tools and equipment here. That is why it is guarded. I am from a salvage firm. We will be removing everything soon."

"And you said there was nothing here," said Strabo, playfully punching the man in the arm and offering him a big, conspiratorial grin.

The man was not amused. "Just go home, please," he said, his face turning aggressive.

"Whatzat? What'd you say? Go where?" said Whatzat. "I ain't going nowhere till I have a look-see what you got in that hut there."

"*Señor!*" said the man in the suit, and he put a hand on Whatzat's arm.

"Whatzat?" said Whatzat. "Can't hear you."

He walked into the hut and the two Mexicans followed him in, shouting angrily.

James could hear an argument inside, then there was a crashing noise, and the man in the suit flew out of the window in a shower of glass and splintered wood. He tumbled down the slope and lay still. A moment later the two guards came out with their hands up and Whatzat prodding them from behind with his gun.

"They finally saw sense," he said. "We're free to look around."

Strabo checked the man in the suit. His neck was broken. He rolled him out of sight under some bushes, and then unhooked the chain across the track. The two scared guards climbed onto the back of the truck with the children, and sat down with their hands on their heads.

They started down the track. For several minutes they weaved their way between the stagnant pools of water and mounds of discarded earth and stones that had been dumped here when the central area was leveled. Finally they crossed the stream on a rickety wooden bridge and arrived at the derrick and the collection of long, low sheds, their woodwork rotting and collapsing. There was a desolate, bleak air about the place. Rusting machinery was standing abandoned, and there were piles of empty oil drums and a big pile of ashes and blackened wood where something had been burned.

As James climbed down from the truck his foot went into a puddle and was gripped by the waterlogged slime beneath the surface. It took him some effort to tug it free, and it came loose with a squelching, sucking noise, leaving his shoe encased in stinking, yellow-gray mud.

He wiped it clean on the rear wheel of the truck as Strabo shot the padlock off the double doors of one of the huts and pulled them open. While Whatzat, Sakata, and Mrs. Glass went off to explore the other buildings, Strabo motioned the rest of them inside.

This had been a storage shed. There were still some cans of paint in there and some old sacks, spilling their contents out onto the concrete floor. They were mostly full of lime and cement, which must have been used to make the foundations for the buildings and the derrick. The air smelled of chemicals, and it caught in the back of James's throat, but it was good to be out of the sun.

Strabo found some fencing wire and tied the two guards to a wooden roof support. They seemed resigned to their fate and sat slumped against the post with sad expressions on their brown faces.

Strabo inspected the paint cans, then clapped James on the back.

"You kids can keep busy painting the truck so's it's not so conspicuous." He pulled his hunting knife from his belt and handed it to James. "Just in case," he rasped, and winked. "I don't reckon they'll try running off, but it's best to be prepared."

James smiled and nodded, acting the tough.

Whatzat called to them from outside and Strabo went out with Garcia. James walked over to the doors and watched as the gang reversed the truck up to another shed and manhandled the safe off the back and inside. A few minutes later there came the sound of hammering and drilling.

James and Precious made sure that JJ was comfortable, and took the paint over to the truck.

"Why are we helping them?" said Precious. "Why don't we just pour the stinking paint into their gas tank?"

"We need to keep them sweet," said James. "Until we can see our chance."

The paint was thick and black, designed for weatherproofing external metalwork. It left big drips and lumps all over the truck, but it very effectively covered over the army markings and the original olive-green finish.

They worked all afternoon to the accompaniment of a relentless, dreary clank, clang, clang from the shed where the gang was working. They stopped when it grew too dark to see, and soon afterward Whatzat and Strabo came back out, their hands and faces streaked with grime.

"Whoever designed that safe was one sadistic son of a snake," said Strabo.

"Ah. Those tools are useless," said Whatzat. "If we had us some explosives I could get the blamed thing open in five minutes."

"We'll take another look around in the morning," said Strabo. "For now, let's eat."

Whatzat made a fire and cooked supper. Garcia and Precious sat with JJ. Sakata amused himself showing James some more jujitsu moves. Strabo got drunk. Mrs. Glass sat by herself smoking. The moon shone down on them as it had done every other night. Insects and frogs filled the night with their racket.

The next morning dawned dull and overcast. The sky was a flat, gunmetal gray. There was no breeze and the utter stillness was oppressive. James was up before anyone else, and he searched the area for anything that might be of use. Walking helped to clear his head a little, and the pieces of a plan started to form in his mind.

Hidden behind a mound he discovered a concrete bunker built into the side of the hill. There were two lurid warning signs on the door, one with a picture of an explosion, and it was locked with a heavy chain and padlock.

As Whatzat prepared breakfast, James told him all about it, shouting to be heard and repeating himself often.

"Sounds like an explosives dump," said Whatzat with a weaselly grin. "Just what we been looking for, kid."

James took Strabo and Whatzat over to the bunker. The men hacked the padlock and chain off and gingerly opened the door. Sure enough, there inside were crates of dynamite. Whatzat cleared everyone else away and went in alone to inspect them. He came out a little while later buzzing with nervous excitement.

"We need to be careful," he explained, scratching his red neck. "They been there a while. The dynamite's pretty unstable. Sweating. That's probably why they left it behind. We try and use it like it is, we run the risk of blowing ourselves to hell and back."

"So whadda we do?" said Strabo.

"Whatzat?"

"I said whadda we do," Strabo shouted.

"We boil it."

"I ain't going near the stuff," said Strabo, backing off with his hands up. "I seen what that stuff can do."

"The kid can do it," said Whatzat.

Strabo and Sakata fixed up an old oil drum over a fire, well away from the buildings, and half filled it with water from the stream. Whatzat stayed at the bunker with James, supervising him.

"Three sticks should do it," said Whatzat. "Bring 'em out one by one. The gunk that's leaking out of them is nitroglycerin. It's the devil's sweat, Corona, more dangerous'n you can imagine. You just have to knock it and it goes off. One slip and—bang—instant sausage meat. That's why they invented dynamite. To make the stuff safer to use. They mix it up with this chalky powder and make it into sticks. But leave it sitting around too long and the nitro starts to ooze out. So, be nice to it."

He gently shoved James into the bunker and retreated to a safe distance.

James went over to the nearest open crate, the blood pounding in his ears. There were about twenty sticks in it, each a dull, reddish brown color and sticky. Encrusted with white crystals. They looked rotten and evil and deadly. If anything went wrong there wouldn't be enough left of him to bury.

Best not to think about that. Clear your mind. Concentrate.

His hands were shaking.

He wiped the sweat out of his eyes, took a deep breath, and picked a stick up.

Nothing happened.

He went back out into the sunlight, holding the horrible thing in front of him at arm's length.

"Take it over to the fire and put it in the drum," Whatzat yelled at him.

James walked slowly and carefully. He could see Strabo and Sakata hiding behind a rock. He made it without any mishap and lowered it into the boiling water.

Feeling more confident now, he returned for the next stick, and soon there were three of them bobbing in the water.

Whatzat joined him and peered down at the boiling dynamite.

"The water'll force the rest of the nitro out," he said. "Then we'll skim it off the surface. But don't get too cocky. The whole lot could still go up at any moment. Learned all about it in the army, in the war in Europe. I was in the engineers. Blowing up bridges mostly. To me, there's no more beautiful sight than a big explosion."

"That how you damaged your hearing?" said James, hardly bothering with a Mexican accent.

"Whatzat? No. That was later. After the war I turned to blowing up safes. One time in Iowa I got the fuse wrong on some dynamite. Was too close to it when it went off. Had a ringing in my ears ever since. Drives me crazy."

As they worked, Whatzat told James all about dynamite. How much to use. How it was made. How it worked. How to cut a fuse. And all the while he delicately skimmed the nitroglycerin off the surface of the water and transferred it to a glass jar.

"When we've got enough I'll pour it into some holes we've drilled around the safe's lock. Like I said, nitro detonates with percussion. That means you hit it to set it off. I'll probably shoot at it with one of those rifles we took from the soldiers."

"How long will that take to get ready?" said James.

"About an hour to set up so's it's safe, then about a second to blow the lock."

At lunchtime James sat apart from the others with Garcia. "Once they get that safe open, who knows what they'll do," he said. "If they find what they're after, they might not have any more use for us."

Garcia nodded. "We cannot wait any longer," he said.

"We'll have to make our move while they're inside, working on the safe," said James. "We just need to get Precious and JJ up to the car by the entrance."

"Is a long walk," said Garcia. "JJ will not make it."

"We can carry him," said James. "The two guards can help. Between us we can do it."

"It hurts me to see how sick he is," said Garcia. "There is a hospital in Veracruz. In the car we can be there soon."

When they got the opportunity, James explained the plan to Precious, and Garcia spoke to the guards, who visibly cheered up when they discovered that they were going to be freed.

After lunch, Mrs. Glass and the others went over to the shed to get the safe ready. James and Garcia were just about to put their plan into action when Strabo returned.

"We need your help, Garcia," he said in his harsh, rasping way. "We got to move the safe."

"Sure," said Garcia. "I just finish my coffee and I will come."

"Yeah, well, be quick about it. I know what lazy slobs you beaners are."

Strabo went back and James joined Garcia.

"Now what?" he said.

"Maybe it is better this way," said Garcia. "I can try to make sure they stay here and don't come after you."

"We can't do this without you," said James.

"Sure you can," said Garcia. "You can do it, James. You are a brave kid. The guards can get you to Veracruz. I will see you there when this is all over."

James gripped Garcia's hand briefly.

"Thank you," he said.

"No problem," said Garcia, and he strolled over to the other shed.

James was moving fast. He used Strabo's knife to cut the wire holding the guards.

They hugged him and thanked him, babbling away in Mexican, and James told them to keep quiet.

Precious was shaking, but she had a determined look about her. She would fight her fear to help her little brother. JJ was sweating and very feverish. He didn't really seem to know what was going on. James helped him on to the back of the younger guard. JJ cried out feebly as the wound in his leg was knocked, but Precious soothed him and he calmed down, his eyelids drooping closed.

All set, James went outside to see that the coast was clear. There was Whatzat. Striding toward the truck. James hastily signaled to the others to stay back and walked over to him.

"How's it going?" he said.

"Whatzat?"

"How's the work going?"

"Slowly. You can't rush nitro . . . Hey, whatzat?"

"What?" James turned and, to his horror, saw the elderly guard poking his head out of the doorway.

He quickly ducked back inside, but not before Whatzat had spotted him.

"You're supposed to be keeping an eye on those guys," he snarled, and pushed James out of the way before hurrying over the muddy ground toward the shed.

James picked up a rock and ran after him. He hated to do it, but he swung as hard as he could and struck Whatzat in the base of his skull. He went down like a felled tree, and James ran past him into the shed.

The Mexican was gabbling an apology. James told him to shut up and get going, but the next thing they knew Whatzat was in the doorway brandishing his gun.

James hadn't knocked him cold, only stunned him.

He looked furious.

"You shouldn'ta done that, Corona," he said. "I don't know what your game is, but I aim to put a stop to it— *permanently.*"

CHAPTER 14—A HOPE IN HELL

There was no time to worry. No time to think. James had to act.

He picked up a handful of lime, and before Whatzat could fire his gun, he threw it hard into his face. Whatzat yelled and clutched at his eyes, the powder burning into the soft flesh.

"Run," James shouted as Whatzat started firing blindly.

The bullets punched through the flimsy wood of the shed creating bright spots in the walls.

James and Precious threw themselves to the ground while the two guards darted outside carrying JJ.

There were tears streaming down Whatzat's face, and his eyes were a livid red. He was roaring in pain and anger. As James scrambled to his feet he pulled the frightened Precious after him. They barged into Whatzat and ran out into the light.

Whatzat was on their tail, though, still wildly firing his pistol.

Hand in hand, James and Precious zigzagged to avoid the bullets as well as the pools of oily water. Whatzat stumbled after them.

A bullet hit the ground at their feet with a wet smack. James let go of Precious's hand and they separated.

James had only run on a few paces when another bullet whined past his ear, dangerously close, and he dropped to his knees in a sticky patch of wet clay, losing sight of Precious.

Whatzat's shooting had alerted the rest of the gang, and Strabo burst out of the other shed, closely followed by Sakata.

"Watch where you're going, Whatzat!" Strabo yelled.

"Whatzat! Who's shouting?"

Half-crazed, unable to see or hear properly, Whatzat turned and fired toward the sound of Strabo's voice.

It was Strabo's turn to drop to the ground now, and Sakata ducked behind a pile of rubble.

"It's me, you idiot!" Strabo shouted. "Strabo! It's Strabo. Stand still and stop shooting. Let me deal with them."

"Whatzat? Whatzat?"

James tried to stand, slipping and slithering in the wet clay. Whatzat was slowly emptying the magazine in his automatic. A steady stream of bullets was whacking and zinging all around as he marched in a big, clumsy circle.

At last the shooting stopped—he had emptied the gun. He fumbled in his pocket for a fresh ammunition clip and kept on walking.

Strabo jumped to his feet and ran over to him.

"Don't move, Whatzat," he shouted. "Just stay put—"

It was too late, though. Just as Whatzat snapped the clip into his gun, he blundered straight into a pool. He toppled forward with a splash, his arms waving uselessly. He brought his head up, spitting and swearing, but found that he couldn't lift his body out of the sucking embrace of the thick mud that lay just beneath the surface of the oily water.

"Whatzat?" he shouted. "What's happening?" He wiped his eyes but only succeeded in smearing them with filth.

"Hold still," shouted Strabo. "Don't struggle, you'll make it worse."

But Whatzat couldn't hear him. He was in a blind panic, and the more he twisted and turned, the farther he sank into the foul mud.

"Hold still, goddammit!"

Mrs. Glass had come out of the shed and was hurrying over with Sakata.

James was stuck fast himself now, half-buried in the boggy patch of ground he'd blundered into. He lay there, unable to tear his eyes away from the grisly spectacle.

"Fetch a rope," Strabo shouted. "Anything."

Sakata found a plank and picked his way carefully to the edge of the pool.

Whatzat's head and shoulders were the only part of him above the surface now. His hands were scrabbling at the sloppy muck.

"Grab hold of this," said Sakata.

"Whatzat?"

Sakata just managed to get the tip of the plank to Whatzat, who batted it away in fear.

"Help me, oh God, help me," he screamed. "Get me out of here."

"I am trying," said Sakata. "You must hold on."

"Whatzat? Speak up, I can't hear you. I can't see you."

Whatzat fired his gun; whether it was on purpose or not, it was impossible to tell. But Sakata backed off for fear of getting shot. He turned to his companions with a despairing look on his face.

James saw that Mrs. Glass was completely impassive, watching Whatzat sink, almost with fascination.

Whatzat's chin was under now, and then his lips. He coughed and spluttered and tried to scream, but the mud was filling his mouth, and no sound came out, just a huge bubble, then a smaller one, then a long stream of tiny ones as his nose slipped under. For a moment only his eyes showed, red and wide, staring into hell.

Then they were gone too.

Soon all that was left was his right hand, still clutching the gun. The gun that had killed so many people. The gun that could end lives so easily, but was useless when it came to saving one.

Whatzat started firing, straight up into the sky. Bang, bang, bang . . .

Then the gun slipped under.

There was silence. Nothing moved.

Strabo and Sakata went over to the side of the pool and peered down. There was no sign of their friend. Then one last bullet shot out from underwater, and it was over.

"Poor devil," said Strabo. "What a way to go."

"What happened here?" said Mrs. Glass, staring at James, and then she realized something.

"They're gone," she said. "The kids are gone."

There was a brief explosion of noise and movement. Mrs. Glass shouted some orders, then jumped into the truck with Strabo, and they thundered off up the track. The truck rattled and banged across the uneven ground and took the old wooden bridge at such a speed that James felt sure it would collapse.

They disappeared from view, and an unbearable stillness settled across the camp. Garcia pulled James to his feet, and they stood alongside Sakata, staring fixedly ahead. James didn't want to catch Garcia's eye for fear of what he might see. Hopelessness? Despair?

They waited in frozen silence on the gray landscape under a gray sky. The only movement was from the flies. James barely noticed them buzzing around his face and crawling across his skin. He was holding his breath, his ears straining for any sound. His entire attention was focused on what was going on past the mounds of earth and stone that blocked the view of the entrance.

Did Precious, JJ, and the two guards have a hope in hell of getting away?

How much of a head start had they had? Would they make it to the car before the truck caught up with them?

Like the others, James had been so caught up in the death of Whatzat that he hadn't been paying attention to what Precious was doing. If only he could have given one of the guards the gun he still had hidden in the waistband of his trousers, they might have had a chance.

Finally they heard it. A distant crack, and then another. Two shots and no more. The guards were unarmed. It could only mean one thing.

Unless . . .

Unless they had guns hidden in the entrance hut? Or in the car? Perhaps they had lain in ambush? Waited for the truck to drive up . . .

James turned and looked at Sakata. He avoided James's eyes, ashamed.

Presently there came the growl of an engine, and the truck came into view. It seemed to take forever, crawling slowly toward them along the track.

James wanted it never to arrive, and he wanted it to be here now, both at the same time.

When at last it stopped, he could see Strabo sitting on the back and Mrs. Glass sitting up front in the driver's seat next to Precious.

There was no sign of either JJ or the guards.

Mrs. Glass got out of the cab and strode over to James and Garcia.

"What the hell happened here?" she said.

"One of the guards had a hidden knife," said James. "He must have cut through the wire in the night. They overpowered me."

"Yeah? Well, that was their mistake. We should have shot them straight away instead of keeping them prisoner. Well, they're shot now."

James tried not to show any emotion. He looked over at Precious, who was getting out of the cab. She looked defeated, but she wasn't crying. Maybe there were no more tears inside her.

Mrs. Glass gripped James by the bicep.

"You screwed up, Corona," she said. "Screw up again and I'll cut your guts out."

"Sorry," said James.

"Yeah? Well, being sorry won't bring Charlie back."

"Charlie?" said James, momentarily confused.

"That was his name," said Mrs. Glass, glancing over at the mud hole. "Charlie Moore."

Strabo picked up something from the floor of the truck and hopped down. It was JJ. He looked unconscious. Strabo brought him over to Precious and dropped him at her feet.

"He's all yours, darling," he rasped. "Next time we won't go so easy on you two."

"Next time?" shouted Garcia angrily. "There won't be a next time. The boy is nearly dead."

"That's not my problem, *muchacho*," said Strabo, turning away, chuckling to himself.

Garcia stepped forward, grabbed him by the shoulder, and spun him around.

"You scum," he said. "You filthy, crawling pig. Don't ever touch the boy again."

"Watch who you're talking to, greaser," said Strabo, half-laughing.

Garcia didn't hesitate. He slapped Strabo across the face with the back of one hand. The blow was so hard it knocked Strabo off his feet. He fell on his side and lay there stunned, his eyes wide, not quite believing what had happened.

Garcia spat on him, hitting him full in the face. This brought Strabo back to life. He got to his feet and pulled his Colt from his belt. But Garcia was ready for him. He swatted Strabo's wrist and the gun flew off, skittered across the ground, and sank into a mud hole.

"That's right," said Garcia. "Pull your gun. That is all you know. Guns and killing. You are not a man. You are a piece of worthless dirt."

As he said this, Garcia hit Strabo repeatedly with the

back of first one hand and then the other, whipping Strabo's huge square head from left to right.

Garcia had worked hard all his life, hauling in nets and lifting heavy crates of fish. His arms were immensely strong. Strabo could do nothing to resist. He staggered backward under the relentless hail of blows.

James looked at Mrs. Glass to see what she would do. She was watching the attack just as she had watched Whatzat die, with fascination, amusement even. It was clear she wasn't going to do anything to stop Garcia.

Strabo sank to his knees, woozy and confused. Garcia grabbed him by the lapels and hauled him over to a pool of filthy green water. He thrust his head into it and held it underwater for a few seconds before letting go.

Strabo came up, choking and spluttering and dripping slime. He got to his knees and was sick over himself.

"Stand up, *cabrón*," said Garcia, and Strabo forced himself to his feet.

Garcia hit him again. And again. His knuckles were bleeding and Strabo's face was red and raw looking. His eyes, though, for the first time in his life, were focused. He had lost his squint.

Garcia beat him until he was exhausted, then he tossed him to one side, where he slumped in a lifeless heap.

Garcia went to JJ and knelt by him, stroking his face.

"You will be all right," he said. "I will not let anything happen to you, *mi niño*. I will find a doctor for you."

Gently he scooped the boy up in his muscular arms and stood.

He walked over to Mrs. Glass.

"I am taking the boy to the car," he said. "Do not try to stop me, or I will kill you with my bare hands."

Mrs. Glass said nothing, but she held Garcia's stare.

Garcia turned away and started walking down the track toward the entrance. Mrs. Glass lit a cigarette and watched him go.

He grew smaller and smaller.

James felt a warm glow of relief pass through him. He wished he were as brave as Garcia, but he had done nothing for the boy.

Then he froze. His world fell in on itself.

A gunshot had split the air. Garcia had fallen.

Strabo was standing there holding a rifle, his face a bloody, bruised mask.

He was smiling.

Precious screamed, and she and James ran to where Garcia was lying.

He was just alive. He took hold of James's hand.

"It's up to you now," he said. "God has chosen. You must be *valiente*. Look after JJ for me."

Garcia closed his eyes, and Precious clutched his handsome head.

"No, no, no, no, no . . ." she murmured. "Please, no . . ."

Precious buried Garcia by herself. She wouldn't let anyone else help her. James watched as she dug the trench and dragged the body over to it. He watched her gently roll him in and cover him over with earth. Then he watched as she sat there, all alone, the light fading from the day.

He barely noticed the gunshot and the small explosion

from the work shed when Mrs. Glass and Strabo finally got the safe open. They came out soon afterward and joined James where he was helping Sakata to make a fire. The two Americans looked tired and none too happy. Strabo's face was a mess, covered in cuts and bruises, his right eye completely swollen. He grabbed a bottle of whisky from a bag and took a long, noisy swallow. Mrs. Glass adjusted her wide-brimmed hat and stared at the flames that were curling up out of the fire.

"I hope it's worth it."

Everyone looked around to see Precious glaring at Mrs. Glass.

"You talking to me?" said Mrs. Glass, taking the bottle from Strabo.

"Yes, I *am* talking to you," said Precious. "I want to know if the money in that safe is worth all the lives you've taken. How many is it now? Twelve? Thirteen?"

"I'm not counting," said Mrs. Glass.

"I am," said Precious. "And I am going to make you pay for every one of them."

"Fine words, honey," said Mrs. Glass. "But in the end, just words. What are you going to do, huh? What do you seriously think you are going to do, sister?"

"You never answered my question," said Precious.

"Is it worth it?" said Mrs. Glass. "That's a good question. The men who drilled this oil well? Working themselves to death eighteen hours a day for the promise of wealth? Did they think it was worth it? The generals back there in the war, when they sent thousands of young men off to die? Did they ask themselves if it was worth it? God, up there in heaven? When he sent the storm to wipe out Tres Hermanas—"

"I'm not asking God," said Precious. "I'm asking you. Is the money in that safe worth all the blood you've spilled?"

"In a word, honey, no."

"So, why did you do it, then?" asked Precious.

"The thing is," said Mrs. Glass, rubbing her tired eyes, "we didn't expect to find a whole lot of money in that safe."

"What? You're saying there's no money in it?"

"Oh, there's some cash in there, but that's not what we were looking for."

"So you'll just throw it away?"

"Of course not. We'll spend it, and enjoy it. It's the least we deserve after all the trouble we've been to. But it won't last long. Your daddy didn't have a lot of cash."

"He's a rich man," said Precious, and Mrs. Glass laughed quietly.

"Oh, sure, your daddy likes to give the impression he's rich," said Mrs. Glass. "Living in that fancy house with all those fancy things. He's got a front to keep up. The great American war hero, rewarded by his country. But the house is rented, the furniture, too. His cars borrowed."

"That's not true," said Precious. "We live in the finest house in Tres Hermanas."

"You think he could afford all those servants if he lived in America? Why do you think he moved down here in the first place?"

"Because of the oil boom. He works for the big oil companies. Scouting for new fields."

"That's right. Allows him to fly wherever he likes. All

over Mexico, in and out of the States, down into South America, over to the Caribbean. Good old Jack Stone: flyboy, war hero—free to travel the heavens, no questions asked."

"What are you talking about?" said Precious.

"Your daddy," said Mrs. Glass. "Seems I know him a whole lot better than you do. Maybe that's because he's one of us."

"No, he is not!" Precious shouted. "He is a hero! He won three medals in the war. He had dinner with the president."

"Many crooks have had dinner with the president," said Mrs. Glass.

"Have you?" said Precious scornfully.

Mrs. Glass smiled.

"Matter of fact, I have," she said.

"Shut up," said Precious. "I don't believe you."

"Have it your own way," said Mrs. Glass. "It's no concern of mine."

"Why?" shouted Precious. "Why would you rob a safe that had no money in it? Answer me that."

"There are some things more valuable than notes and coins."

"Daddy doesn't have any jewels, if that's what you think, or gold."

"Never said he did, sugar. Never said he did. But, pound for pound, some things are worth a whole lot more than gold."

"Like what?"

"Secrets."

"Let me tell you a story," said Mrs. Glass, warming her hands by the fire. "About a war hero. About a famous air ace. About a guy who traveled the world and met kings and queens and movie stars, a walking commercial for the United States of America. A guy who found out that when the fighting stops, a country doesn't have much need of heroes; it needs businessmen and factory workers and farmers. The world is always changing, sweetheart, and as it changes, people change too. Time don't stand still, and men will do desperate things to cling on to what they got. The taste for barnstorming air shows and flying daredevils didn't last. Airplanes are expensive machines to run. Your father's money began to disappear. He hired himself out as an expert aviator to whoever needed him, and yes, when the oil boom hit Mexico, like so many other adventurers that sniffed a quick buck, he moved south.

"He sold up and brought his family down here, to El Dorado, hoping to get rich from the harvest of black gold. But he soon found out it wasn't that easy. Sure, people were getting rich—the men who owned the oil companies—but everyone else, as usual, was getting screwed. He did what he could. He worked as a scout, a spotter, a taxi service for the rich executives. But no taxi driver ever got rich. His dreams were coming to nothing. But he was Jack Stone. He had to keep up the pretense of being a rich, successful swashbuckler. He had a big house to maintain. He had servants to pay and a wife to keep happy. It was a lie, though."

"It *wasn't*," said Precious. "It's *not* true."

"Oh, come on, sugar," said Mrs. Glass. "You're telling me you never suspected anything? You never wondered why your mother left home?"

Precious looked away, not wanting Mrs. Glass to see what she was thinking.

"Your father's a good actor, but you must have known that something was wrong," Mrs. Glass went on. "You must have noticed the worry in his face. Secret meetings with strange men?"

"Go on," said Precious, holding her voice steady.

"Your father found a way to make good money. Smuggling. He had the perfect cover. He was a clean-cut American hero, and he could fly wherever he wanted without suspicion. It started small. Some guy would approach him in a bar and ask if perhaps he could fly something over the border for him. This guy would have a friend. His friend had a friend. Word got around. Soon he was at the center of a major smuggling operation. Built a false bottom in that plane of his. Secret compartment to stash hot items in.

"Some of the most valuable things he carried were ancient artifacts. The Incas, the Mayans, and the Aztecs all left a lot of treasure behind, objects made of gold and studded with jewels, hidden in the forests and the jungles. Your father would spot forgotten ruins. He'd fly men there, open the temples, the graves, and the treasure-houses, and rob what was in them. Then he'd fly the stolen treasures to where the money was. To collectors in Brazil and America and the West Indies. I'm sure he reckoned he wasn't doing no harm. Nobody was getting hurt. Along the way, though, he met a lot of guys, some of them pretty bad pieces of work, and through them he heard about a great treasure. It wasn't gold, nor silver, it wasn't jade: it was words on paper. An American naval officer had stolen some secrets. Somehow he'd got his hands on a great deal of information about the U.S. Pacific Fleet. Details of the ships, their movements, their construction, their armaments, their secret radio codes even. And there was more. There were all the plans for new ships. Everything was in these papers. The officer well knew the value of it all and he escaped across the border into Mexico, starting a trail of greed and betrayal. He asked around and eventually he turned up on your father's doorstep. They struck a deal. In return for a handsome sum of money, your father would fly the officer to Argentina, where he had a buyer for the information.

"On the flight south, though, your father faked engine trouble. Told the officer that he'd have to set the plane down for repairs. He landed on a secret airstrip he knew in the heart of the rain forest, miles from anywhere. He tricked the officer. Left him there and flew home with the stolen documents. The poor schmuck ain't been seen since."

"You're lying," said Precious. "How do you know all this?"

"It's my job to know," said Mrs. Glass.

"If my father took those papers, it was so he could return them," said Precious. "He's not a traitor."

"Gold makes traitors of us all, honey," said Mrs. Glass.

"Your father set about trying to see who would pay the most for what he had, but he was playing a game that was too big for him. He'd strayed into very dangerous waters, and he got too greedy. His price kept going up. He'd make an agreement and then break it. In the end, one of the bidders ran out of patience."

"Who?" said Precious.

"Who would dearly love to control the Pacific Ocean? Who would pay most for American naval secrets?"

James looked at Sakata. "The Japanese," he said.

"Exactly," said Mrs. Glass. "America's rival in the Pacific. They got scared that the documents were gonna slip through their hands, so they sent a man."

"Sakata," said James.

"Sakata," said Mrs. Glass, nodding.

"My people knew of Mrs. Glass," said Sakata. "They told me where to find her."

"He came to me and asked if I'd care to steal the documents. The Japs were willing to pay a lot for them. I put together a team. It should have been easy. All we had to do was force Stone to open his safe, and that would be that. Sakata would take the documents with him back to Tokyo. What could your father do? He couldn't go to the police. He couldn't tell anyone. As I say, it should have been easy. But things went wrong from the start. First of all, Stone wasn't there, and nobody else knew the combination. Then the storm hit. And now . . ."

Mrs. Glass looked at James and Precious.

"The papers weren't in the safe, were they?" said James.

"Nope," said Mrs. Glass. "Which means that Jack Stone

has them with him." She stared at Precious and lit a cigarette with a glowing piece of firewood. "Which means that this ain't over for you yet, honey."

"What do you mean?"

"I mean that your daddy might see fit to hand over those papers in exchange for you."

"But JJ," said Precious. "He has to get to a doctor. He will die."

"I only need one of you," said Mrs. Glass.

"But you can't just let him die," wailed Precious.

"Why not? It might just focus your daddy's mind," said Mrs. Glass. "With one kid dead, he ain't gonna risk anything happening to the other one, is he? Now, there's only one thing I need to know."

"What?"

"Where is your daddy?"

"You think I'd tell you that?"

Mrs. Glass nodded to Strabo, who went into the storage hut and returned a little later carrying JJ in his arms. He laid him on the ground next to the fire.

Mrs. Glass stood and pulled her pistol from her belt. She aimed it at JJ's sleeping body.

"Where's your daddy?" she said calmly.

"This is not right," said Sakata.

"Where's your daddy?"

"Stop it! Stop it!" Precious screamed. "He's near Palenque. His plane is damaged. There's a jungle airstrip there."

"See," said Mrs. Glass, putting the gun away. "It wasn't so bad, was it? In the morning we're getting out of this dump.

Corona, you're going to get us to Palenque. Wherever the hell that is."

That night James felt too sick to eat. He sat out alone under the stars and thought about everything that had happened. Mrs. Glass's story. The death of Whatzat. And the death of Garcia. He had lost a friend today. He had only known Garcia a short time, but he knew that he had been a decent man. A good man. James had seen enough of the world, however, to know that good men die as easily as bad.

He told himself that he would not give in to despair. Deep inside, a tiny hard nub of hope kept him going, and right next to that nub of hope sat something cold and dark.

Revenge.

He had been to chapel enough times at Eton to know that a good Christian was supposed to turn the other cheek. That forgiveness was better than revenge. Well, maybe that was good enough for other boys, but it didn't work for him. He wouldn't be going to heaven when he died, but if he could only take some of these people to hell with him, then so be it.

Slowly everyone else in the camp settled down until he was the only one awake. He didn't want to sleep. Sleep was a healer. He wanted to feel his anger. He didn't want the comfort of dreams. Dreams would only lie to him and take him somewhere pleasant. They would take him home, back to Eton or Aunt Charmian's cozy little cottage in Kent.

Sometimes he dreamed that his mother and father were still alive.

He had no use for dreams.

He heard a noise and saw someone come out of the shed and walk quietly away.

It was a man, too tall to be Strabo. It must be Sakata.

James watched as he began to pace up and down.

"What are you doing?" he said, and Sakata stopped dead.

"I didn't know you were there," he said.

"Can't sleep," said James.

Sakata came over. He had a concerned look on his face.

"I am sorry about Garcia," he said.

"Feeling sorry won't bring him back," said James.

"I do not want you to think that I am like those other two," said Sakata softly.

"Aren't you?" said James. "You seem to go along with them quite happily."

"Until a month ago I did not know them at all," said Sakata. "I was sent because I can speak good English. I did not know what they were like. They have no honor. They leave a trail of senseless death behind them everywhere they go. I do not pretend to be a good man. I am a gangster too. Yakuza. But Mrs. Glass and Strabo have no allegiance. They serve no one. They have no code—"

"Please," said James. "I'm not sure I can bear to hear one murderer saying he's better than another because he kills people politely. You're all as bad as each other."

"Perhaps you are right," said Sakata with a sigh. "But perhaps I can change things for the better."

"It's a little late, don't you think?" said James. "The damage is done."

"We shall see," said Sakata. "I have had enough of this. It is not the fault of the children. They are innocent."

176

"You want to help Precious and JJ?" said James. "Then get the boy to the hospital in Veracruz. Otherwise just shut up. Shut up and leave me alone. I'm sick of the lot of you."

In the morning Sakata was gone. And he had taken JJ and the Chevrolet with him.

Strabo was furious. He stamped about the camp yelling obscenities and kicking things. The combination of his anger and the bruising had turned him a virulent purple color. He was so hoarse from shouting that his rasping voice had nearly fallen silent. The foul insults he hurled at the name of Sakata were the worst that James had ever heard.

Mrs. Glass remained quiet. James could see she was angry, angrier even than Strabo, but she refused to show it. Instead she turned in on herself and retreated into moody silence. She sat on a rock next to the truck and lit a cigarette, watching the smoke drift off into the still air around her. She gave off an atmosphere of coiled, poisonous menace. James noticed that Strabo was careful not to go near her.

Precious and James watched and waited by the truck to see what would happen now.

James could see that Precious was confused about JJ's disappearance. Different emotions fought to gain control of her features—hope, despair, happiness, fear, anger.

She put a hand on James's arm.

"Where do you think Sakata's taken him?" she said. "Where's JJ gone?"

"I think our man Sakata had a sudden attack of the morals," said James. "He turned out to be the Japanese equivalent of the Good Samaritan. The good samurai perhaps."

"You mean JJ's going to be all right?"

"I think so. I think Sakata must have taken him to Veracruz. He didn't want to watch him die. He'd probably have taken you too if Mrs. Glass hadn't been keeping such a close watch on you."

James told Precious about his conversation with the big Japanese man the night before, and she slowly broke down into tears.

She wept for a long time, and then she dried her eyes and wiped her nose.

"I'm not going to cry anymore," she said. "I won't give them the satisfaction."

James smiled at her. "The odds are much better now," he said. "It's two against two."

Eventually Strabo's anger died away, and Mrs. Glass flicked her cigarette into a mud hole. This act seemed to clear her mood, and she straightened her hat and came over to James with her usual air of cool detachment.

"Strabo, you get everything together and load up the truck," she said. "And you, Corona, you show me where we're going."

She took an old crumpled map from her jacket and unfolded it on the bonnet of the truck.

"Far as I can tell we're somewhere here," she said, jabbing at a spot just northwest of Veracruz.

James tried to remember what Charmian had showed him on her map when they were on Garcia's boat.

"You must continue south," he said, following the road with his finger. "Palenque is in the jungle, here, near to the border with Guatemala. It is an old Mayan city."

"That's three, maybe four hundred miles," said Strabo, who had joined them, "and all in the wrong direction. I wish we was goin' home."

"Home?" said Mrs. Glass.

"The States," said Strabo.

"The States haven't been our home for a long time," said Mrs. Glass. "We are no longer Americans, Strabo, and now that Sakata's gone, we're free to do what we like. We don't need to sell the plans to the Japs anymore. We can sell to the highest bidder."

A smile spread across Strabo's face.

"I'm beginning to see what you're getting at," he said. "So, where do we go? South America? Over to Europe, maybe?"

"No need," said Mrs. Glass. "I know where we can get a good price and keep clear of the law at the same time."

"Where?"

"Lagrimas Negras," she said, pointing to an island off the coast of the Yucatán Peninsula.

"You serious?" said Strabo. "I didn't think that place really existed. Like the Big Rock Candy Mountain, or El Dorado."

"Oh, it exists all right."

"I don't know—"

"Strabo, my friend," said Mrs. Glass, "we've been running around, putting our butts in harm's way for too long. Don't you think we've earned a rest? Don't you think that maybe it's time we put our feet up for a while and enjoyed some of the good things in life?"

"Yeah. I like the sounda that. Cocktails and fat steaks

and long, lazy evenings counting our money."

"So let's pay us a visit to the land of milk and honey," said Mrs. Glass. "We'll sell our booty to the old goat who runs the place, and take ourselves a nice long vacation."

"Now *that*," said Strabo, "is a plan."

"We'll have to ditch the truck at the first opportunity, though, and boost a car," said Mrs. Glass, folding the map. "Even with this paint job we could be recognized. It's been a coupla days since we killed those soldiers, and word might have got around."

"If only I hadn't let that greaser escape," said Strabo, and he spat onto the ground.

"What's done is done," said Mrs. Glass. "Now, let's saddle up and get out of here. I can tell you I will not be sorry to say good-bye to this place." She opened the passenger-side door and nodded to Precious and James to get in.

"I am *not* sitting with you," said Precious. "I refuse, and you can't make me. I will scream and yell and fight you every inch of the way."

"I'm too tired for this," said Mrs. Glass. "Get in, or I'll—"

"Or you'll what?" Precious cut her off, hands on hips, head tilted to one side. "You can't shoot me, I'm all you've got."

Mrs. Glass sighed. "Put her in the back and tie her to the bench," she said to Strabo, who grabbed a rope and hauled Precious around to the rear of the truck. "You'll have to sit up there with her, see she doesn't get any ideas."

"Is that a good idea?" said James, and Mrs. Glass looked at him from under the brim of her hat.

"You got a better one?" she said.

"Maybe I should sit with her."

"You?"

"Give me another chance," said James. "Strabo will be noticed. They will be looking for men. Who will look at a couple of kids?"

"You've got a point," said Mrs. Glass, and then she put a hand on James's shoulder and gripped it hard, staring into his face with her ice blue eyes. "You've got another reason for wanting to be up there in the back with her, though, haven't you?"

James tried to look as innocent as possible. He shrugged. "What do you mean?"

"I've been watching you, Corona. You can't hide anything from me. I know what you're up to."

James put on a big, foolish grin. "I'm not up to anything, *señora*," he said.

"Sure you are," said Mrs. Glass. "You're not just a thief, are you, Corona?"

"Well, I—"

"You're a lover too, aren't you, kid?"

James blushed.

Mrs. Glass laughed.

"You've taken a shine to that gal, haven't you? Don't think I haven't seen the two of you together. Can't say as I blame you. She's a pretty little thing. Now, I don't want to break your heart, blue eyes, but I don't think a girl like that would look twice at a *Mexicano* like you if things were different. If she was back home in that fancy house of hers, with all her pretty dresses and her servants."

"She's okay," said James. "But she has a sharp tongue on her."

"Don't I know it," said Mrs. Glass, handing him a water canteen. "Okay. You ride in back with the girl. But don't let her sweet-talk you into doing nothing stupid."

"You can trust me."

"Can I? I trusted you to watch the guards."

"It won't happen again."

"Damned right it won't." She walked off. "I like you, Corona," she called back over her shoulder, "but it won't stop me from killing you."

CHAPTER 16—NOW OR NEVER

The truck trundled slowly out of the oil field, past the deserted guardhouse at the entrance, along the pitted dirt track, and onto the road. James sat in the back opposite Precious, who was tied to the bench but looking strangely happy. She grinned at him.

"You're looking at me like I have a plan," said James.

"It's going to be all right," said Precious. "We're going to get away and we're going to help Daddy."

"Are you sure you want to?" said James. "After what he's done."

"Oh, but don't you see?" said Precious.

"See what?"

"See why he didn't sell those plans? Why he wouldn't do a deal?"

"He got too greedy," said James.

"No," said Precious, as if she were talking to a stupid child. "He was never going to sell them all along. It's obvious. He stole them off that naval officer just so that he could give them back to the American government."

"Maybe," said James, who didn't want to argue with the girl. If it helped her to believe this story, then he wasn't going to interfere.

"Daddy would never betray his country," said Precious. "He never would."

"No . . ." said James. He couldn't blame her for thinking this way. It must have been painful hearing that the father she had worshipped as a hero had proved to be as weak and as human as anyone else. "I'm sorry," he added.

"Sorry for what?"

"I didn't know . . . about you and your father and everything. I didn't know your mother had left home."

"That was another lie," said Precious harshly. "She travels to America a lot. That's all. She has family there. She likes the shops. It's too hot for her in Mexico. . . ."

James nodded and turned away. People were very complicated sometimes.

"*You* may not have a plan," said Precious after a while, "but I do."

"Oh, yes?"

"Yes. We get off this truck. We flag down a car, and we go and get help."

James looked at her. Her eyes were shining, her face open and excited.

"Okay," he said. "It's as good a plan as any. The only thing is—if it goes wrong and they catch us at it, they'll probably kill me."

"Are you scared?"

"No," James lied. "Are you?"

"Not anymore."

"Good," said James, taking Strabo's hunting knife from his belt. "Here's what we do . . ."

There were no other vehicles on the road. Occasionally

they passed people on foot: peasants and farmers, once a family with a donkey. If they did escape it might be some time before they found anyone to help them. But for now James just wanted to concentrate on getting off the truck. Once he'd sawed through Precious's ropes, they carefully got up, leaning on the back of the cab for support.

They studied the way ahead, waiting for their opportunity.

It took a while, but eventually they came to a wooded area where large trees overhung the road.

"Get ready," James said to Precious, bracing himself. "Don't make a sound. You go first. I'll help you."

Precious gave a quick, tense nod of her head.

The first few trees were no good. Their branches were too flimsy or too far away. Then the truck was going too fast. Finally, they came to a sharp bend. The truck slowed to a crawl, and James spotted exactly what he was looking for: the perfect tree.

"There," he said, and Precious understood.

He waited until the last moment before hoisting Precious into the air. She grabbed hold of a good thick branch, then quickly pulled herself up and lay flat along it, so that she wouldn't be seen in the truck's rearview mirrors. James looked back. In a moment she had disappeared from view.

Now it was his turn. It was going to be difficult. The trees were thinning out and the truck was picking up speed. He would have to hurry. He couldn't spot the ideal tree, though.

Hell. He couldn't waste any more time. He was going to have to risk it. He tightened the strap of the canteen across his chest and climbed higher onto the side of the truck, balancing unsteadily. A branch was heading straight for him. But the truck was going much faster, now. He heard it shift gear. Strabo gunned the accelerator.

It was now or never.

James threw himself into the air and the branch thudded into his chest like a giant's club. Somehow he hung on, and, without even knowing what he was doing, swung his legs up and wrapped himself around the branch. He was dizzy and sick, his head swimming, black spots weaving before his eyes. He couldn't breathe. He was dimly aware of the truck rolling on, kicking up dust as it went. He waited until it had passed out of sight around another bend, then slipped into unconsciousness and dropped to the ground.

He was awakened by the feel of water on his face and looked up to see Precious kneeling over him.

"Don't waste the water," he croaked.

"Is that all the thanks I get?" she said.

"Sorry," said James, sitting up. He took a drink. The canteen was nearly empty. "Thank you."

"Are you hurt?"

"I don't think so. At least nothing's broken." James struggled to stand. "We need to get off the road," he said, wincing. His chest was burning and he felt very short of breath. Precious helped him. She put an arm around him and they hobbled to the verge.

James looked around. The countryside on the other side of the road fell away into open scrubland. If they went that way they could be easily spotted. On this side the ground rose through the trees and up a steep, rocky slope.

"We need to get as far away from here as we can," he said, although it hurt him to talk. "It's only a matter of time before they find we've gone. They'll be bound to come back and look for us. We'll have to climb up there."

"Will you be able to?"

"Yes," James snapped. "Don't worry about me. Let's go."

The going was quite easy at first. Under the trees it was cool and shady, and the ground was soft. But, as they climbed higher, the trees thinned and gave way to rocks and cactus. Soon they were out in the open, baking in the midday sun. The rocks were hard and sharp, and there was no obvious path. They moved from one hiding place to another, trying to keep to the shadows. James checked all the while to make sure they couldn't be seen from the road below. It was slow work, hot and painful. James felt awful and was sure that at any moment he would be sick. He prayed that he hadn't damaged anything inside.

"How far do we have to go?" Precious whined.

"As far as we can," grunted James. "The more distance we put between us and the road the less chance they have of finding us."

"I don't think they'll come back," said Precious. "They're in too much of a hurry to get to Palenque. This is a waste of time."

"Save your breath," said James, and then he suddenly grabbed her and pulled her down behind a rock.

"What are you doing?" Precious gasped, and James clamped a hand across her mouth.

"Listen," he hissed.

From down below they heard the sound of the truck chugging along the road. It passed on by. A minute later it returned and they heard it stop.

"Don't move," James whispered, letting Precious go. She stayed in the shadow of the rock, trembling with fear.

"If I had a gun I would go down there and I would kill them," she murmured.

James felt the Mexican officer's pistol still tucked into the waistband at the back of his trousers under his shirt. He thought it best not to tell her about it. If they tried to take on Mrs. Glass and Strabo in a gun battle, he knew all too well who would lose. He had seen enough dead bodies in the last few days to show him just how deadly the gang was.

"We can't take them on by ourselves," he said.

"I will see them hanged for what they did to Garcia," said Precious.

"I still can't believe he's dead," said James.

"That poor man," said Precious. "He was kind to me and JJ. He didn't have to be. He saved JJ's life in the flood. He tried to take him away to safety, and he paid for it with his own life. Well, I am going to make *them* pay for that."

"I don't like them any more than you do," whispered James. "But there's nothing we can do now. We just have to try and stay alive. So, keep still and keep quiet."

They waited like that for nearly an hour before they heard the truck start up again and move off. James felt very tired, and for a moment he let his head drop down to his chest, and he nodded off.

It was Precious who woke him up.

"What do we do now?" she said. "Have they gone?"

"I think so," said James.

"Do we go back down?"

"Too dangerous."

"Are you proposing we spend the night here?" said Precious.

"No. We need to find shelter and water. What's left in the canteen won't last long."

"All right, don't rub it in. I was only trying to help. Would you rather I'd left you lying there in the road?"

"No. Obviously," said James. "I didn't mean anything by it. Do you have to be so spiky all the time?"

"I'm hot and I'm tired and I'm hungry," said Precious sadly.

"Me too," said James. "We'll wait here until it cools down a bit, then look for somewhere to hole up for the night."

So they sat there and waited as the sun slowly dropped behind the Sierra Madre and their side of the hill was cloaked with purple shade. They watched the line of shadow creep down the hillside and march out across the flat green lowlands to the distant silver ribbon of the sea.

The air cooled rapidly, and James was feeling stiff all over.

"Come on," he said, "let's move on."

It was torture having to get up and walk again, but somehow he managed it, and Precious trailed behind him, grumbling quietly to herself. They followed a little gully upward and presently heard running water. They headed for the sound and eventually crested a ridge to find a large basin in the rocks. It was carpeted with greenery, and there was a thin, silver waterfall tumbling into a pool.

Precious laughed and they hurried down the slope, threw themselves on their bellies, and drank in great mouthfuls of cold water.

"We'll make camp here," said James, rolling onto his back and looking up at the darkening sky. "It's perfect."

"James?" said Precious.

"What?"

"I can't stop thinking about JJ. Worrying about him. Do you really think he's all right?"

"I'm sure he is," said James, although he was as worried as the girl. "He'll be sitting up in his nice comfy hospital bed eating ice cream."

Precious laughed. "JJ loves ice cream. Strawberry and chocolate."

"In the morning," said James, "we'll flag down a car and hitch a ride into Veracruz. You'll be together again, and we can try to get in contact with your father on the radio. We have to try and warn him about Mrs. Glass."

"Yes . . ." said Precious, and she fell silent, hardly daring to hope that James's words might come true.

Before it got too dark, they collected ferns and leaves and moss, and made a bed of sorts. They were both exhausted, sleeping would not be difficult tonight, but James sat and watched over Precious until he was sure she was asleep, then lay down and closed his eyes. He was too tired to think about tomorrow, and in no time at all he was dead to the world.

But Precious had been faking. When she heard James's breathing become slow and deep she opened her eyes and looked at him.

A thin sheen of moonlight lay across his skin. She

pushed back the untidy lock of hair that always fell into his face, and wished him good night.

Precious awoke to the smell of wood smoke. She was chilled to the bone, but James was already up and had made a fire.

His hair was wet and plastered to his forehead. He had been for a swim in the rock pool and was wearing just his underpants. The rest of his clothes were hanging out to dry on branches. There were livid blue-and-brown bruises on his ribs.

"Did you sleep all right?" he asked.

"Yes, thank you," said Precious, and her stomach gave a long, noisy growl. They both laughed.

"I am *so* hungry," she said. "I don't think I shall be able to walk a single step today."

"We have to get back down to the road," said James.

Precious groaned. Her hunger was making her miserable. She looked at the jagged hem of her dress. At her dirty hands. She remembered that she had promised not to cry again, and instead she clenched her fists and punched the earth.

"Oh, I hate this," she said fiercely. "I need a proper meal and a hot bath and a change of clothes."

"Well," said James, "I can't offer a hot bath, but there's a perfectly serviceable cold shower just over there. You can wash your dress in the pool."

Precious jumped up, cheerful again.

"You mustn't look."

"I won't," said James, walking off to fetch his clothes. "I'll go and see if I can't find something to eat."

Precious went down to the pool, stripped off her dress,

and dived in. The water was icy and clear as crystal, and for a moment, she forgot everything except the feel of it on her skin and the sound of it in her ears.

She came up grinning from ear to ear and swam over to the waterfall. The water pounded down on her head and neck and shoulders. It was the best massage she had ever had. She untangled some of the knots from her hair and let the water wash away all her frustration.

James, meanwhile, was following an animal track up the other side of the crater and into the rocks. In his hand was the pistol. He wasn't sure if he'd find any edible wildlife, but he wanted to be ready if he did.

A small brown bird flew up from the undergrowth and rattled off into the sky, and apart from the insects, it was the only living thing he saw for the next few minutes.

He spotted a stand of the big cactuses known as prickly pears. They would not bear fruit until later in the year, but he remembered seeing some cooked on a roadside stall in Tampico and sold as *nopalitos*. He cut off a couple of smaller, flat, padlike growths, being careful not to spike himself, and sat down on a rock in the sun to scrape away the big spines and the nasty little furry ones with Strabo's knife. It felt good to warm his body. His damp clothes were sticking to him, and they made him uncomfortable and chilly.

As he was sitting there, lost in his work, he realized that he wasn't alone. Another creature had come out to warm up in the morning sun. It was a huge, ugly lizard. An iguana. Looking like a prehistoric beast. Being cold-blooded it had no way of warming its blood up by itself, so it was letting the sun bake its loose, wrinkly skin.

It had a two-foot-long tail and a body the size of a large cat. As James looked at it he saw that there were two more iguanas sunning themselves on rocks about ten feet away, their heads erect, alert for danger.

Moving ever so slowly, never taking his eyes off the nearest big lizard, James carefully picked up the pistol. He raised it and gently eased back the hammer, anxious that it didn't move too quickly and snap into place with a loud click. He leveled the sights at the lizard, which had eyes in the side of its head, giving it a very wide field of vision.

James released the safety catch, holding the heavy gun as steady as he could.

He held his breath, closed one eye, and squeezed. The trigger was stiff and needed more strength than he had counted on. He squeezed harder . . . harder . . .

The bang was incredibly loud, and the gun jumped in James's hand. For a moment he was stunned, his ears ringing and the muscles in his arm tingling.

There was no sign of any of the three lizards. He must have missed.

He stood up and went over to where the one he had shot at had been lying, and looked around.

He spotted the mottled black-and-gray body lying behind a rock.

Its head was missing, and though James looked for it he never found it.

He picked the lizard up. It was warm and dry and its legs were still twitching slightly.

He reckoned that Precious would be pretty squeamish about eating it, and he didn't want to make it any harder for her than he had to, so he took out his knife, slit its belly open, and gutted it on the rocks. He then cut off its feet, with their long rattly claws, and most of its tail.

Precious ran up just as he was impaling the thing on a long straight stick.

"What's going on?" she said. "I heard a shot."

"It's all right," said James. "It was only me. I was shooting our breakfast."

"You've got a gun?"

James shrugged. "I took it off the Mexican officer."

"You've had it all this time?"

"Precious," said James indignantly, "what would have happened if I'd tried to use it? I'd have ended up as dead as this lizard."

Precious was about to say something else when she looked at the iguana for the first time and made a horrified face.

"I hope you don't expect me to eat that," she said, backing away and putting a hand to her mouth.

"Suit yourself," said James, and he picked up the lizard and the prickly pear and set off back to their camp.

After her swim, Precious had stoked the fire with some large pieces of wood and got a good hot blaze going so she could dry her clothes, and now the logs were glowing red-hot.

James sat down and held the skewered lizard over the flames, ignoring the protests from Precious. As the heat got to it, the skin bubbled, cracked, and darkened. James had to keep turning it so that all sides were evenly done.

Soon a pleasant smell of roasting meat wafted around the

crater. James's mouth began to water, and he noticed the hungry look return to Precious's face. She shuffled nearer and sat down next to him.

Once the lizard was done, he peeled off the crisp skin with his knife and cut the animal up into pieces. It looked like any plate of meat now, and when he tasted it, it was not unlike a tough chicken. It felt good to have some warm meat inside him.

In the end Precious couldn't resist it. She gingerly picked up a scrap, popped it in her mouth, screwed up her eyes, and chewed it. She relaxed. Took a larger chunk of flesh. Soon she was tucking in with gusto.

She ate greedily, meat juices dribbling down her chin. Squatting on her haunches she looked like a wild animal. All the carefully arranged curls and waves had fallen from her hair, and the makeup had long since been scrubbed from her skin.

James smiled. She was changing, toughening up, growing up. She was starting to understand that many of the things that she thought were important were not important at all.

In no time the meat had gone—all that was left was a pile of thin bones and burned skin. James browned the *nopalitos* over the hot embers and cut them into slices. They were quite tasty, if a little slimy.

Afterward they lay back on the grass, contented, and for a brief moment they forgot all about their troubles.

But the moment soon passed. A cloud plunged the crater into shadow, and Precious shivered.

"I suppose we should get going," she said, remembering all they had to do today if they were to get to JJ in Veracruz.

"We better had," said James, licking his greasy fingers and rolling onto his feet.

They doused the fire, filled the canteen with fresh water, and began the long slog back down the hillside to the road.

An hour later they were sitting under a tree, ready to flag down the first vehicle that came along.

The minutes ticked by. A man on a donkey appeared and slowly walked past them, man and beast looking hot and bored. They heard a car's engine, but it was going the wrong way. It sailed northward in a cloud of dust and fumes. They heard another car, and this one was heading in the right direction. They jumped up and waved at it, but it didn't even slow down. The driver sat staring straight ahead.

Precious shouted after it, but it was no use. They returned to their spot under the tree and sat there in gloomy silence.

"We could be here for days," said Precious, "and all the time Mrs. Glass will be getting farther away from us. We have to warn Daddy. We have to get help."

"I know," said James. "We must be patient. Someone will come along eventually."

Even as he said it they heard another engine approaching from the north. A car. They stood up and stared along the road, willing it to appear. At last it came into view: it was a black Dodge sedan, traveling fast.

They weren't going to take any chances this time. They stood in the middle of the road, waving their arms like mad and shouting for it to stop.

"It's slowing down," said Precious. "I think it's going to stop."

Sure enough, the Dodge pulled up before it got to them.

"Looks like our prayers have been answered," said James.

He went over, putting on his most friendly, open face. But when the driver got out of the car, the smile froze on James's lips.

He had last seen the man in Tres Hermanas, suspended in the air outside the Stones' house. Their eyes had locked then, and they locked again now.

It was Manny—the youngest member of Mrs. Glass's gang.

Manny, who James had pushed out of the window.

And he was holding a gun.

Everyone stood very still.

CHAPTER 17—MANNY THE GIRL

Manny was sweating heavily and had a wild look in his red-rimmed eyes, which darted about as if he were watching a particularly manic fly zigzagging through the air.

He frowned at James, then looked over to Precious and frowned harder, trying to make sense of what he was seeing. He blinked. He rubbed his mouth.

"Hah!" he shouted finally, and slapped his leg. "I know you."

"I don't think so," said James. "How could that be?"

"I know you," said Manny, slowly shaking his head. "And I know the girl." He aimed his pistol at James with a trembling hand. "She's the Stone girl," he went on. "Yes. I know her. Jack Stone's little girl. And *you* . . ." He squinted at James. "I know your face. I saw it in the storm. It was you. Yes. You pushed me out the window, didn't you?"

"No," said James. "You're mistaken."

"No, no, no, no, no . . ." said Manny, and he grinned. "Oh, I got you, now. I got you good. Where's the other one? Where's the shrimp?"

"Just leave us alone," said Precious.

"Oh, I should kill you," said Manny. "I should shoot you here and now." He groaned and clutched his head. "Goddamn," he said. "I got such a headache." He screwed his eyes shut, forgetting about James and Precious for a moment.

When he opened them again, he looked calm and relaxed, all the pain gone from his face. He looked off toward the sea then back at James, not recognizing him.

"There was somebody else here," he said. "I was talking to somebody else . . ."

James was staring at him, openmouthed. When Manny had turned his head, James had seen for the first time that he was badly injured. A section of his skull above his right ear had broken away and was hanging loose, still attached by a flap of hair-covered skin. As he moved, the flap swung backward and forward like a door opening and closing. And as it opened it revealed a glistening patch of pinkish gray brain behind a rubbery membrane.

His shirt collar was stained with blood, but the flow had stopped, and the edges of the wound were black and scabby. James was half-revolted and half-fascinated by the wagging piece of skull.

Manny peered at the gun in his hand as if he had no idea how it had got there. He stuffed it in a pocket.

"I'm trying to get to Veracruz," he said. "Is this the right road?"

"Yes," said James.

"At last someone who can speak American," said Manny. "I been up and down this road. It's the only road open."

"Yes," said James and he pointed. "You want Veracruz? It's that way."

"It sure is good to meet a friend all this way out here," said Manny.

James turned to Precious with a questioning look.

"We can show you the way," she said.

"Sure." said Manny. "Get in."

As Precious passed James on her way to the car he gave her another look.

"It's a ride, at least," she muttered. She was right—it *was* transport, even if the driver did seem to have scrambled his brain. It was dangerous, very dangerous, but this might be their only chance of getting to Veracruz.

When Precious got a glimpse of Manny's wound, however, she clamped a hand over her mouth and tried not to gag. She backed away from the car in horror.

Manny glared at the two of them, the madness coming back into his eyes.

"Get in," he snapped, and they obeyed.

James climbed into the front seat next to Manny, and Precious got in the back. Before setting off, Manny gave them the once-over.

"I know you from somewhere," he said, putting the gun in his lap and releasing the brake.

"We're your friends," said James. "Remember?"

"Sure," said Manny, and he gave a happy smile. "We're all friends. We're family. Yeah. Mama's gonna be so pleased when she sees us. I'm gonna tell her all about what's happened. She'll laugh. She always laughs. Makes everything A-okay. Man, that was some storm back there, wasn't it? You shoulda seen me. I think I hit my head something bad. I don't remember most of it. Woke up in the bushes. Didn't know where I was. They left me behind. Can you believe that? That witch left me to die back there. Well, I don't give up that easy. I walked and walked. Couldn't walk no more. Borrowed a car."

James noticed a small hole in the windscreen. He touched it.

"Yeah," said Manny, and he laughed. A crazy high-pitched laugh, almost like a scream. "That was me. Mama's little boy. Shot a hole right through the windshield. Bam! Driver didn't want to stop. Now, don't you think that was rude? I need a car and he won't stop. Well, he's stopped now. Ha, ha, ha, ha, ha, ha. He's one dead Mexican."

Manny suddenly stamped on the brake, snatched up the gun, and held it to James's head. "I know you," he said, cocking the hammer. "You're the rat who pushed me out that window. Oh, Mama, you're gonna wish you never did that. . . ."

James could see the confusion in his eyes. It was like looking into the eyes of an animal, rather than a human, and he knew he would have to treat Manny like a wild dog.

"I'm gonna blast your brains out," said Manny, pressing the gun barrel painfully into James's forehead.

"No," said James calmly and firmly, and Manny frowned. "Put the gun away, Manny," James went on, as soothingly as possible. "You don't need to shoot me. I'm your friend, remember? You don't need to shoot me."

Manny struggled to stop his mind from wandering. Tears filled his lower lids.

"I'm so mixed up," he said. "There's somebody inside my head, whispering and whispering, and sometimes they shout, they shout so loud I can't think. Oh, Geecries, you don't know what it's like."

"It's not me you want to shoot," said James. "It's Mrs. Glass, remember? She left you behind, Manny. She left you for dead."

"Mrs. Glass?" Manny was thoughtful, turning the name over in his damaged mind. At last he gave a long sigh of relief and wiped away the tear that was crawling down his cheek. "Yes," he said. "Mrs. Glass. That's it. We'll find her. Don't you worry."

"Let's drive," said James. "It's getting late."

"Yeah . . ." Manny started the car up again and they set off.

James noticed that as long as he was driving, Manny could concentrate and hold his thoughts together. So James got him to talk about himself, to stop him from thinking about who his passengers were and what had happened at the Stones' house.

It all came out in a jumble as his memory jumped about from one incident to another, but James managed to piece together a rough picture of Manny's grim little life. His father had been a small-time thief in New York who had spent most of Manny's childhood in prison. He had finally died of blood poisoning from an infected stab wound he'd earned in a street brawl when Manny was ten. Manny had followed in his father's footsteps. He'd been a pickpocket, a numbers runner, a lookout for the gangs, a housebreaker; then when he was old enough, he'd graduated to bootlegging, and armed with a rifle, had gone on beer runs up into Canada and back.

"I wanted more, though," he explained. "I wanted my own gang. I wanted to be remembered for something. To make a name for myself. Wasn't going to happen in New York. The whole town was carved up by the big gangs and the local political machines. There wasn't room for a new face. But out of town, in the Midwest, in Kansas and Nebraska, Michigan, and Ohio, things were starting to happen. Guys were making names for themselves as bank robbers—Machine Gun Kelly, Pretty Boy Floyd, Baby Face Nelson, John Dillinger, Bonnie and Clyde. Yeah, not just guys, gals as well, like Ma Barker. Yeah, that was the place to be, and that was where I went. You probably heard of me. Manny the Girl!"

Manny laughed and looked around at James. "Manny the Girl. That's what they call me. On account of how I dress up as a girl to pull bank jobs. I make a very pretty girl. . . ."

James looked at Manny's soft, unlined face. He could just about imagine him disguised as a girl, but it was not a pretty picture.

"What I do is this," Manny went on. "I go in the bank, flutter my eyelashes at them dumb tellers, and get them on the back foot; then I pull my gun from my purse and clean the place out. Works every time. Change my outfit in the car, and the stupid coppers bust their guts searching for a female bank robber. The newspapers are crazy for me. They call me the Black Widow, or Deadly Nightshade, the Poison Blonde. The pros, though, they know who I am. They all know my name: Manny the Girl. But it's getting tougher 'n' tougher, let me tell you. The banks are on the lookout for me. They're suspicious of every woman that steps inside their doors. So I got my brother Louis helping me out now."

As Manny got excited in the telling of his story, his driving slipped out of control. He was swerving crazily down the road, switching sides, driving sometimes on the left and sometimes on the right.

"Slow down, Manny," said James. "We don't need to go so fast."

"Yeah," said Manny, and he laughed. "For a moment there I thought we was running from a job. Thought the cops were on our tail. Could hear the sirens and everything."

James saw that the car was stuffed with banknotes. He didn't know where Manny had got all the money from, but he guessed that he had stolen it somewhere along the way. He doubted that Manny would even be able to remember. His memory of recent events was shot to pieces, but distant events seemed clear and sharp in his mind, as if they had happened only yesterday.

"What about Mrs. Glass?" said James. "How long have you been with her?"

"This is my first job with her," said Manny. "Strabo's the only one of us she's worked with before. We was in Texas, me an' Louis. We'd turned over a bank in San Antone, and it had got messy. There was a lot of shooting. I slipped over the border to Monterrey. Was hanging out there till the heat died down a little, keeping my ears to the ground. Met up with a half-deaf safe buster called Whatzat. He told me about some broad who was looking for muscle. You couldn't rightly say in the end whether we found her or she found us, but there she was, with a Jap and a dwarf, talking big bucks and an easy job down on the Gulf Coast. Still can't believe she lit out on me, Whatzat too. Ran off and left me to rot in Tres Hermanas. Well, I ain't gonna stop until I find her, and when I do, whooo boy, you watch the fireworks! If she thinks she ain't gonna give me my cut, she's got another think coming. If she thinks . . . if she thinks . . . Well, damn her to hell. Where is she?"

James could tell that Manny was about to have one of his fits, unless he could head him off.

"It's all right, Manny," he said. "Where would you go if you were her?"

"Only one place," said Manny. "Veracruz. Take a boat out of this stinking country."

"Exactly," said James. "That's where you'll find her. That's where we're going. Remember? We just need to get to Veracruz. We don't need a change of plan."

"Yeah," said Manny, and he sniggered. "I knew all along. See. She can't fool me. Manny the Girl don't take things lying down. Yeah, Manny the Girl, that's what they call me, on account of my disguise. . . ."

He was off again. He'd been over this part of the story at least three times now, and James knew it back to front, which was how Manny told it mostly.

The great peak of Mount Orizaba, tipped with white snow, passed to their right, and as they neared civilization the roads steadily improved, and they began to see buildings and people. They passed through some small villages and then a couple of larger towns, all the time getting closer to Veracruz.

Thank God. They were almost there.

Then all they would have to do was ditch Manny at the first opportunity, which shouldn't be too hard, considering the confused state he was in, and they were home and dry.

And not too soon. Manny was sweating badly, and the inside of the car felt damp and claustrophobic. Flies had got in and they crawled on his wound, which was starting to smell.

In the late afternoon they saw a sprawl of white buildings on the coast up ahead, but the Dodge was beginning to falter.

"We're running low on gas," Manny explained. "We need to fill her up."

"We're nearly there," said James. "Just a few more miles."

It would be awful to get this close, only to grind to a halt.

They were fine on the downhill slopes. Manny could cut the gas and freewheel, but if they had to use the engine on flatter sections of the road, the car would judder and falter. Luckily it was downhill nearly all the way.

"Come on, baby, you can make it," said Manny.

Then, at a junction, James spotted a small roadside shack selling farm produce and gasoline.

"We're saved," he said, and Manny whooped with delight.

They coasted to a stop by the pump. It was very quiet. There didn't seem to be anybody around.

"Why is everything always closed in this goddamn country?" said Manny. "How's a man supposed to go about his business?"

He shoved his door open and got out, then stood and stretched, his muscles cramped from the long drive. He twisted his neck and grunted as it clicked.

"*Hola!*" he shouted. "Shake a leg. You got a customer."

A swing door opened and a tired-looking Mexican woman came out.

"There you are!" said Manny. "Fill her up. Full. *Entiendes?*"

"Full?" said the woman.

"You got it," said Manny, and turned to look up the

road. As he did so the woman got a look at the wound in his head. She gasped and said something under her breath that sounded like a prayer.

"Whassamatter with you?" said Manny. "Why are you staring at me?"

The woman was shaking her head and backing away from Manny, still muttering.

"I said what's the matter with you?" said Manny, advancing on her. "You look like you seen a ghost or something."

James got out of the car.

"What's eating her?" said Manny.

"Get back in the car," said James. "I'll sort this out."

"Don't treat me like a kid, Louis," said Manny, and he rubbed his temple.

"I'm not Louis," said James. "I'm not your brother."

Manny laughed. "Sure you are. Don't try and kid me, Louis. You always was a kidder. Oh, this is giving me a headache." He let out a long animal moan that ended up as a sort of growl.

The woman backed in through her door and James heard the lock slide shut.

"Now, you get back out here," yelled Manny. "You hear me? I need some gas. *Gasolina*."

He pulled out his pistol and started firing at the building, laughing wildly. James ducked back into the car.

"What are we going to do?" said Precious.

"If we can just make it as far as Veracruz," said James.

"Should we make a run for it?"

"It's too risky," said James. "He'd try and shoot us."

"I can't stand it a moment longer," said Precious. "Being

shut up in here with him. That hole in his head is making me nauseous."

"Hold on," said James. "We're so close."

Manny walked over to the car, put his gun on the roof, and unscrewed the petrol cap. He then took the hose from the pump and started to fill the tank.

He leaned in through the window. "Why'd she stare at me like that, Louis?" he said. "I don't like people staring at me."

James heard a rumble and looked around to see a police car driving toward them. There were two policemen in it, probably alerted by the gunshots. They pulled onto the verge a little way off and got out. They said something to each other and walked cautiously toward Manny, who had his back to them and hadn't seen them.

"Manny," said James, "I think we'd better go."

"She's not full yet," said Manny.

"Never mind," said James. "Let's go."

Manny finally heard something and turned around to see the two policemen approaching from the rear.

He grinned at them. "*Buenos días*," he said. "Just filling the ol' jalopy."

One of the policemen said something in Spanish.

"*No entiendo*," said Manny. "*No hablo español.*"

The other policeman moved a hand toward the gun on his belt, but Manny was too quick for him. He dropped the hose, snatched his pistol from the car roof, and fired. The policeman threw himself to the ground just in time and avoided being hit. The other policeman also dived for cover. Manny fired off a couple more shots and jumped into the car.

"Let's get out of here," he said.

They screamed off down the road, Manny crunching through the gear changes, forcing the Dodge to her limit. A siren started up behind them, and James looked in the rear-view mirror to see the police car pulling out.

Manny still had his gun in his hand.

"Take the wheel," he said, and without slowing down, he leaned out of the window, twisted around, and let off a volley of shots.

There was a deep thud and a bright flash. He had hit the petrol pump. A boiling, orange-and-black ball of flame rose up and filled the sky behind them.

CHAPTER 18—CHANGE OF PLAN

A cloud of thick, purple smoke with a raging orange heart filled the road. In a moment the police car burst from it like a bat out of hell, its siren blaring.

"*Hoowee!*" shouted Manny, taking charge of the wheel again. "This is more like it, Louis."

One of the policemen was shooting at them out of his window now. They were going too fast for him to aim accurately and every bullet missed, but James knew that if they couldn't pull ahead, it would only be a matter of time before the shooter got lucky. He scrunched down in his seat, trying to make himself very small. There was a little figure of the Virgin of Guadalupe fixed to the dashboard, and he was seriously considering sending out a prayer to her.

Manny was a good driver, and had had a lot of practice escaping from the police. They tore down the road, feeling every bump and dip, skidding and sliding in the loose grit, but slowly, ever so slowly, the police car fell behind, until at last, it disappeared from view.

"Looks like we burned our bridges," said Manny. "We ain't gonna be very welcome in Veracruz."

James was seething. Veracruz had meant safety. It had meant help. It had meant finding JJ and an end to this ordeal. Now they were racing south down the coastal road with no destination and no hope of rescue. There were a few large towns ahead. They could try to steer Manny into the next one they came to, but if the Mexican police telephoned ahead, they would be welcomed by bullets. He felt the gun pressing into the small of his back. Could he get it out? Shoot Manny? No. Not traveling at this speed. And Manny had his own gun still in his lap.

And the simple truth was that Manny was used to shooting people, and James wasn't.

They were driving through fertile green lowlands, close to the ocean. There was evidence that the storm had struck here, although nowhere near as severely as farther north. There was water everywhere, but people seemed to be getting on with their lives as usual. As day slipped into evening they passed farmers returning from their fields, clogging the roads with donkeys and mule wagons.

Eventually Manny had to stop the car. There was a flock of sheep crossing the road.

"Damn," he said, wiping his face. "I sure wish I knew this place better."

"Where are we going?" said Precious miserably from the back, and Manny looked startled, as if he had forgotten all about her. He turned around in his seat.

"What did you say?" he asked.

"I said, where are we going?" Precious repeated.

"Where are we going?" said Manny. "I'll tell you where we're going . . . we're going to . . ." The wild look came back into his eyes. As long as they'd been driving he hadn't needed to think. Now his poor, damaged brain was struggling to make sense of it all. He began to shake. "There was a storm," he said. "A kid . . ."

"We're going to find Mrs. Glass," James said hurriedly, hoping to distract Manny from thinking about what had happened.

"That's right," said Manny, and he struck the steering wheel with his fists. But then the haunted look returned. He became like a little boy lost. "Where is she?" he said. "I don't know where she is."

"Don't worry," said James. "We'll find her."

Manny snatched up the gun and started waving it around inside the car.

"Where is she?" he screamed. "Where's that devil-woman gotten to? Tell me. Tell me or I'll shoot your face off, I swear to God I will."

He grabbed James by the throat and forced him back against the side of the car, jamming the gun into his cheek with his other hand.

James thought quickly. Should he tell Manny the truth? Get him to drive them to Palenque, and hope they arrived before Mrs. Glass and Strabo? Then they could maybe warn Jack Stone . . . ?

No. It was too risky. What if Mrs. Glass was already there?

He had spent so much energy trying to get away from her, it would be madness to go rushing back into her arms, and with Manny in tow it would be like sticking your head into a hornet's nest.

So what should he say? He had to say something, or Manny was going to shoot him. If he said the wrong thing, though . . .

"Palenque," Precious shouted before he could speak. "She's gone to Palenque."

Manny calmed down. Lowered the gun. "Palenque, huh? Okay, can you get us there?"

James nodded, rubbing his sore neck. So, Precious had made the decision for him. She must have been thinking along exactly the same lines as him.

The hornet's nest it was, then.

Manny started the car up.

"That woman," he said. "She thought she could run out on me. Nobody does that to Manny the Girl."

"Tell me about her," said James.

"Who?" said Manny.

"Mrs. Glass. Tell me about Mrs. Glass."

"She don't say a lot, keeps tight-lipped," said Manny. "Not like most broads I know. Yack, yack, yack. You know what I'm saying? But one night Strabo told us some about her. She's a Kraut, apparently."

"A German?" said James.

"Yeah. Was born in Cincinnati. Theda Horowitz was her name. The daughter of German immigrants. Moved to L.A. when she was a kid."

Telling the story, Manny became calm. James had observed how easily he slipped in and out of confusion. Now, remembering what Strabo had told him, he was relatively lucid.

"Theda grew up an all-American girl, but when we joined the war in 1917, things changed for her family. A lot of Yanks turned against the Krauts. You know, a funny thing, the Germans in America started changing their names. The Schmidts became the Smiths, the Silbermanns became the Silvers, Garfinkles became Garfields. Look at us! We're all patriotic Yanks! Didn't work out for Theda's pa, though, lost his job. Her world fell apart. Started getting into fights. Hurt another girl at school real bad with a knife. Said she was only sticking up for herself, but they sent her to prison. Was only seventeen. Well, that was the start of her criminal career. She fell in with some real bad types.

"Six months after she came out of the slammer she was married to a local hood called Billy Grosman. Who can say if she was born bad, or just turned bad, but she proved real good at *being* bad. Billy Grosman worked the border between the U.S. and Mexico. He was a smuggler of drugs and drink and guns and people, and with Theda at his side he terrorized all of Los Angeles. But one day Billy's luck ran out. He was ambushed in a hotel by a *Mexicano* gang and shot to pieces. Theda was with him. Was badly wounded. Tommy guns can do a lot of damage. Strabo reckons her body still carries the scars from that night, but I ain't never seen 'em.

"After that she went into hiding, and somewhere down the line she married some guy called Glass. Don't know what happened to him. Died probably. A lot of the guys she hangs around with seem to wind up in the morgue. Was with Legs Diamond for a while. Rumor was she helped set him up when he took his fall. She's poison, Louis. We shoulda never gotten mixed up with her."

Manny suddenly moaned and shook his head, the loose section of skull flapping open and shut with the movement.

"You all right?" said James.

Manny was looking around in an agitated fashion.

"I don't know the way, Louis," he said fearfully. "I don't recognize this road."

James had stopped trying to explain that he wasn't Manny's brother Louis. As long as Manny didn't think about the incident at the Stones' house, he and Precious were relatively safe.

"It's the right way," he said soothingly. "Just keep driving."

"The right way home?" said Manny.

"Yes."

This seemed to cheer Manny up and he drove on with more confidence.

"When I get there, Louis," he said, "I'm gonna give Mama a big kiss and a hug, and damn, will she be pleased to see her little boy. Hoowee! I'm coming home, Mama. Me an' Louis are coming home. They didn't kill him, Ma, he's right here with me. You can touch him and talk to him and everything. It's a miracle, Mama, a goddamn miracle. I tell you it is, I done it, it was me, your little boy, I can raise the dead. I don't know if I ain't maybe some kind of a miracle worker, or a saint, or something!"

Manny ranted on like this for several miles until he ran out of steam and lapsed into silence, muttering occasionally to himself, lost in his thoughts.

Darkness came down fast, and the headlights chewed up the seemingly endless and unchanging road. Apart from muddy farm tracks there were no exits to either side. Manny began to grow tired. He had been driving for about eight hours. Even though there were no other vehicles about, James was worried that they might crash.

Eventually Manny nodded off, and James had to grab the wheel to stop them from piling into a tree.

Manny woke up, pulled over, and sat there yawning. The noise of the engine ticking over was the only sound in the night.

"I'm beat, Louis," he said, picking up his gun and checking it. Then his head dropped to his chest, and he closed his eyes. "Could sleep for a thousand years," he sighed.

"You sleep. I'll drive," said James.

"Sure, Louis. You drive some."

Manny got out and came around to the passenger side.

James slid over and took the wheel.

When Manny settled into his seat, however, there was an intense look on his face.

"Don't try any more tricks," he said.

"What do you mean?" said James.

"I know who you are," said Manny, sticking the gun in James's stomach.

"I can get you there," said James, desperately changing the subject. "I can get you to Mrs. Glass."

"Yeah," said Manny, smiling. "Mrs. Glass. Yeah."

James shifted into gear and they set off. He drove steadily, holding the car at a regular speed, hoping to lull Manny back to sleep. Every time he looked around at him, though, he could see the black holes of his eyes, and the ugly gun still aimed at his guts.

"I miss Ma so bad, Louis," said Manny after a long period of silence. "I never shoulda shouted at her, you know. I never shoulda argued. I never shoulda raised my fist in anger to her. She was the only one could hold me and make everything all right." Manny gave a soft sigh in the darkness. "It's gonna be just like it always was, Louis, when we was kids. You remember? Playing in the yard without a care in the world, and Ma would call us in for supper. I can still hear her voice—'Boys! Chow time!' I never shoulda struck her down, Louis. But we'll be a family again, won't we? The three of us. An' we'll sit down to eat and I'll say grace, an' the Lord will smile on us and forget all the bad things I done. Tell me it's gonna be all right, Louis, tell me . . ."

"Don't fret," said James. "Go to sleep."

"Yeah."

Eventually James gave up checking on Manny and concentrated on the road ahead, until he heard Precious's voice.

"He's asleep."

Sure enough, Manny's head was lolling back, his mouth hanging open, his eyes shut. His gun, though, was still firmly gripped in his hand.

"Do you think we can make it to Palenque before Mrs. Glass?" said Precious.

"She had a head start on us," said James, "but that truck was pretty slow, and they would have had to change vehicles. We've a chance."

"We've got to do something about Manny, though."

"I know," said James. "And now might be our only chance. While he's asleep. I'm worried that if I stop the car he might wake up."

"You've got a gun," said Precious. "Give it to me and I'll shoot him."

"Could you really do it?" said James.

"No," said Precious, quietly.

"Me neither," said James. "Not in cold blood."

"What then?"

"The door," said James. "Can you reach the handle without waking him?"

"I think so."

"I'll count to three," said James. "Then you open the door and I'll shove him out."

"I'm not sure I can—"

"One . . ."

"James—"

"Two . . ."

"Wait—"

"Three!"

It all happened very fast, and James recognized the look on Manny's face. It was the same startled, disbelieving look he'd had when James had pushed him out of the window in Tres Hermanas.

One moment he'd been dozing peacefully in the car, the next he was flying out into the night, flapping his arms.

There was a second's silence in the car, and then James and Precious erupted into screams of triumph and crazy laughter. James stamped on the accelerator. Behind them they could hear distant gunshots, but they were clear. They had done it. Manny the Girl had been left for dust.

They drove on, chatting excitedly, until James couldn't keep his eyes open any longer, and they pulled off the road under some trees. They searched the car, and James stuffed Manny's stolen banknotes into his pockets. They had been hoping to find some food, as well, but all they turned up was some half-rotten fruit and a sack of dry biscuits that had gone soggy. They were too hungry to be fussy, though, and crammed handfuls of them into their mouths.

Before going to sleep James studied the map he had taken all those days ago from the Duesenberg. There were very few roads in this region, and their route took them southwest into the Chiapas highlands, a remote, jungly area that stretched all the way down to the border with Guatemala.

"Is it much farther to Palenque?" said Precious.

"I don't think so," said James. "A day at the most."

They settled down on the ground, the bright stars twinkling between the black leaves of the overhanging trees, and James was too tired to feel anything at all. Neither hope nor fear nor excitement.

When he woke it was morning. It was barely light, and the day was dawning gray and cold and drizzly. Half an hour later they were back on the road, which began to climb slowly upward into the Chiapas. The sun burned off the clouds, and it became warm and humid in the car.

They scrounged some petrol in a little settlement, where the village chief was the proud owner of an ancient Model T Ford, and drove all morning on winding back roads that took them deeper and deeper into jungle. It was difficult to follow the map, which was only a rough approximation of this out-of-the-way part of the country. Several times they reached a dead end and had to backtrack, and they would have been altogether lost if they hadn't eventually stumbled across a logging camp where they got directions. In midafternoon, to their intense relief, they spotted an old hand-painted sign for Palenque.

It took them another hour to find the airstrip, half-hidden among the trees. They had almost given up hope when they rounded a bend, the vegetation opened up, and there was a wide, bright patch of closely cropped grass under a clear blue sky.

And sitting out on the strip, tilted to one side, its landing gear broken and the tip of one wing stuck into the ground, was Jack Stone's plane.

"We're there," said Precious as they drifted to a halt. "We made it. I can't believe it."

James said nothing. He was too tense. *Yes*, they'd made it. But now what?

There was no sign of Mrs. Glass. Had she been and gone? Had she not arrived yet? There didn't seem to be anyone around, but he wasn't going to take any chances.

He picked up his gun from where he'd left it on the floor, opened the car door, and stepped out.

Off to one side was a long, low hut with a roof of thatched palm leaves. He took a step toward it.

A bird screeched.

He sensed movement and froze. There was a sudden loud bang as a bullet punched into the front of the Dodge with a dull clank, and a jet of steam hissed out of the punctured radiator.

James threw himself flat as a second shot sent a bullet whistling over his head and off into the trees.

CHAPTER 19—PALENQUE

"**S**tand up and put your hands on your head, *señor*!"

James looked up. A lanky Mexican had come out of the hut holding a shotgun.

"Drop your gun and get up!"

James let go of the pistol and stood.

"This gun is loaded with buckshot, *señor*," said the Mexican. "At this range it will cut you in half where you stand. Now put your hands on your head."

James did as he was told.

Two more Mexicans appeared from the bushes. It must have been one of them who had shot at him.

"Who are you?" said the first Mexican.

James heard the car door opening behind him and wanted to shout at Precious to stay where she was, but he couldn't risk it. The man with the shotgun seemed in control, but the other two looked nervous and jumpy.

"Beto!" Precious called out. "It's Beto, Dad's copilot."

The man lowered his shotgun.

"Precious? Is it you?"

James let out his breath as Precious ran across the grass toward the others.

He sat down. He wasn't sure how much more excitement he could stand.

Later on inside the hut, while James and Precious had their first proper meal in days, Beto told them what had happened.

The plane had been badly damaged in the storm, but Stone had managed to land it safely. With the landing gear broken, there was no way of taking off again, though, so they were stranded here until spare parts arrived. Using the plane's radio, they had eventually made contact with the port authority in Veracruz, and a day later they got word via Garcia that Precious, JJ, and James were safe and had gone inland to Puente Nuevo. Stone and Charmian had wanted to set off back, but they had no means of transport and were miles from the nearest town. Stone had radioed for help and arranged for a car to drive over from Tabasco to pick them up. But the car never arrived. Nor did the other members of Charmian's expedition. The storm had changed everything.

"Then we got word from Veracruz," said Beto. "A Japanese man had turned up there with JJ."

"JJ?" Precious exclaimed. "Is he all right?"

"I think so," said Beto, showing a broad, gap-toothed smile and a shining gold tooth. "The message was from the hospital. He had hurt his leg, but he was okay."

"Oh, thank God," said Precious, and she burst into tears.

"Your father, he went crazy, though," said Beto. "He didn't know what to do. In the end he set off on foot with Charmian and the guide, Mendoza. They were hoping to find a car, some way of getting to Veracruz."

"When was this?" said Precious.

"Two days ago," said Beto. "I tried to tell them not to

go. These are dangerous parts. The roads are not safe, even with Mendoza helping. I couldn't stop your father, though. He told me to wait here and guard the plane. These other two *muchachos* work here. Your father said that if anyone tried to take anything from the plane, we should shoot them."

"Has anyone else been here?" said James. "A man and a woman?"

"Nobody has been," said Beto. "Yours are the first new faces I have seen since we arrived. I am glad you are safe, Precious. Your father will be pleased. Every morning at eight o'clock I warm up the radio. I leave it on only for a few minutes to save the battery. Maybe tomorrow Señor Stone will make contact."

"There are others coming," said James, and he told Beto about Mrs. Glass and Strabo. When he had finished, Beto looked worried, but he shrugged. As if the matter was out of his hands and in the hands of God.

"When will they get here, do you think?" he asked.

"It's only a matter of time," said James. "We have to get away."

"I cannot," said Beto with a sad smile. "I promised Señor Stone I would stay."

"But what can be so valuable on his plane that you should guard it with your life?" said James. "Surely not Charmian's supplies?" Even as he said it, though, he knew the answer.

After they had eaten he took Precious outside.

"The stolen plans," he said, once he was sure that their conversation could not be overheard.

"What about them?" said Precious.

"They must be on the plane," said James. "They must

have been there all along. It was too risky for your father to take them with him to Veracruz."

"On the plane?" said Precious. "But where? That would be even less safe."

"What did Mrs. Glass say?" said James. "Your father fitted secret compartments. Come on."

They climbed into the Tin Goose. Behind the cockpit was a seating area for six passengers, and then a storage hold, which was still filled with the boxes and crates for Charmian's now-abandoned expedition. It was difficult moving about, as the plane was on such a tilt, but they clung to the bulkheads and explored as best they could.

It was Precious who spotted it, underneath one of the boxes: a square metal plate held down by four screws that didn't match the others on the plane. They shifted the box for a better look and then poked around until they discovered a tool kit strapped to the side of the fuselage near the tail. James took it down and selected a screwdriver.

The screws came up easily, and when they lifted the panel clear they found several carefully wrapped items, neatly stowed in a hidden storage space.

There were a couple of small jade statues, some Mayan gold jewelry, and a crocodile-skin attaché case, inside which was a bulging leather pouch stuffed with papers and bearing the unmistakable insignia of the U.S. Navy.

Precious sat there on the sloping floor with the papers in her lap. She looked deflated, as if she might start to cry.

"Half of me was hoping not to find anything," she said. "I wanted to believe that Mrs. Glass was lying."

"No," said James. "Remember what you said? You could still be right."

Precious stared at James. There was a glimmer of hope in her hollow, red-rimmed eyes.

James gripped her by the shoulders.

"Your father was intending to return them," he said firmly, almost believing the lie himself.

Precious brightened and became brisk and businesslike. "Yes," she said, standing up awkwardly. "And we've got to keep them out of Mrs. Glass's hands until we can get them back to him. It's up to us now."

"Do you think Beto knows?" said James as they jumped down from the plane.

"I don't know," said Precious, "but we shouldn't say anything. The fewer people who know about this the better."

"The first thing we have to do is get well away from the landing strip," said James. "It's only a matter of time before Mrs. Glass shows up with Strabo."

"I cannot leave here," said Beto when they told him they were leaving. "I gave Señor Stone my word."

"It's just an airplane," said Precious. "Nobody can steal it. Wouldn't my father rather you took us to him than stayed here?"

"*Sí, sí,* I am sure," said Beto, his face serious. "But your car is broken and we will need to walk. It is late now. Soon it will be dark. We must wait until the morning."

"It's too dangerous," said James. "They could turn up at any minute."

"It will be too dangerous to leave tonight," said Beto.

"And the radio is here. I am sure that Señor Stone will call in the morning. Then I can tell him what we are doing. I can ask him if it is all right to leave the plane."

"If Mrs. Glass arrives before then, she'll kill us all," said Precious.

"All right, all right," said Beto, putting his hands to his temples. "Let me think." He was silent for a long while before coming to a decision.

"This is what we will do," he said. "You two will go from here to somewhere safe. You will hide. I will stay with the guards. We will be ready if they come. We have our guns. If all goes well, I will speak to Señor Stone on the radio at eight o'clock, then I will come for you, and we will leave together."

"All right," said James, who could see that there was no point in arguing with him.

"But where will we hide?" said Precious.

"In the jungle," said Beto. "Go to the city of Palenque. There is a track that runs from behind the hut. It is a half hour walk, no more. I will give you a flashlight and some food and water. You keep to the path and you will get there, no trouble."

Fifteen minutes later James and Precious were walking down a narrow path that had been hacked out of the rain forest, the stolen plans safely tucked inside a leather satchel they had found in the hut.

The sun was going down, and it was the noisiest time of day. Every animal and insect for miles around seemed to be calling to its friends, so that the air was filled with a tinkling, zizzing, chirruping cacophony.

"I don't understand," said Precious, slapping away a mosquito. "If Palenque's a city, and it's only half an hour away, why couldn't Dad go there for help?"

"Oh, Palenque's a city, all right," said James. "But nobody's lived there for nearly a thousand years. It was built by the Mayans, who abandoned it when the jungle took over. Charmian told me all about it. I was quite jealous when I realized I wouldn't be coming down here with her. It's funny how things change. She's abandoned her expedition and here *I* am trekking into the unknown."

When they arrived at the ruined city it was more amazing than either of them could have imagined. Standing half-swallowed up by the jungle were the remains of many huge buildings—pyramids and temples and palaces—their intricately carved white stonework glowing golden in the dying rays of the sun. Everywhere they turned there was more to look at—chambers, terraces, staircases, mysterious grassy mounds—and in the center, on a raised, stepped platform, was a crumbling mass of buildings topped by an open-sided, four-tiered tower.

"We should try and get up there," said James, pointing. "It'll be safe and will make a good lookout."

They climbed the steps and at the top were faced with a maze of corridors, courtyards, and interlinked halls.

"What do you think this building was?" said Precious, marveling at the carvings and glyphs on the walls depicting an ancient, long-vanished civilization that looked utterly alien.

"Maybe a palace," said James. "It's certainly the most important-looking building here."

They found their way to the base of the central tower but discovered they could only climb up to the first level.

"Never mind. This'll do very well," said James, scanning the clearing below. The sun had gone down and the sky was darkening rapidly. From up here they could see out over the treetops. Palenque was built on a high ridge and had a commanding view of the countryside for miles around. They were surrounded by a black blanket of vegetation that seemed to go on forever.

They shared out their food, and, to the accompaniment of frogs and crickets, they ate sitting on the hard stone floor. Afterward they settled down to try to sleep. They had brought blankets with them from the airstrip, but it was desperately uncomfortable and horribly cold, and they lay there looking out at the stars twinkling in the sky and listening to the ceaseless chatter of the wildlife.

"I feel so ashamed," said Precious quietly.

"Of your father?" said James.

"No," said Precious. "Of myself. My behavior."

"You're doing fine," said James. "Most people would have given up a long time ago, and not just girls."

"I've found out a lot about myself," said Precious. "And when I think back to how I used to behave I feel terrible. The way I treated the servants. I learned it from my mother, I suppose. She never wanted to move to Mexico. She missed America. The fine shops, the restaurants, the people. She hated it here, and I guess she took it out on the servants. I thought that was how you were supposed to behave. I started doing it to try and impress her, and it became a habit. It made me feel important to tell the servants off. I would never do it again. *Never.* I have seen how kind and brave the Mexicans are. Whenever I close my eyes I see that poor man, Garcia, falling down dead with JJ in his arms."

"I think about it, too," said James. "It was horrible."

"And now Beto," said Precious. "He doesn't have to stay and guard my dad's plane. He's loyal, a man of his word."

"He's also stubborn," said James. "And I hope it doesn't cost him his life."

"Oh, don't say that," said Precious, propping herself up on one elbow. "I couldn't bear for anyone else to be killed."

"It's more than likely," said James, "until we get the papers back to where they belong."

"We will do it," said Precious, lying down again. "I know we will."

CHAPTER 20—DEATH IN THE JUNGLE

James slept badly; his sleep was shallow and troubled by unsettling dreams in which he was trying to escape from some dark thing, but kept getting pulled back. Sometimes he dreamed of his mother. She was reading him a bedtime story, but whenever he looked at her she turned into Mrs. Glass.

He awoke just as the first shafts of sunlight lanced over the treetops and in through the open sides of the tower. He could see squares of pinkish gray sky framed by the corner supports.

He groaned. His body always felt worst first thing in the morning. He was aware of every bruise, scrape, and cut. His head throbbed. His ribs ached all over. He was cold and damp and more tired than when he'd gone to sleep.

But he was alive, and with a bit of stretching and light exercise things wouldn't seem so bad. He forced himself upright and rolled his shoulders, loosening his stiff neck.

Precious was still sleeping, her head resting on her forearm, her face squashed out of shape. He let her sleep on, and sat with his legs dangling over the edge of the platform watching the new day form itself. It was almost as if he was still dreaming. There was something so unreal about the place. The big, square pyramids topped by fantastically carved buildings, the jungle trying to fight its way back where it had been cleared, the eerie dawn light that made the tops of the structures bright and shining and left the ground dark and murky and lifeless.

Presently he heard movement behind him and turned to see Precious stirring. She opened her bleary eyes and blinked at him.

"It's morning," she said. "Any sign of Beto?"

"It's too early," said James.

They drank some water and ate more of their food, and then decided that they should go down and wait for Beto where he could find them.

They climbed down the tower and made their way through the rooms of the ancient Mayan palace toward the steps. The ground was still in shade, and a light mist lay across the grass. The morning was very still and quiet. They went down the steps, which ran the whole length of the palace, and shivered as they entered the shadows at the base.

"We'll head for the entrance to the track," said James. "There was a small building there we could hide in. Just in case."

"I'm getting fed up of running and hiding," said Precious.

"It's nearly over," said James, but he couldn't have been more wrong.

As they rounded the end of the palace they came face-to-face with Manny, who looked almost as surprised to see them as they were to see him.

James's mind was spinning. How on earth had Manny got here? He couldn't have followed them all the way on foot. It was impossible.

He was still trying to come to terms with this apparition when Strabo and Mrs. Glass stepped into the light.

"Morning, Precious," said Mrs. Glass with a thin smile. "We picked us up a hitchhiker. Sure had a lot of interesting stories to tell." She shifted her gaze to James. "Well, would you look at who it is. Good old Angel Corona. If that really is your name. Manny, here, tells me he saw you at the Stones' house, that you pushed him out of the window."

"He also says he can raise the dead," said James, using his Mexican accent for the last time. "He's crazy."

"What difference does it make?" said Mrs. Glass. She walked over to James and studied him. "I set out from Tres Hermanas with a gang of four. I'm down to two because of you, and one of them, as you say, is crazy. I need to put a stop to you before you foul up any more of my plans. So why don't you tell me just who the hell you are?"

"My name's Bond, James Bond."

"No, no, no, no, no," said Manny, shaking his head, the flap of skin and bone waving and slopping against his skull. "He's my brother Louis."

"Cut the gags, Manny," said Strabo.

"We robbed a bank," said Manny.

"What're you talking about?" said Strabo.

"We was getting away, and all. Me and Louis and the—"

"Can it, Manny," said Strabo, but Manny grabbed him by the shirtfront.

"Don't you talk to me like that," he snarled. "Don't you never talk to me like that, d'you hear?"

Strabo shoved him away and looked at Mrs. Glass, who raised an eyebrow.

Manny clutched his head. "I get confused," he said.

"It's okay, Manny," said Mrs. Glass. "We'll look after you."

Manny brightened, a look of childish delight on his face.

"I knew you would," he said.

"You can't trust her," said James. "She left you behind, remember?"

"Yeah," said Manny. "That's right." He confronted Strabo and Mrs. Glass. "You left me for dead. You want all the dough for yourselves. I never shoulda trusted you."

"Now, there's an idea," said Strabo with a grin. "Maybe I will just pop you now and keep all the loot."

"Leave it, Strabo," said Mrs. Glass. "And you, Manny. If anybody dumped you it was the kid. Pushed you outta your car, if you recall. It was us who picked you up wandering in the road. It was us who rescued you."

Manny looked more confused than ever, looking from Mrs. Glass to James and back again. James tried not to catch his eye.

"What have you done with Beto and the guards?" said Precious anxiously.

"Beto? That his name? He didn't say much."

"You killed him?"

"No," said Mrs. Glass. "It took us forever to find this place. We need someone to show us the way out. We left him tied up back at the airstrip and came to find you. He put up a good fight, not like the other two. Ran off like jackrabbits at the first sound of gunfire. As I say, Beto didn't want to talk much, so perhaps you can tell me, honey: where in the hell is your father?"

"He's gone," said Precious defiantly. "Back to Veracruz. So you've wasted your time coming here."

Mrs. Glass sighed.

"What do we do now?" said Strabo.

"We'll have to take 'em with us," said Mrs. Glass, walking away. "But search 'em first."

Strabo nodded to Manny, who handed him his gun and frisked James. He soon found the officer's revolver and Strabo's knife, and James gave them up without a fight. When Manny turned his attention to Precious, however, she protested and struggled as he took the leather satchel from her.

"There's nothing in that," she said. "Leave it—"

"What's this?" said Manny, pulling out the pouch.

Strabo gave a long, low whistle and then roared with laughter. He called Mrs. Glass over and they checked through the papers, murmuring in amazement.

"Now, honey," said Mrs. Glass, putting the pouch back in the satchel and strapping it over her shoulder. "You have saved one hell of a lot of effort." She slapped Manny on the back. "Keep an eye on the kids," she said.

"Don't worry, Ma," said Manny. "I'll watch 'em."

"Funny guy," said Strabo, and he walked a little way off with Mrs. Glass, where they started a whispered conversation. Occasionally they looked back at Manny. Strabo kept shaking his head and laughed once. Mrs. Glass was, as usual, cool and unreadable.

James and Precious sat on the steps of the palace. Clouds had come from nowhere and there was a light drizzle, but they hardly noticed the rain. Soon flies appeared and buzzed around their heads, attracted to Manny's wound. James felt almost too miserable to bother swatting them away.

"What now?" said Precious after a while.

"Keep quiet," said Manny.

"You can't trust them," said James. "They've got what they want. They don't need any of us anymore."

"Shut up."

"They're going to get rid of us, Manny. You as well. Isn't it obvious?"

"I'm one of the gang," said Manny, sounding less sure of himself.

"They won't want you around," said James. "You're hurt. You'll only slow them down."

"They wouldn't try nothing," said Manny. "I still got my gun."

"Where?" said James, and Manny frowned, feeling all over his body with panicked hands.

"My gun?" he said. "Where's my gun?"

"Strabo took it," said James.

Manny looked like a lost schoolboy. He glanced over at Strabo. He held his head. Groaned.

"Come on," said James, grabbing Precious by the hand. "Let's get out of here."

They were running. Bobbing and weaving. Across open ground, toward the tree line about fifty feet away. They heard yells behind them, and then shots. First a warning shot. And second a shot that was intended to stop them dead.

James felt the bullet crackling through the air past his right ear.

He risked looking back. Manny was behind them, with Strabo catching up fast, his short legs pounding like steam hammers.

He raised his gun.

James pulled Precious to the side, and they zigzagged as another shot ripped past them.

And then they were into the jungle.

It was dark under the trees and very quiet. They followed an animal track deeper into the thick vegetation, pushing aside lianas, and trampling ferns and low-lying shrubs. Huge spiderwebs hung across the track, and they blundered through them without thinking.

They passed several ruined buildings—parts of the Mayan city that hadn't yet been excavated—then a beautifully carved stone pillar, and a little farther on, a statue of a jaguar half-buried in the earth.

They ran on blindly. The track twisted and turned before straightening out and running between high rocks covered in tough, thorny creepers. Then they could go no farther. The way ahead was blocked by a big fallen tree, half-rotten and crawling with beetles, caterpillars, spiders, and a thousand other tiny creatures that seemed to be hurrying over it toward them.

From the other side there was a rustling sound, and James thought it must be a small stream or river.

"I'm not climbing over that," said Precious. "I hate bugs."

James wasn't sure he could do it either. The surface of the bark was alive with insects, some of them very large and poisonous looking.

"Back," he said quickly, and they retraced their steps, hurrying along between the rocks. As they rounded a bend, however, a shot exploded by their heads, and a branch shattered, scaring up a cloud of angry flies.

"That's far enough," said Strabo, advancing toward them, panting and sweating.

James and Precious stood still, hand in hand.

A slow smile spread across Strabo's big, wide face, which still showed the signs of Garcia's attack.

"I been looking forward to this moment for a long time," he rasped.

A large, blue-black wasp with orange wings had been disturbed when Strabo fired into the tree. It was making a loud buzzing noise and circling the air, looking for something to attack. It made straight for Strabo, who tried to shoo it away with his free hand.

"Get off," he snapped, and the next moment the wasp darted in and stung him on the neck. He screamed and pressed his hand to the sting, dropping his gun into the undergrowth.

The wasp was a tarantula hawk wasp, and its sting is more painful than any snakebite. Its venom is meant for killing tarantulas, and while it isn't deadly to a human, it will lay a man out in a few minutes. Strabo pulled the hunting knife from his belt and staggered forward, gasping for air. Already his face and neck were beginning to swell up.

"We'll have to see if there's another way," said James, and they turned and ran back toward the fallen tree.

James scanned the rocks, seeing if there was somewhere they could climb, but the barbed creepers on them were almost as uninviting as the insects swarming over the tree.

He tried pulling some creepers away but only succeeded in cutting his hand. He swore, then Precious grabbed his arm and pointed.

Strabo was charging down the track, his face a vivid purple color and bulging grotesquely. His yellow eyes seemed to be bursting out of his head. From his thickened, blubbery lips came a horrible, growling, wheezing sound.

In his hand was the hunting knife, its vicious blade glinting as he passed through shafts of light.

"Get to the side," said James, pushing Precious against the rocks, and he braced himself, running quickly through his options in his mind.

Strabo came on, like some ravening jungle beast, clawing at the air with his knife.

James never took his eyes off him.

At the last minute he dropped backward, raised a knee, and grabbed Strabo's jacket all at the same time. He fell to the ground, pushed up with his foot, and shoved Strabo skyward, trying to remember everything that Sakata had taught him.

Strabo gasped in surprise as he was thrown along the track. He did a lazy somersault in the air, struck the back of his head on the fallen tree, and landed with a heavy thump on the other side.

James picked himself up, brushing loose dirt and twigs off his clothing.

He snatched up the knife that Strabo had dropped, and waited, tensed and alert, ready for anything.

There was no sound from the other side of the trunk, except for a soft rustling sound. Maybe Strabo had landed in the stream.

No. There hadn't been a splash. James had heard a distinct thud.

Maybe the blow to his head had knocked him unconscious, or perhaps the wasp venom had paralyzed him.

There was only one way to find out. James cautiously approached the trunk, all the while expecting Strabo's ugly face to appear over the top of it, spitting obscenities.

James *had* to look.

He ignored the teeming insects, which were still spilling over the trunk, and scrambled up, feeling brittle bodies pop and crunch beneath him. He was bitten three times and stayed there just long enough to get a glimpse of what was on the other side before dropping back down.

"What is it?" said Precious when she saw his pale face. "What happened to him? Is he gone?"

James nodded.

Nothing could ever have prepared him for the sight that had met his eyes. The image, seen for only a brief moment, was burned on his retinas.

A river of insects, perhaps twenty feet wide, the individuals swarming together like a single, giant creature, devouring everything in their path. It was a colony of army ants on the move. There must have been a million of them, and nothing could stop them. Spiders, scorpions, lizards, even a snake, were struggling to escape, but sinking under a boiling, seething mass of black bodies and red heads with huge, slicing mandibles. The ants latched on to anything they could hold—a leg, a wing casing, an antenna, an eye—and after paralyzing their prey with their bites they cut them into pieces.

And lying in the middle of all this was Strabo. James had been right about him. The combination of the wasp sting and the blow to his head had paralyzed him as effectively as the ants' bites paralyzed the smaller creatures. His body was twitching and racked with spasms, but he couldn't get up. The ants flowed over him, crawling into his clothing, his mouth, his ears, his nose. Biting at his eyelids and his lips. He was disappearing under a living carpet of ants.

James had heard tales about army ants. How they would march like this all day until nightfall, when they would nest in readiness for another expedition the following morning. The insects scurrying over the trunk had been trying to get out of the way. They were the lucky ones. They had escaped the juggernaut. The unlucky ones, the ones that hadn't been quick enough, didn't stand a chance.

"James?" said Precious. "What happened to him?"

"He won't be any more trouble," said James. "He's out cold. Let's get away while we can."

He took Precious's hand, and they once more went back the way they had come. Going cautiously, not knowing what to expect. When they came to the spot where Strabo had dropped his gun, they stopped and looked for it, groping around in the tangled vegetation by the side of the path. It was hot, dirty work. Water dropped from the leaves overhead, and they were soon both soaked and filthy.

It was Precious who eventually found it. But no sooner had she jumped up, triumphantly clutching it in her hand, than Manny came thundering down the track.

"They're coming, Louis," he yelled.

"Who?" said James.

"I dunno," said Manny. "The cops, I reckon, maybe."

"Who's after you, Manny?" said James. "Is it Mrs. Glass?"

Manny thought for a moment, his face clouded. "Yeah," he said finally. "It's her. It has to be."

Before James could stop him, Manny had grabbed the gun off Precious and fired wildly back down the track. He then shouted, "This way!" and pulled her deeper into the bushes.

James had no option but to follow.

They ran through the jungle, pushing branches and lianas out of their way, dodging between the tall, bare trunks of the trees. They were heading down the side of a hill into deeper jungle, and try as he might, James could not get Manny to stop. In the end, he physically took hold of him and pinned him to a tree.

"Wait," he said. "This is stupid. We'll get completely lost."

"They're coming," said Manny, looking around nervously. "They're after me."

"I don't think there was ever anybody after you, was there?" said James.

"I don't know," said Manny fearfully. "I don't know anything anymore."

James didn't want to upset him. For now Manny seemed to have forgotten all about being pushed from the car. James needed it to stay that way.

"It's all right, Manny," he said. "We'll look after you. Just calm down."

James slapped his arm where a mosquito was feeding on him. He hated mosquitoes. Last summer he had been so badly bitten by a swarm he had nearly died. Now their bites hardly itched at all, but he still hated the evil little things.

"I need to rest," said Precious, flopping to the ground.

"We can't stay here," said James. "We have to keep moving. We have to find food and shelter and a way out of this mess."

"We need to go back," said Precious. "We have to stop her."

"Which way is back?" said James. "We're lost. If we ever get out of this jungle we can worry about Mrs. Glass. In the meantime our main concern is survival."

"We had the papers, James," said Precious. "We had them in our hands. And now she's got them. I handed them to her on a plate."

"There was nothing we could have done," said James. "Don't be so hard on yourself."

"I'm going to get them back," said Precious. "I won't rest until I do."

"All right," said James hotly. "But as long as we're in the middle of this jungle, miles from civilization, there's nothing we can do."

It was a sullen, silent group that set about trying to find a pathway or track of some sort, and three hours later they were still wandering completely disorientated in the forest.

They were just about to give up all hope when they came across their first sign of civilization. James spotted a big old tree, the bark of which had been cut in a herringbone pattern. A sticky, rubbery substance was oozing out of it and dribbling down the trunk into a burlap bag.

A little farther on they found another tree that was being similarly harvested, and then they stumbled upon a crude path that had been chopped through the jungle. They followed it, passing several more trees dripping sap. At last they caught the odor of wood smoke and cooking, and through the foliage up ahead they could make out a camp in a clearing.

James put a hand on Manny's arm.

"Keep quiet," he said. "Don't say anything. Let me do the talking. Please. Whoever they are, I don't want to scare them, and for God's sake, put Strabo's gun away. If you start waving that around, we're sunk."

Manny nodded mutely, like a little child told to behave by his father, and James led them into the camp.

CHAPTER 21—THE CHICLEROS

The camp was primitive but looked comfortable enough. There were mosquito nets draped everywhere and hammocks slung from trees. Metal boxes held provisions, and there was a tank for freshwater.

Four men stood around a large iron pot set over a fire. It was filled with a thick, sticky, gluelike substance, and one of the men was stirring it with a pole. They looked fierce and half-wild, as if they had been living there in the forest for months. They had long black hair and the dark skin of Indians.

A woman sat by another fire, preparing food, with a small grubby-faced boy.

The men stared at the newcomers, and one of them idly slapped a machete against his leg.

"*Hay alguien que hable ingles?*" James asked, and after a pause one of the men stepped forward.

"*Sí,*" he said. "I speak a *leetle Ingleesh.*"

"We are lost," said James. "*Perdido.* We had an *accidente.* . . ."

The man frowned and peered at the gash in Manny's head. He whistled and beckoned his friends over. They crowded around Manny, staring and talking quietly to each other. James was worried that they would set him off.

"Be careful," he said. "Not too close."

While Manny wasn't looking, he tapped his own skull to indicate that Manny wasn't quite right in the head. The man nodded in understanding and waved his companions back.

"Please," said Precious, "we are very hungry. *Memuero de hambre.*"

"You want eat?" said the man, and mimed taking food to his mouth with one hand.

James nodded wearily.

"We need food, and we need a guide," he said. "Someone who can show us the way to a village or town."

"*Un guía?*" said the man.

"*Sí,*" said James. He wasn't sure if he could trust these men, but, right now, they were his only hope, so he added, "We have money, we can pay. Pesos."

The man smiled. "First eat," he said.

James sank to the ground, relieved. The smell of the cooking was delicious. It may have only been a clearing in the jungle, but this place suddenly felt like the best restaurant in the world.

The woman served up a meal of beans, rice, tortillas, and fiery chillies. James ate every scrap of it and washed it down with cold water. When the three of them had finished eating, they sat in a sort of stunned silence, letting their bodies regain their strength.

James felt lazy and contented. His spirits had been lifted by the simple food, and he could look on the bright side again.

Once more they had escaped death. Mrs. Glass had the

papers, but she was alone now. There was none of her gang left. That was justice of sorts.

He turned to Precious and smiled at her.

She smiled back at him. It was the first time he had seen her smile all day.

She looked quite beautiful.

James watched the men working. They had removed the giant pot from the fire to let it cool, and they were now stirring the rubbery contents and pulling out thick strands with a paddle, as if they were making toffee. When they were satisfied that it was the right temperature and consistency, one of the men rubbed a soapy paste onto his arms to protect them, and scooped out a blob of the warm gum with his hands. He quickly dropped it into a wooden mold and spread it smooth. There was soon a mounting stack of golden brown blocks, and as each block cooled, the man carved his initial on the top of it.

James was curious to know what the stuff was, and he forced himself to his feet and went over to join the men.

"What is it?" he asked.

"*Chicle*," said Elijio, the man who spoke English. "We are *chicleros*."

"*Chicle*?" said James, who had never heard the word before. "What is it? What's it used for? Is it like rubber?"

"*Leetle*," said Elijio. "Is for *gom*."

"*Gom*?" said James. "You mean gum?"

"*Sí*," said Elijio. "Chewing *gom*. We sell to the Yankees."

"Chewing gum?" said James. "You're harvesting chewing gum!" He laughed. He had chewed gum before, but had never wondered where it came from.

One of the other *chicleros* broke off a piece of *chicle* and gave it to James to try. It was hard and almost tasteless, but after some vigorous chewing he managed to soften it.

He was still chewing it that evening as they sat around the fire watching the bats dart through the air, chasing the insects that were attracted by the light. He had been negotiating a fee with Elijio for guiding them to safety and had agreed on two hundred pesos. The woman, meanwhile, had been preparing a paste from leaves and berries she had picked in the forest. James thought it was for another meal, but it turned out to be for Manny's wound. They persuaded him that it would be all right, and she gently folded the flap of skin and bone back against his skull and smeared the paste all over it. Then she bound it tightly with a clean bandage and said some words to him that he didn't understand.

James was glad that the gaping hole was hidden. The sight of it had been making him feel sick. It didn't make any difference to Manny's mental state, however. He seemed to be slipping in and out of reality and didn't really have a clear idea of where he was and who these people were.

It rained in the night. James woke up soaked to the skin and covered in seed ticks that had got in through the mosquito net and were having a morning snack of blood. After their own breakfast of beans and tortillas and several cups of strong, bitter, black coffee, they set off with Elijio leading the way. It was cold this morning and a thin, damp mist hung in the trees. The *chiclero* knew the forest intimately and led them through its heart as easily as if they had been strolling through a well-laid-out city.

It was tough going; the paths weren't straight, and they

frequently had to hack at huge leaves and vines that were blocking their way. When they at last stopped to eat, Elijio explained that they were still only about halfway to their destination: a small settlement on the banks of the Rio Usumacinta from where they could take a boat out of the jungle.

Lunch was more beans and cold tortillas. Last night this simple food had tasted like the food of the gods, but James found that he was already growing bored of the monotonous diet.

As they ate, a group of howler monkeys yelped and whooped at them from the branches above, and a brilliant scarlet macaw swooped past, adding a thrilling splash of color to the unbroken grays and greens of the forest.

When they set off again Precious quizzed James about where they were going.

"As far as I can tell, the river goes all the way to the Gulf of Mexico," said James. "We should be able to get a boat up to Veracruz from there."

"Not Veracruz," said Precious.

"What do you mean?" said James.

"JJ is safe," said Precious. "Dad's with him. We don't need to go there."

"What about you?" said James. "You're not safe. Don't you want to go to your father?"

"I can't," said Precious quietly. "Not without fixing everything first."

"You've got to stop thinking about Mrs. Glass," said James. "You'll only make yourself miserable. Put her out of your mind."

"I can't," said Precious. "She has to be stopped. It's fate, James. It's like God asked us to do his work."

"You're sounding as crazy as Manny," said James with a smile. But Precious did not smile back. He realized she was serious about this.

"Think about it," she said. "Every time we've tried to get away we've been thrown straight back at her. After the storm, in Puente Nuevo, she found me and JJ; then, when we got away from her, there was Manny. We got away from Manny, and there she was again, in Palenque. But each time, each time there was one less of them. Whatzat, Sakata, Strabo. I tell you, this was meant to be. We're going after her, James. We can do it. We can get the papers. We can make everything all right again."

"She'll be halfway to her island by now," said James.

"You see, James?" said Precious. "We know where she's going. We can follow."

"I'm not sure this island she talked about, this Lagrimas Negras, is somewhere we'd want to be," said James.

"If you won't come with me, then I'll go alone." Precious sped up and walked ahead of James, as if she were in a great hurry to get on. James caught up to her.

"You're just a girl," he said. "What do you think you can do?"

"I don't know. But before this started I didn't think I could do half the things I've done. You just point me in the right direction."

It was dark when they arrived at a ramshackle collection of huts and tents on the river. The settlement was inhabited by rough-looking men, most of whom seemed to be headed for the only building of any size: a rowdy bar from which yellow light spilled out into the muddy street.

They had been walking all day and James was too exhausted even to talk. Manny was red-eyed and feverish, more confused than ever, and Precious, after her brief blossoming of nervous energy earlier, had retreated into the sullen mood that James knew so well. He could hardly blame her.

James paid Elijio his two hundred pesos, and he introduced them to a French logger who would take them on down the river. The tough little *chiclero* then bade them farewell and slipped back into the jungle. James wondered if he was intending to walk all the way back through the night. The journey certainly didn't seem to have tired him out at all.

James was still chewing his gum, and he knew that whenever he chewed gum again he would remember Elijio and the *chicleros* working away in the jungle, tapping the trees for *chicle* and boiling it up, miles from civilization.

There were rooms to rent behind the bar, and James paid far too much for three beds for the night. The locals were content to carry on drinking, arguing, and singing until daybreak. James spent another sleepless night.

He wasn't alone. Manny kept getting up and pacing the room. At one point he walked out, and James got up to follow him.

He found him outside, sitting on a step, smoking a cigarette he'd bought in the bar.

James sat down next to him.

"Have you ever heard of an island called Lagrimas Negras?" he asked.

"Sure I have," said Manny. "Everyone's heard of it, but it's a fairy tale, it don't exist."

"Mrs. Glass thinks it exists," said James. "She said she was going there."

"We all dream of going to Lagrimas," said Manny. "Every bad man with a big score and nowhere else to go. It's a paradise for lawbreakers, where you can live like a king and nobody bothers you none. No cops. No judges. No nothing. But you gotta have a big pot of gold to get in. I tell you, if I had the dough, that's where I'd be, Louis. That's where I'd be."

They talked some more until Manny's mind slipped out of gear, and James took him back into the room and put him to bed. He sat by him until he dozed off.

The next day they bought some basic provisions in the store, and the French logger loaded the three of them on to a raft with a fat middle-aged Mexican and his donkey. Then they set off down the river with a flotilla of mahogany logs that were being floated to the timber yards in Tabasco.

Manny sat at the back and muttered quietly to himself, and James and Precious sat and watched the scenery drift by. The river water was thick and brown as tea. A fishing eagle splashed down onto it and came away with a fat silverfish. A great blue heron flew past. A crocodile wriggled out of the bushes and crashed into the water.

"Do you really mean to go after Mrs. Glass?" said James.

"I've never been more sure of anything in my life," said

Precious. "I once swore I'd kill her, and I *will* do it. She thought she could destroy my family and everything I love; well she can't. Do you know the story of the Greek Furies?"

"Vaguely," said James. "Weren't they female demons of some sort? With snakes for hair?"

"Yes," said Precious. "And when they were unleashed, you couldn't stop them until they had finished their task, until they had chased down the wrongdoers and punished them. Well, I may not have snakes for hair, but I am not going to stop, and you had better believe it."

"I believe it," said James. "But I'm not letting you go off by yourself. It looks like we're in this together. We're stuck with each other till the bitter end."

"Till the death," said Precious.

"Let's hope it doesn't come to that," said James, looking into the rushing, turbulent water of the river.

CHAPTER 22—"YOU KNOW THE TYPE OF PLACE YOU'RE GOING TO?"

They drifted sedately along for the rest of the day and all through the night, and as the sun came up they found that the river was dividing into three branches, and men were strapping the floating logs together into huge rafts and sending them in different directions. James, Manny, and Precious transferred to another raft and took the easternmost branch. A couple of hours later they arrived in the small port of Carmen.

They found a bustling *cantina* and had a good lunch of *huevos rancheros* and *tamales*. The *cantina* was popular with truck drivers. After a few times of asking they eventually found one who would, for a fee, take them up the coast to the larger port of Campeche, on the western side of the Yucatán Peninsula.

The three of them crammed into the cab, trying to ignore the stink of the pigs being carried in the back. Manny seemed to come alive. Maybe the poultice was working. He still had the bandage around his head and didn't complain so often of headaches. Or maybe it was because this was all more familiar to him than the jungle and the river. He took a lively interest in the scenery. The light sparkling on the bright blue water of the ocean to their left, the low hills to their right, and ahead, the road running along a flat, dry plain.

"This is a fine country, Louis," he said. "An' I am so glad you're here to share the adventure with me."

"Me too," said James, humoring him.

"You know I had no choice back there in San Antone, don't you?" Manny added.

"What do you mean?" said James.

"I had to leave you behind," said Manny. "How was I to know the cops would be waiting for us?"

"You couldn't have known," said James.

"Exactly," said Manny. "I knew you'd understand. If I'da stayed I'd be dead too. You *do* understand, don't you?"

"I understand," said James. "You had no choice."

Manny laughed. "It sure is a weight off my mind, Louis. See, I was beginning to wonder whether you hadn't come back for a reason. If maybe you were one of them ghosts that can't sleep because somebody done 'em wrong. You swear you're not sore at me, Louis? You swear?"

"Don't worry about it," said James.

"When I heard you was dead," said Manny. "When I heard the cops had shot you twenty-three times. I didn't know what to think. I thought I was gonna go crazy. I blamed myself. But then I thought and I thought and I looked into my heart and I reckoned I didn't have no choice, Louis. I just didn't have no choice. Same as it was with Ma. She should nevera shouted at me like that. I didn't have no choice."

Campeche had once been a major seaport, but a newer port at Progreso at the tip of the Yucatán Peninsula had taken over most of the traffic. There were still a few cargo ships in and out, though, so James and Precious thought they would have a fairly good chance of finding a captain who would be prepared to take them to Lagrimas Negras.

They booked two rooms in the Hotel Cuahtemoc, and the next day they started asking around. They tried the shipping office, the port authority, and the numerous bars and cafes.

Most people they spoke to had never heard of Lagrimas Negras, others laughed and treated them as if they were crazy; some cursed darkly and told them to get lost.

Finally, at ten o'clock that night, following a tip-off from a group of sailors, they found a drunken English first mate in a seedy bar who said his captain would take them if they could pay their way.

James had to offer most of the money he had left, and when the man went away into the night chuckling to himself and counting the notes, James fully expected never to see him, or his money, ever again.

But at five o'clock the next morning, as arranged, a lighter was waiting for them on the small stone pier in the bay, and the first mate, still evidently drunk, took them out to his ship, which lay at anchor in deeper waters.

"You know the type of place you're going to?" he said as they chugged slowly out to sea.

"Yes," said James.

"I won't ask why you three want to go there."

"And we wouldn't tell you if you did," said James.

The first mate laughed and belched and didn't say anything else until they pulled up alongside the ship, a cargo vessel called the *Lady Gray*.

She was carrying sisal and animal hides, and the captain, who met them on deck, was a gruff, bearded Yorkshireman with a fat belly and a cigarette permanently hanging from his lower lip.

"So, you're my passengers," he said, giving them the once-over. "A rum bunch, if ever I saw one. Now, this is not a passenger ship, I've no spare cabins. You can eat with the men, but it'll be tomorrow by the time we get to the island, so you'll have to sleep where you can. On deck or in the hold. Makes no difference to me. Happy sailing."

The three of them tried to make a nest among the hides in the hold, thinking it would be soft and comfortable, but the overpowering animal smell coming off the skins made it very unpleasant, and they moved to a spot on deck beneath the lifeboats.

The voyage was dull and uneventful, and James took the opportunity to get some rest. He sat out on the deck in the sun, listening to the chug and thump of the diesel engines and smelling the fumes mixed with the ozone-rich spray from the sea.

He wondered if this wasn't all part of his dream. It was crazy to be sailing off into the unknown with this obsessed girl and cracked bank robber. What would they find on the island? All he had to go on was what Manny had said. And Manny was unreliable at the best of times. Certainly they were being treated like criminals, and strangely, he felt closer to Manny than he did to these sailors.

Day faded slowly into night, and a roof of stars appeared.

Precious emerged from under the lifeboat and paced up and down the deck. She had been keeping to herself, lost in her own thoughts. Perhaps she too was wondering if they were doing the right thing. She was a very different person from the one he had first met the other day at her house.

How long ago was that? It seemed like years.

Precious stopped her pacing and approached James.

"I can't sleep," she said.

"You should try," said James, standing up.

"I know," said Precious, and before James realized what was happening she gave him a hug.

"Thank you," she whispered in his ear.

"What for?" said James, taken aback.

"For helping me," she murmured. "I know I said a lot of things back there in the jungle, but I really don't think I would have been brave enough to do this by myself."

She kissed him quickly and crawled back under the lifeboat.

James settled down on the deck with his jacket for a pillow and looked up at the stars, trying to think of nothing. Slowly sleep crept up on him, and he lay there, rocked by the waves, untroubled by dreams.

He was awoken by a boot in the side at daybreak. The first mate was standing over him, chuckling.

"Wakey, wakey, rise and shine," he said. "We're there."

The sky was a dull, lifeless gray broken by thin streaks of lurid salmon pink. James felt queasy and disoriented. He sat up, rubbing his eyes and scratching his head. Precious and Manny were emerging from under the lifeboat, looking as dazed and confused as James felt.

Off the starboard side of the ship was the crouching, black shape of an island, but in the dim early-morning light James could make out no features.

"How long till we put in to the harbor?" he asked.

"Put in to harbor?" the first mate laughed. "You must think us daft. This is as close as we're getting, my friend. You know what that place is? No one ships there unless they got bad business. Well, it ain't my business, it's your'n. From

257

now on, you're on your own." The mate spat over the rail.

"A rowing boat, then?" said James. "You'll at least row us to the shore?"

"I'm not a pirate," said the mate. "I've little sympathy for you, but I'll not see you drown. Come along."

They clambered over the side of the ship and down a rope ladder to a waiting rowing boat where four sleepy sailors sat ready at the oars.

They pulled steadily across the dark water until they were within a couple of hundred feet of the shore.

"This is the end of the line," said the mate. "It's too dangerous to go in any closer. There's submerged rocks here and a very nasty reef. You can swim, I hope."

"Yes," said James, "but—"

"There's no 'buts' about it," interrupted the mate. "You can swim ashore or you can return to the *Lady Gray* and sail with us to Kingston."

"I paid you to take us to—" said James, but it was all he said before the mate pulled out a pistol and waved it at him.

"Get in and swim," he said unpleasantly.

James took Precious by the hand and jumped before she could protest; a moment later they heard a splash as Manny joined them.

James kicked and felt sharp rocks below the water, which was churning and surging over the reef.

The rowing boat was already a small shape heading back toward the ship.

He looked at Precious's frightened face. Manny was nowhere to be seen.

If they made it to dry land, it would be a miracle.

PART 3—LAGRIMAS NEGRAS

Dear James,

As your classical tutor I thought it my duty to write to you and bring you up to date with all things Eton. I'm afraid that I can never stop being a schoolmaster, and even from a distance of some five thousand miles I am worrying about your education. I am sure that your admirable aunt will be doing her best to school you, but I know how you always did prefer outdoor pursuits to dry and dusty learning. I realize that you find lessons pretty beastly at the best of times, but it won't stop me from trying to drum some education into you, and I only hope that something is sinking in.

As you have no doubt already discovered, I am enclosing in the package a couple of school books I would like you to look over, as well as some test papers for you to complete. On another sheet you will also find some "homework". It is merely a few construes and some passages to translate from Latin into English and vice versa, just so that you don't become completely rusty. You will be familiar with all this from work we have done before, and I don't think you will find any of it too taxing. As I say, though, I don't want your brain to turn to complete mush while you are away in the land of the sombrero. I trust you are enjoying yourself in Mexico, and despite this letter and all my efforts, don't work too hard!

261

I have been mulling over your return to Eton in the summer half. I think it would be pleasanter for you if you could ease gently back into school life. To that end, I wonder if you would like to join the school party in Kitzbuhel at Easter. The Alps will be rather lovely at that time of year. There will be rock climbing, walking in the mountains, tobogganing, and skiing (weather permitting). I feel sure that an adventurous, outdoors chap like yourself would rather enjoy that sort of thing. Anyway, have a ponder and get your aunt to write to me when you have made a decision.

I can hardly believe that a year has passed since you first arrived here at Eton. Time seems to be slipping through my fingers like desert sand. The months just gallop past. I remember your arrival as clearly as if it were yesterday. Standing outside my room one morning was a tall, quiet boy. He seemed a little unsure of himself, as all new boys must, but how quickly he learnt! You soon became a confident, self-sufficient young man, and I could see that you were going to be a credit to the school. Not least because of your athletic achievements. Remember all the excitement of the Hellebore Cup and your triumph in the cross-country? You had all the self-assurance and guts of someone twice your age. It's a shame you are missing out on all the running at the moment, but I am sure that you are keeping fit out there in Mexico.

I am pretty confident that books and learning and the world of academia are not going to figure very heavily in your future, but I am also confident that you are destined for great things! For my part, I am doing my duty and sending you this, no doubt unwelcome, reminder of school. You, as usual, will do with it what you please.

I will sign off now. I am sure you are not at all interested in the ramblings of an old schoolmaster. Good luck with the "homework".

Yours sincerely,
Michael Merriot

CHAPTER 23—INTO HIS MOTHER'S ARMS

James struggled toward consciousness, like someone clawing his way through a sticky, silver spider's web. As he pulled aside the last strands, he became aware of light and sound and a soft breeze stroking his naked skin.

He could hear two things, a rasping breath and a repeated harsh trumpet blast. As he tried to make sense of them he realized that one was the sound of surf breaking lazily on a beach and the other was the cry of a seabird.

Now he tried to make sense of what he could see. It looked like a pile of glittering gold, spread out before him in a vast undulating heap. The nuggets closest to him were sharply defined, but the rest were hazy and out of focus. He twitched his nose; something was pressing against his face. Then he understood that he was looking not at gold, but at sand. He was lying on his stomach with his face half-buried in the stuff.

So he was on a beach, then? Yes. He could feel warm sun on his back, and as he shifted his gaze he saw a large piece of smooth, bleached driftwood a few feet away.

It all came back to him, now. Plunging into the cold water of the Caribbean. Fighting the waves and the current. Swimming hard toward the island, but with every stroke being pulled farther out. The gray-black sea smashing into him and trying to force him under. Refusing to give in to it, his arms hacking away at the water. Then the reef scraping his legs and stomach. Tearing at his shirt. Trying to find a way through. Being thrown this way and that. Against the rocks. Precious tiring, calling for help. Holding her. Pulling her along the reef, looking for an opening, a way through to the sheltered waters on the other side. Losing all sight of Manny. Not caring. Only hoping that he and Precious could make it safely ashore. How long were they in the water? It felt like hours. Then there was the agonizing memory of larger waves, and being hurled onto the rocks. He must have hit his head. After that his memory was blank, and his thoughts were spun into the suffocating spiderweb.

He was in one piece. Even if that piece was battered and bruised. Where was Precious, though? Had she made it ashore? He moved his elbows forward through the warm sand and pushed himself up. He checked the damage. His shirt was gone and his trousers were in tatters. He had scraped the skin off his arm and shoulder. The right-hand side of his chest was caked with dried blood. There was a hideous purple blotch lower down around his hip. But at least he was all there. Arms, legs, hands, feet. And his heart was beating and his lungs still pumping.

A small red crab was curiously picking at a scab on his ankle. He plucked the creature off and threw it into the sea.

The effort of this small movement exhausted him, and he sank back into the sand and closed his eyes.

In a moment he was asleep again.

He was woken by a shadow falling across his face as the

sun was blotted out. He shivered and opened his eyes. Someone was standing over him.

"Thought you could trick me, huh?" said a man's voice.

James squinted up into the sun. The man was in silhouette, but it was unmistakably Manny, and he was pointing Strabo's gun at him.

Now what?

"Manny?" James said feebly. "You made it, then. Where's Precious?"

"Never mind the girl," said Manny. "This is between you and me."

With a huge effort, James rolled on to his side and sat up.

"You tried to fool me, huh?" said Manny. He was damp, and had lost his jacket and the bandage from around his head, but he looked like he'd had an easier time of it than James.

His eyes were clear and burning.

"Me!" he shouted. "Nobody can make a mug out of Manny the Girl."

James hung his throbbing head in his hands and was sick into the sand.

He needed to get out of the sun.

He needed food and water.

What he didn't need was Manny going crazy on him.

"Not now, Manny," he said.

"You tried to pretend you was my brother Louis," said Manny. "All these days you been pretending. I don't know how you did it. You musta put some kind of hoodoo on me. Used some kinda magic. But I seen through it. You ain't Louis. You never was. I know who you really are. Yeah. You didn't expect that, did you? You're the guy tried to kill me back in Tres Hermanas. You're the guy pushed me out the car. You and Precious have been working together."

At the mention of her name, James came alive. He stood up and looked along the beach in both directions, ignoring Manny.

There was no sign of her. There was only golden sand and palm trees and the surf whispering on the shore.

"Where is she?" James asked. "Where's Precious?"

"Don't worry about her," said Manny. "I took care of her."

"What?" said James angrily. After everything they had been through he hated the thought that Manny would harm her in some way. "What have you done to her?" he shouted.

"I told you," said Manny. "She's taken care of. Now tell me *who*? Huh? Who is ever going to know? You tell me that. Who is ever going to know?"

"Know what?" said James.

"Know I shot you," said Manny. "You and the girl. I'm gonna shoot you and leave you on this beach to be eaten by the crabs. You thought I didn't know what was going on, just because I hit my head. Well, I ain't stupid, boy. I may be crazy but I ain't stupid."

James was getting desperate. What had happened to Precious? He looked past the line of palms at the edge of the sand. The land rose sharply toward a bare hill, broken here and there by jagged, rocky outcrops. A group of big saguaro cactuses stood looking down at them like men standing and pointing. A gull screamed. Like the scream of a girl.

"What have you done with her?" James yelled.

"Shut your mouth," snapped Manny. "I don't want you

trying to put another hoodoo on me. You ain't Louis, you won't fool me again."

"No, I'm not Louis," said James, with all the venom he could muster. "You left Louis to die, remember? Back in San Antone. You left him behind to be shot twenty-three times by the police. So, no, I'm not him, and I'm glad of it."

"Shut up," shouted Manny. "Just you shut up."

"No. I won't shut up," James yelled. "I know all about you, Manny. I know all about how you killed your own mother, your precious mama."

"No, you're lying," said Manny. "I never did. I never did. Not my mama."

"Maybe you didn't mean to kill her," said James coldly. "Maybe you only meant to hit her, but you did kill her. You hit her and she fell, and she died. She isn't waiting for you, Manny. Because if she's in heaven, you're going to hell."

"No," said Manny, fearfully shaking his head, which caused the flap to come loose again. "You're lying, and your dirty lies are giving me a headache. Just you shut your mouth, you liar."

"Here he is, everybody," said James. "The great Manny the Girl! Who killed his own mother and left his brother behind to die."

Manny closed his eyes, fighting back tears. It was all that James needed. He squatted down, grabbed a piece of driftwood and swung it at the gun in Manny's hand.

There was a loud crash as the gun went off, and then it spun away over the sand. James and Manny both dived for it at the same time, and scrabbled to get their fingers around it, rolling in the sand.

"Oh, I'm gonna make you pay for your dirty lies," said Manny, getting his fingers around the trigger.

"Put a sock in it," said James, and just then the gun went off.

James felt the heat of it, searing across his chest, but it was Manny who took the bullet. It hammered into his shoulder and he collapsed onto his back with a sigh.

He lay there, white with pain and shock and bleeding heavily.

Despite everything, James suddenly felt sorry for him. He tore off part of Manny's shirt and used it to try to stem the flow of blood.

Manny's eyes had become unfocused. He looked frail and haunted.

"It hurts, Louis," he said, the loss of blood tipping him back into fantasy. "I thought they got you, but they got me. I don't understand."

"Just be quiet for a moment and lie still," said James. "I may be able to get help."

But Manny pushed him away, picked up the gun, and lurched clumsily to his feet. He looked around, his eyes darting crazily, and saw the big cactuses up on the rocks.

"Who are those people, Louis?" he said, shielding his eyes from the sun, his shirt rapidly staining crimson.

"There's nobody there," said James. "Sit down and rest."

"No," said Manny. "Look at them! Can't you see them? What do they want? Why are they staring at me?"

James tried to pry the gun out of Manny's fingers, but he was holding on with a clawlike grip.

Manny shoved James away again and strode, stiff-legged,

across the beach. James hurried after him into the tree line and up the hill. As Manny got up among the rocks he began firing at a cactus, knocking its "arm" off. Then he carried on firing at its body until it was turned into a flayed and mushy pulp.

"They won't stop staring, Louis," he said. "How do they know me? How do they know what I done?"

"There's no one there," said James. "They're just cactuses."

Manny froze, momentarily unsure of where he was, and there came a distant shout from the trees.

Manny spun around, his cheeks streaked with tears. "Can't you hear it, Louis?" he cried. "What's the matter with you?" Then he broke into a smile, and his face lit up with the big, open grin of a child.

"I heard *something*," said James.

"I think it's Mama, Louis. I think she's calling out. She's calling us home to dinner. We're all going to be together again, Louis, the three of us."

He turned away from James, who scrambled up onto the rock behind him. On the other side was a low depression, filled with more cactuses: maguey, prickly pear, agaves, and some big round barrel cactuses like giant pincushions. In the center was another tall cactus, which, indeed, seemed to be beckoning them with outstretched arms.

"I'm coming," Manny called out. He looked like a little boy. "I'm coming, Ma—"

"No," said James, but he couldn't stop him.

Manny staggered down the slope, got up onto a big rock, and stepped off it, straight into the "arms" of the cactus.

He screamed.

"It's a trap, Louis," he roared. "They tricked us. They was waiting for us. Get away! Oh, damn, but it hurts."

As he struggled to free himself he stumbled deeper into the thicket of spiky plants and started firing again.

James ducked down so as not to be hit by a stray bullet.

He heard voices and the sound of hurrying footsteps. A moment later a group of Indians with long black hair emerged from the bushes. They were wearing matching white outfits and carrying modern rifles. They shouted something to Manny that James couldn't understand, but Manny was lost in a world of pain and confusion, thrashing wildly in the cactuses, screaming and firing the last of his bullets.

James watched as one of the Indians calmly raised his rifle and fired a single shot. Then Manny was silent.

The men spoke quietly to each other, and the shooter shook his head.

James stayed down, hoping they hadn't seen him, trying to flatten himself on the rocks and ignore the way they cut into his bare flesh.

Then he felt something cold and hard press into the back of his neck, and a soft voice said, "Don' move, or I kill you."

CHAPTER 24—PINAUD ELIXIR

El Huracán was sitting at the huge mahogany table in his dining room, taking his morning coffee. The windows to the balcony were open, and the thin white curtains were flapping in a cool ocean breeze. The sun was riding high across a blue sky decorated with puffy clouds. All the scents of the island drifted in—the smell of the trees and the rotting vegetation in the jungle, the sharp tang of the sea—and from closer to hand, the smell of breakfast being prepared. He himself had been up for hours, but many of his "guests" slept in and ate their breakfast late.

He was looking forward to spring, when the island would come alive with bright flowers and fruit and heavy scents. He knew that it would be upon them all too soon. Time passed quickly now. There was no escaping the fact that he was growing old.

There came a knock, and presently one of his men put his face around the door.

"What is it?"

"We found the others."

"Bring them in."

"There is only one. A boy. We had to shoot the man."

El Huracán grunted and nodded. Then he sat back in his chair, stretched his legs out under the table, and lit a cigar.

The boy they brought in was tall with black hair falling untidily over his forehead. His skin was tanned from the sun and covered in cuts and bruises and insect bites. He was half-naked, and but for his cold, gray-blue eyes, El Huracán would have taken him for a wild boy, a savage from the jungle.

Those eyes were strong and bright and sharp, and seemed to say that, despite what had happened to the outside of him, inside the boy was unchanged. His heart beat strongly.

El Huracán smiled. He liked the boy.

"Bring him something to cover himself," he said, and one of his men hurried out. "Sit down," he went on.

Warily the boy sat at the table, ever watchful and alert, like a jaguar.

"Are you hungry?" he asked, and the boy nodded. El Huracán gave a sign to another of his men, and he too slipped quickly out of the room.

El Huracán sat there watching the boy and smoking his cigar. For his part, the boy watched him back.

"I have many questions," said El Huracán. "But they can keep until after you have eaten. I will ask one thing, though. Did you mean to come to Lagrimas Negras, and do you know what this island is?"

The boy nodded "yes" to both questions without hesitation.

"Do you know who I am?" asked El Huracán.

This time the boy shook his head.

"I am the ruler here. This is my island. They call me El Huracán."

"The Hurricane?" said the boy, raising an eyebrow.

"Yes. And just like a real hurricane you cannot argue with

me. I am king, chancellor, judge, jury, and executioner. There is no law but mine. My word is absolute. I was named after a Mayan god—Hurakan—the god of wind and storms. And *here* I am God."

The first of the men returned with a brightly colored, native blanket. He moved silently to the boy and draped it over his shoulders. The boy wrapped it closer about himself. A minute later a tray of food and drink was brought in, with bread and cold meat, cheese, fruit, nuts, a glass of orange juice, and a jug of iced water.

El Huracán watched as the boy greedily set to, working his way methodically through the food until all the plates were empty.

"So," said El Huracán when he had done, "why are you here?"

The boy straightened in his chair and pushed back from the table.

"I followed someone," he said.

"Ah," said El Huracán.

"Mrs. Glass," said the boy. "Mrs. Theda Glass."

"And what did you mean to do with the *señora* when you caught up with her?"

"She has something that doesn't belong to her."

"You were taking a great risk coming here."

"I know."

El Huracán let out a great puff of blue smoke. "You should know that I have several rules," he said.

The boy looked at him coolly, waiting, not afraid but listening closely.

"I have a strict rule that only people with money can stay

on my island," said El Huracán. "By the look of you, I would say that you have nothing."

The boy shrugged. "Not a single peso," he said. "What are you going to do about it?"

"Normally I would send you back. Hand you over to the police, or the army, or whoever you were running from."

"I'm not running from anyone," said the boy. "I told you—I came here to find Mrs. Glass. That's all."

"You present me with a problem," said El Huracán. "I have never had anyone like you turn up here before. You are not a policeman. You are too young. So, what are you?"

"I'm just a boy."

El Huracán laughed quietly. "I can see for myself that you are not just any boy," he said. "I'll tell you who you are. Your name is James Bond. You tricked Señora Glass into thinking that you were a Mexican pickpocket so that you could try to rescue two American children that she had kidnapped."

"You know a lot about me," said James.

"It is my job to know everything," said El Huracán.

"So she's here, then?" said James.

"Who?"

"Mrs. Glass. She must have told you all that. And I suppose she's already sold you the stolen naval documents."

El Huracán looked at him without saying anything.

This all felt slightly unreal to James. He had had no clear idea of what to expect on the island, but he could never have imagined this. The place felt more like an expensive hotel resort than a criminals' hideout.

And he had certainly not been expecting to meet this

elegant, clever man, who looked half Mexican Indian, half African, and wholly unlike anyone he had ever met before. There was a coldness, a stillness, and a watchfulness about him that made him seem more reptile than human.

James remembered the big iguana he had shot, how it had looked like something unimaginably ancient and alien. He could have looked into its shiny black eyes for all eternity and still not known anything about what was going on inside its mind, or its chilly heart.

This man was the same. His name, El Huracán, put one in mind of raging destructive chaos. But his eye was the eye of the storm. Dark and deceptively calm.

"Can I ask you something?" said James.

El Huracán took a sip of coffee, delicately wiped his mouth on a crisp white napkin, and nodded.

"The girl who was with me?" said James. "Precious Stone? Do you know where she is?"

El Huracán clicked his fingers and said something to one of his men, who bowed and backed out of the room. "She arrived this morning," he said. "Wandered into the square, looking like a drowned rat. She was asking for help, saying her friend was unconscious on the beach with a crazy man, but she would tell us nothing more, not who she was, where she had come from, or what she might be doing here. Now I know."

"Where is she?" said James. "Is she all right?"

"Do not worry yourself, James," said El Huracán. "She is safe."

A moment later there was a happy cry from across the room, and there was Precious, wearing a simple peasant dress. She ran across the polished marble floor and threw her arms around James.

James hugged her back.

"How touching," said El Huracán. "So you are Precious Stone? I should have realized."

Precious looked around at him, frowning.

"Mrs. Glass is here," said James. "She's told him everything."

"She told me a story that she thought had ended," said El Huracán. "It seems it is far from over. It seems there is one last chapter to tell."

"What are you going to do with us?" asked Precious.

"That is enough talk for now," said El Huracán, clapping his hands. "My men will take you to your rooms. They will bring you clean clothes. You will bathe and my doctors will tend to you. Then you must rest. I will see you later and we can talk some more. We will have a civilized dinner, and I will tell you what I have decided to do. Now, run along."

The next few hours passed in something of a blur. James and Precious were taken to adjoining rooms in one of the blocks off the main plaza, with a shared balcony and views out toward the sea.

James took a scalding hot shower, ignoring how much it stung, and scrubbed his sore and aching body with coarse soap. It felt so good to be clean again. He washed his hair with a gloriously rich shampoo, and was delighted to see rivulets of filthy gray foam snaking down his body into the drain. He noticed the label on the shampoo, Pinaud Elixir, and promised himself that he would only ever use that brand from now on in memory of the best shower he had ever had. Then, although he was by now spotlessly clean, he climbed into the bath and lay stretched out flat in it until the water had grown nearly cold.

At last, smelling of roses, wrapped in a huge, soft dressing gown, and feeling heavy and sleepy, he was taken to the medical block, where a doctor and two nurses took his temperature, his pulse, and his blood pressure. They felt his bones and dressed his cuts and went over every inch of him, checking that he was all right.

"What's this?" the doctor asked, feeling a bump on James's shoulder.

"It's just an insect bite that won't clear up," said James. "I've had it for days. It's very painful."

"As if some creature were chewing away at your flesh under the skin?" said the doctor.

"Yes," said James. "Exactly like that."

"It is *Dermatobia hominis*," said the doctor, wrinkling his nose.

"What's that when it's at home?" asked James.

"A nasty little bug called the botfly, or beef fly," the doctor explained. "The adult captures a mosquito and lays an egg on its proboscis. When the mosquito next takes a feed it injects the egg under the skin of its victim. A maggot hatches out of the egg and feeds on the muscle tissue of its host."

"You're telling me I've got a maggot growing in my shoulder?" said James.

"Yes," said the doctor, "and another one on your back. Don't worry, it is painful, as the maggots are covered in spines, but it is not serious. Here . . ."

James watched as the doctor taped a piece of raw bacon over the lump.

"What's that for?" he asked.

"We have to lure him out," said the doctor. "The maggot breathes through a tube that he sticks through your skin. This way, he will eat his way up out of his hidey-hole into the bacon, but the tape will suffocate him. In a few days we can remove the tape and the bacon, and squeeze the little monster out like toothpaste."

Feeling slightly sick, James was returned to his room, where he settled down on his bed. The last thing he heard before he fell asleep was the key turning in the lock of his bedroom door.

This may feel like a hotel, he thought as he drifted into unconsciousness, but I must never forget that it is nothing of the sort.

"What happened to you this morning?" James asked.

"You knocked yourself out trying to get me past the reef," said Precious.

The two of them were sitting out on their shared balcony in big wicker armchairs, looking at the view and chatting.

"Then we were washed over by a big wave," Precious went on. "I managed to get you to the beach, but I couldn't wake you. I was so worried. It was still dark. Manny was already there. He must have found an easier way to get ashore. He was rambling, said he would take care of me. I wanted to go for help, but he wouldn't let me. In the end I had to pretend to go to sleep, and then sneak off when he wasn't looking."

"I thought he'd done something to you," said James. "I was worried."

"I can take care of myself," said Precious.

James couldn't stop himself from grinning. "You know," he said, "I'm beginning to think you can."

"I've been a fool, though," said Precious angrily. "A stupid, little fool. What did I think we were going to do when we got here? I *didn't* think. We had no plan. My head was too full of revenge."

"Don't give up now," said James. "We'll find a way."

James had woken for a late lunch, which he'd eaten with Precious. They had both been given fresh clothes: simple white Mexican outfits, but clean and comfortable. Precious had put a flower behind her ear, and James thought once again how much better she looked without all her makeup and her fancy Hollywood dresses and her hair tortured into an elaborate and unnatural style.

As they chatted, the light slowly faded from the sky, which was streaked with purple and gold. Twinkling lights started coming on all over the island. Insects struck up their music. The air was warm and still. It was like a dream. For the first time in a long while, they felt safe and relaxed. Which was odd considering that they were in a haven for criminals, and somewhere out there, El Huracán was deciding their fate. No matter how friendly and welcoming he appeared to be, James understood that he could kill him without a second thought, and nobody in the outside world would ever know a thing about it.

At last there came the knock on the door that they had been both longing for and dreading. It was time for dinner.

Time to find out what El Huracán had in store for them.

James went indoors and quickly tried to brush his hair into shape. As usual he failed. He studied the face in the mirror. He looked thinner and older. He wondered if he would ever be able to adjust to life back at Eton.

If he ever made it back to Eton.

Strange to think of life going on there without him. All those boys asleep in their rooms, with nothing worse to worry about than winning a House cricket match or translating a few lines of Latin. Since his letter from Pritpal he'd had no contact with the school. He wasn't to know that there was a growing pile of mail waiting for him at the central post office in Mexico City.

Mail that he would never read.

He left his room and marched across the plaza with Precious and their escort. Despite what he'd said to Precious earlier about not giving up hope, he couldn't help feeling like a condemned man on his way to the scaffold.

People were strolling in the plaza. They were mostly men, but there were a handful of women as well. James scanned their faces for a sight of Mrs. Glass, but she was not among them.

They were taken back to the dining room where James had first met El Huracán. They found the room deserted, but four places at the table were set for dinner with heavy silver cutlery and crystal glasses. They sat down and waited, too anxious to talk to each other.

James looked at the pictures on the walls. They were mostly framed plans and drawings of the island, relating to its long history. There were some pieces of Mayan art, a couple of detailed maps, some old designs for the prison, architects' drawings of El Huracán's redevelopment, and a row of documents concerning the slave trade.

His attention strayed to the table, and he noticed that Precious was staring at the other two place settings. He had wondered about them himself. One, he presumed, was for their host, El Huracán, but who was the other one for? And what might it mean for their future?

Their questions were soon answered as El Huracán strolled in with Mrs. Glass on his arm. She was wearing an expensive evening dress with matching jewelry, and her hair was tied up in a silk turban with a diamond brooch pinned to the front of it.

She was laughing and chatting breezily, but when she saw whom she was going to be dining with, the smile died on her lips.

"Well, hello there," she said icily as El Huracán escorted her to her seat.

"Hello," said James.

Precious said nothing. She had a face like thunder.

"I believe you all know each other," said El Huracán. "We have a great deal to talk about, and I thought it was for the best if we did it face-to-face."

"I have nothing to say to her," hissed Precious.

"Don't worry, sweetheart," said Mrs. Glass with the hint of a mocking smile, "the feeling is entirely mutual."

"Please," said El Huracán, "I would ask you to leave all your guns at the door. This room is neutral territory. I won't have any ill feeling in here. This is to be a civilized dinner."

He clicked his fingers and a servant poured chilled white wine for Mrs. Glass.

CHAPTER 25—A CIVILIZED DINNER

Fish soup was served, and for a few minutes the four of them ate and talked with strained politeness. El Huracán asked if James and Precious were happy with their rooms, and how they had spent the day. He was interested in the gruesome details of the botfly maggots that James had picked up, and told him how he had spent many years in the jungle when he was younger and was very familiar with the "hungry little devils," as he called them.

Suddenly Precious threw down her spoon.

"I can't stand it," she said. "How can we sit here and pretend that nothing has happened when this woman has ruined my life? She killed all those people. She stole from my father. I can't stand it a moment longer."

"Well, now," said El Huracán, turning to Mrs. Glass with a polite smile wrinkling his ancient face. "What have you to say for yourself?"

"I don't have to defend my actions here," said Mrs. Glass haughtily. "There's men a thousand times worse than me wandering around out there in the plaza, taking the evening air, without having to answer a lot of snotty accusations from a child. What kind of a place are you running here, Huracán? Letting kids like this in."

"I let anybody come here who wants to," said El Huracán calmly.

"That's a damn lie," said Mrs. Glass. "I know full well that if you can't pay your way, you're sent packing."

"I cannot send these children away," said El Huracán. "They have seen too much of my world. They might tell tales of my island and give away my secrets."

"Then why didn't you shoot them on sight?"

"I had to find out who they were."

"I paid my way," said Mrs. Glass. "I gave you the papers."

"Yes. And very valuable they are, too." El Huracán nodded to one of his servants, who placed the leather pouch containing the naval documents on the table.

El Huracán stroked the U.S. Navy insignia. "These will assure you a long and comfortable stay here in Lagrimas Negras," he said, and then looked up at Mrs. Glass. "You know, of course, that you can never leave?"

"I know it now," said Mrs. Glass. "And I think it stinks."

"Oh, you will get used to it," said El Huracán. "In time you will forget that there ever was a world outside these shores."

"Those documents do not belong to her," said Precious angrily. "They belong to my father. If you had any decency you'd give them back to me."

"You know very well that they do not belong to your father, either," said El Huracán. "He himself stole them."

"My father is not a thief."

"Isn't he?" said El Huracán. "I know your father, Precious. There have been occasions when I have had need of his plane and his skills as a pilot. He is not a bad man. He was just trying to get by, like everybody else. But he should never have got involved with these stolen secrets. For him smuggling was a great game. This is different. The stakes are higher. These papers have touched the lives of many people. Touched them with the hand of death."

"Smuggling's one thing," said Mrs. Glass. "Turning traitor and selling state secrets is another. He shoulda left it to the professionals."

"Is that what you are?" said Precious. "A professional? A professional what? Murderer? Crook? Kidnapper?"

"I guess you could call me a spy," said Mrs. Glass.

"A spy for who?"

"Whoever will pay me most."

"Don't make me laugh," said Precious. "Manny told us all about you. How you married some gangster in Los Angeles, how you were nearly killed in a shoot-out."

"He didn't tell you the rest," said Mrs. Glass, "because he didn't know. He didn't tell you about how I went into hiding, traveled down through Mexico into South America, hung out there a coupla years before heading across the Pacific to Japan. I had decided to do a world tour and learn everything I could about crime.

"In Japan I met with the Yakuza, in China it was the tongs. I spent time with gangs in India and the Balkans. In Italy I made friends with the Cosa Nostra, which was how I met dear, departed Strabo. I finally wound up in Germany, where I discovered that it was impossible to tell who were the crooks and who were the politicians. It was a crazy time there. Adolf Hitler's Nazi Party was growing.

"I met an American called Alan Glass. He was a

fascinating guy—smart, ruthless, charming. He taught me everything there was to know about being a spy. He knew everyone and played them all off against each other. In the end I don't think he even knew whose side he was on. He was a double-triple-quadruple agent. He sold secrets to the Russians, the British, the Americans, the Germans, and they all thought they were his best buddies. We married, and for a time we had a ball. But it couldn't last. One day he wasn't there anymore. He'd disappeared. I never saw him again. I reckon it was the Russians took him, but I can't be sure.

"Next morning I was on a plane back to the States. Went straight to Washington. I was welcomed as a heroine. One of their best agents in Europe. Gave them a lot of baloney, kept them happy, told them what they wanted to hear, had dinner with the president. They turned a blind eye to my less than honest past."

"Why?" said Precious. "Why would they? I don't believe you."

"I told you, honey," said Mrs. Glass, taking a sip of wine, "I was a cast-iron, gold-plated heroine, and besides, they knew I could be useful to them. The big problem in America right now is organized crime. The gangs are taking over. And back then in 1930, when I showed up, we still had Prohibition, so things were just about as bad as they could be. They were looking for someone to work with the Bureau of Investigation and infiltrate the gangs.

"I did what they wanted; I went back to my old ways. The first gangster I dealt with was Legs Diamond. Got close to him, set him up, and watched him die. And as I watched him bleed to death I made a decision: this wasn't going to be me. I wanted something better for myself. I had contacts in crime and espionage and politics all around the world. I set myself up as a mercenary, smuggling secrets wherever they were wanted." She paused, and then looked at Precious. "And that," she said, "is how I ended up at your father's house."

Now she turned her attention to James. "I've dealt with New York gangsters, Russian secret police from the OGPU, Japanese assassins, and Mexican bandits, but an English schoolkid came closest to sinking me." She raised her glass in a mock toast. "Here's to you, James Bond," she said. "I hope you're satisfied with what you've done, because you're stuck here with me for the rest of your miserable life."

"I'm afraid that is true," said El Huracán with a shrug. "I can never let you two leave."

James felt a cold, sick feeling inside. He had woken from his dream. Precious had been right. They had come blundering out to the island with no real thought of what would happen when they got here.

Precious hung her head in her hands, and two fat tears dropped into her plate.

James was dimly aware that El Huracán was still talking, his voice calm and even, like a schoolmaster discussing a lesson.

". . . you will have to pay your way. You may stay in your guest rooms tonight, but in the morning you will move to the worker dormitories. We will see where you are best suited. In the kitchens, perhaps, or helping to grow food. You look strong, James: there is always construction work to be done. Or, perhaps, you would rather be a waiter or a barman?"

James said nothing. He would not let his life be decided

for him like this. He was damned if he was going to give up without a fight. They'd got this far. They would see it through to the finish. Now was not the time to say anything, though. He would wait until he was alone with Precious, and then they would think and plan and choose their moment.

At six o'clock in the morning, before any of the "guests" were up, James was taken to the whipping post in the main square, where twenty men were waiting patiently. They were all Indians, dressed in loose, white cotton work clothes. A foreman called Morales divided them up into teams and set them each a task. James was assigned to a gang whose job was to rebuild an old stone bridge near the harbor. They worked steadily until twelve, when they were given a lunch of rice, corn, and beans, and then had to carry on until sunset. The pace was easygoing, the men worked slowly but steadily. James didn't have any trouble keeping up, and he enjoyed the physical labor: mixing cement and carrying stones.

While he worked he took the opportunity to study the comings and goings at the harbor. Two small ships put in during the day and unloaded supplies. Three armed guards patrolled the harbor side and carefully searched each sailor as he got on and off the ship. Two other guards stayed in a stone watchtower, manning a heavy machine gun.

There was no hope of sneaking aboard one of the ships. El Huracán's men watched like hawks, and the visiting sailors were in an obvious hurry to get away as quickly as possible.

The next day James's gang climbed to the highest point on the island to repair a massive steel water tower. From here he got a clear view of the sea. It was obvious that it would be hopeless to try to swim anywhere. There was no other land in sight in any direction, and his experience on the reef that completely surrounded the island had shown him just how dangerous these waters were.

They worked on the water tower for two days, cutting thin steel and aluminium sheets with powerful snippers, and patching up some of the joins where the pipes entered the tank.

Sitting in the sun with an ocean breeze cooling his skin, James could almost imagine spending the rest of his days on the island. He wondered how long it would take him to forget his old life.

No.

That must never happen. He was not going to stay here and rot.

His resolve grew stronger when he was assigned to his next job. There was a narrow canyon in the center of the island, which was crossed by a rickety bridge. The bridge was guarded at either end, and James was intrigued to find out what went on on the other side. A winding path led through a patch of forest to a hidden area. This was where El Huracán grew most of his food. There were chickens, bees in hives, goats, and sheep. What fertile land there was was densely planted with corn and vegetables, mostly tomatoes, peppers, and onions.

James was surprised to see that all the farm laborers were old, in their fifties and sixties, though it was hard to tell exactly, as they were so malnourished and poorly treated that they were old before their time. And unlike the other workers on the island, only a handful of them appeared to be Mexican. They looked worn down and miserable as they toiled with bony bent backs over the crops. He was even more surprised to see that armed guards in little wooden observation towers watched them, as if they were prison laborers.

James and his gang had come to repair some barbed-wire fencing and he had been told not to talk to the elderly laborers. He watched them as they worked on under the sun. At one point one of the workers threw down his shovel and shouted something at a guard. The guard casually strolled over and clubbed him to the ground with the butt of his rifle, and after that none of the other workers looked up from what they were doing.

At lunchtime James's work gang was escorted to a shaded area that overlooked a wide, stony riverbed. There were more old people here, digging up piles of dirt and sieving them over long, wooden waterways. They were skinny and ragged and feeble-looking.

James had made friends with an Indian called Moises, who spoke a little English and some Spanish, and he managed to ask him what they were digging for.

"*Oro*," said Moises quietly, and in such a way as to let James know that he should ask no more questions.

Oro was Spanish for gold. These wretched old skeletons were panning for gold.

They finished work early, so that they could get back across the island before it got dark. As they strolled through the trees, James asked Moises who the people were. Moises was smoking a huge, hand-rolled cigarette, as were most of the other Indians. The path was thick with pungent smoke.

"*Dinari*," said Moises.

"Money?" said James.

"*Sí.* They have no *dinari*. No money. They work for El Huracán."

"What? You mean they're guests who have run out of money . . . ?"

"Don't talk about this," Moises interrupted. "*Silencio.*" And he would say no more.

James knew not to ask him any more questions. El Huracán's men had mastered the art of the stone face. They would not be any help to James if he wanted to escape. They were all either fiercely loyal to their ruler, or too scared of him to say anything.

That night, James was feeling thoroughly depressed and hopeless. A Cuban rumba band was playing in the plaza, and there was a lively atmosphere. People were chatting and dancing, and most were drunk. This was hardly surprising, as there was little else for anyone to do all day except drink.

He looked around at the confident, ruthless faces of the men. If these tough criminals and gangsters couldn't find a way off the island, then what hope did he have? He had tried asking a couple of them if they knew of any way to escape, and they had just laughed in his face.

"Hey, kid!" A fat man with tiny yellow eyes was calling to him.

He went over.

"Get us a dark rum, kid, two glasses. No, better still, bring us a whole bottle."

"I'm not a waiter," said James.

The man raised his eyebrows.

"A little young to be a guest," he said.

James shrugged. The man was sitting at a table under a grapevine with another American, a wiry man with a twitch.

"Tough guy, are you?" said the other man, and again James shrugged.

"Pull up a chair and join us," said the first man.

James sat down. He soon found out that the men called themselves Chunks and Dum-Dum. They were both bank robbers, and they started telling him stories about their exploits in America, each trying to outdo the other. James supposed that everyone else here had already heard these stories. Soon they got on to stories about dead bodies, and the gruesome killings they had witnessed. It was obvious that they were trying to scare James, but he had seen more than most in his short life and didn't scare easily.

"But the cruelest death I ever saw," said Chunks, "was right here on Lagrimas. Guy's name was Bobby King. Didn't know him well. Grifter. Full of himself."

"Killed his wife," said Dum-Dum.

"Didn't take to life on the island," Chunks went on. "Tried to get a message out. Bribed one of the peons. The old lizard found out."

"The Hurricane finds out everything," said Dum-Dum. "You don't get nothing past him. Eyes and ears everywhere."

"He put King in a kinda rat run," said Chunks. "La Avenida de la Muerte, he calls it, the Avenue of Death. Told him if he got to the end he was free to leave."

"Leave the island?" said James, his interest aroused.

"Sure," said Dum-Dum, "but the guy didn't stand a chance." He laughed. "Sure was something to see. I won a stack of dough betting on how far he was gonna get. Chunks, here, he was way off. But, you see, before King went in there, we none of us knew what he was up against."

"The first thing was baby crocs," said Chunks. "Tank full of the little snappers. Boy, that was funny. You shoulda heard him yell."

"Like a baby he was," said Dum-Dum. "Yelling all the way through the scorpions and the spikes."

"Never even made it halfway through the run," said Chunks, sadly shaking his head. "I made a bad bet there."

"Ever seen a man eaten by a jaguar?" leered Dum-Dum, leaning in close to James with wide, bloodshot eyes, and breathing alcohol fumes over him as he laughed raucously. "Neither had I until that day. I seen a lot a things, but I never want to see that again."

"But if he'd got to the end?" said James.

"What of it?"

"El Huracán would have let him go? Is that what you're saying? King would have been free to leave the island?"

"That's what the old lizard said. He also said that nobody had ever got to the end, so . . ."

"Burnt the soles right off his feet," said Chunks. "You could smell him frying."

"Tell me all about it," said James, leaning in closer. "I want to hear exactly what he had to go through. . . ."

"This is the ball court," said El Huracán. "There are ball courts in all Mayan cities, right next to the temples. Do you know about the ancient Mayan ball game?"

James shook his head.

"They took it very seriously," said El Huracán. "It was half religious ritual, half sport. I suppose you could say the same of baseball! The ancient American civilizations had a very interesting approach to life and death and warfare. Warfare became something of a game, and their games became like war."

It was Sunday, a day of rest, and the old Mexican was showing James around the ruins. They were fenced off and out of bounds to the "guests," but he seemed proud of them and was happy to show them off to James. Enough of them were still standing to give an idea of what the place had once been like, and James pretended to be interested in order to get a better look at the rat run.

"For the Mayans," said El Huracán, settling down on the stepped seating that surrounded the court, "the aim of warfare was not to kill men but to capture them. The greatest warrior was the one who could catch the most enemies. The prisoners would then be brought back to the city and taken to the temple, where they would have their living hearts torn out of their chests by a priest, as an offering to the ever-hungry gods.

"The ball game was a religious ceremony played in their honor. There were games at every religious event. Sometimes the players would be captured slaves, but not always. The aim of the game was to keep a ball bouncing against the sides of the court and not let it fall into the middle.

"The players were not allowed to use their hands or feet to touch the ball, which was heavy and made of solid rubber. Instead they used their hips, chests, shoulders, and knees, and they protected their bodies with padding.

"They had to keep the ball moving at all times," El Huracán went on, "as it represented the sun moving across the skies. Do you see those stone rings set high up on the walls?"

James nodded.

"The players had to try and pass the ball through them. Not easy if you cannot kick it or throw it. The losing team in a game would often be beheaded. So you see, James, you must take your sport seriously."

El Huracán laughed and slapped James on the back. Then he got up and led James over toward the pyramid base.

"Even the gods played the ball game," he said. "It was central to the Mayan way of life. Have you ever heard about the Hero Twins?"

"No," said James.

"Perhaps one day I will tell you about them."

They had arrived at the flattened pyramid in which El Huracán had built the start of his run. James could see it snaking through the stones at their feet and leading away toward the second, smaller pyramid.

"This building was once much taller," said El Huracán. "Many layers have been removed. In the past there would have been steps leading right up into the sky."

"Were men sacrificed here?" said James.

"Let me show you something," said El Huracán.

He took James over to a wall that was covered in carvings and inscriptions and the strange pictograms called glyphs that were the Mayans' way of writing.

"See, here," he said, pointing to a row of carvings. "These show a victim being taken to the pyramid. It must have been an especially important sacrifice, because he is wearing a beautiful cape of feathers. They have dressed him to be the living embodiment of a god."

James looked at the carvings. Farther along he could see the victim being given a feast, then he was shown climbing the steps to the altar, and finally, there he was, lying on his back, with a priest cutting out his heart with a stone knife.

"When there was a ceremony," said El Huracán, "the steps of this pyramid would have run red with blood, like a waterfall of death. This pyramid was sacred to Hurakan, the god of wind and storms. He was also one of the gods who made the world and mankind. He was destroyer and creator both at the same time.

"My father, Gaspar, was a prisoner on this island when it was a penal colony. He fought in the uprising when the prisoners took over, and later he was the only one to escape when the American Navy attacked. He hid inside this pyramid where there was a maze of chambers and corridors. The Americans went in after him, and he ran ahead of them, under the ground, like a cornered rat. In the end he found a tunnel that led down to the sea, and he got away. There was a big storm and he was able to steal a boat. That was eighty years ago. He named me in honor of Hurakan, who had protected him. When I came here I opened up the passageways and exposed them to the wind. I use this place now for my own little game. Come." He put an arm around James's shoulders and led him away. "This is not for you."

"These ruins, or the whole island?"

"Both. I like you, James; you should never have come here."

"But not everyone here is a criminal," said James. "Your servants, for instance, the guards, the men who work here."

"No," said El Huracán, "they are Indians, descendants of the men who built this place. Many of these men I have known all their lives. They are loyal to me. I trust them."

"And the musicians who play at night?" said James.

"Study them well," said El Huracán. "They have been handpicked by my men. Every one of them is blind. They are paid well and they are given strict orders not to talk to anyone. They come for an evening and they leave before the morning. They see nothing. They speak to no one. They can tell no tales. But you and Precious know too much."

"What if we promised?" said James. "Never to tell anyone anything? What if we promised to forget that we were ever here? Forget all about you, and Mrs. Glass, everything. It's just not fair, keeping us here. We have family, friends . . ."

"I wonder how many of the captive Mayans who were brought here said the same thing?" said El Huracán. "As they were dragged up the steps to their deaths?"

"I thought they accepted their fate," said James. "I thought it was part of their religion, a fact of life, or death, I suppose. Wasn't it meant to be an honor to be sacrificed?"

"Perhaps," said El Huracán. "But deep down I'm sure they were all crying out for their mothers as they went up the steps."

"Weren't they sometimes given the best food and treated like gods themselves before they were killed?" said James.

"Even so, James," said El Huracán, "would any man willingly allow himself to be sacrificed?"

James studied the long, winding alleyway, which looked so innocent in the bright sun, and he remembered Chunks and Dum-Dum's gruesome story.

If this really was the only way off the island, he wondered if he would have the guts to run it.

"Are you mad?" Precious's eyes were wide and disbelieving. "It's not worth thinking about even for one second."

"There is no other way off this island," said James. "Believe me, I have looked. We can't swim, we can't fly. If we try and stowaway on a boat, they'll shoot us. But anyone who makes it through the rat run is free to go."

"Yes, and you said that nobody ever *has* made it through. What's its proper name?"

"La Avenida de la Muerte," said James sheepishly.

"The Avenue of Death," said Precious. "It's impossible."

"For one person, maybe," said James. "But there are two of us. If we work together we might just make it. We could practice. We could plot a way through. It's worth it, Precious. I'm telling you—it's the only hope we've got."

It was sunset, and they were walking along the beach. They had both been moved out of their luxurious rooms and into worker dormitories. One for the women, and one for the men, but they still met up in the evenings after work.

Precious had been assigned to the laundry. She had never worked before in her life and found it boring and exhausting. The only thing she had to look forward to was seeing James at the end of the day.

They had taken their shoes off and could feel the sand soft and warm between their toes. The palm trees rustled in a breeze. Tiny crabs darted about, popping in and out of their holes on the beach.

"It's no hope at all," said Precious bitterly. "There are snakes and scorpions and a jaguar and God knows what else in there. I won't do it. I can't."

"You've done a lot of things lately that you never would have dreamed of doing before," said James. "You *can* do this."

"I can't," said Precious. "Maybe you can, but not me."

James grabbed her and looked into her face. "Listen to me," he said. "You're strong and you're brave. I've seen it. You want to stay here and rot forever? I don't think so." He pointed out to sea toward where the mainland lay over the horizon. "Somewhere over there is your home, and your father, and your brother. Think of JJ. Will he be happy never seeing his big sister again? Will you be happy never seeing him again? He loves you, Precious. Your father loves you. And I never met her, but I'm sure your mother loves you too."

"No, she doesn't," said Precious flatly.

"Don't say that," said James, taken aback.

"I told you," said Precious. "She's gone. I remember the

first time she went away. She said she was going back to the States to visit her friends, then it was to see her sister or her mother, or to go shopping, and each time she stayed away longer. The last time, I knew she was never coming back. She hates it in Mexico, but if she loved me she would have stayed."

James didn't know what to say. He could run and fight and climb trees. He could get Precious safely out of the jungle and follow Mrs. Glass all the way to hell and back, but when it came to people's complicated feelings and their deepest thoughts, he felt useless.

"Why do you think I was such a little bitch?" said Precious, and she turned away and stalked off up the beach.

James left her alone. He could think of nothing intelligent to say.

The next morning, the foreman, Morales, announced that he needed a repair team to go into the "*túneles*." James asked his friend, Moises, to translate for him.

"The *túneles* beneath the *pirámide*," he explained.

"Tunnels?" said James, thinking that they might be going in to maintain the rat run.

"*Sí. Los Indios* no like to go in there. Is a bad place."

As the other men were reluctant to come forward, James easily got himself on the gang. He soon found out, though, that these were maintenance tunnels beneath the rat run. He also found out why the men didn't like this job. The tunnels were low and cramped and dark and airless. The work crew could only travel in single file, carrying oil lamps, and dragging their tools and heavy materials behind them.

Occasionally they had to squeeze through tiny gaps on all fours.

Part of the tunnels had been built by the Mayans. There were glyphs on the walls and carvings of skulls and mythical creatures. Other parts seemed more recent and had probably been built when El Huracán was creating the rat run. James was impressed by the Mayans, who had constructed this huge building without the use of either wheels or metal tools. It was quite a feat.

They presently came to a series of grilles and shutters built into the roof, and there was a complicated tangle of rusting pipework. After this the tunnel followed the course of a long stone channel that was fed by more pipes along the way. James assumed it must be for drainage. In the rainy season the open-topped rat run above would be liable to fill up with water if there was no runoff. He also knew that there was at least one water tank built into it, which would explain the elaborate plumbing.

Farther on they passed an underground chamber filled with machinery: giant wooden cogs and gears, and spindles linked by long leather drive belts. James peered in; the machinery seemed designed to turn three huge stone wheels set high up in the roof. It reminded James of the workings of a mill. He only got a brief glimpse of it, though, as this was not their destination, and the men pressed on, eager to get their work done quickly so they could get out of the tunnels.

It was hot down there and heavy going. They had all stripped down to their shorts and were sweating and panting. By the time they reached their destination they were exhausted and had to sit down to recover.

They were in a small chamber. To one side a sluice had been carved into the bare rock. It had been worn smooth by water and was covered with thick green algae. James could see it twisting and turning down into darkness. He wondered if this could be the way El Huracán's father, Gaspar, had escaped from the Americans all those years ago.

A stone channel drained into it, as did some more gutters from the surface, and it was directly opposite a metal door set into the wall. This was much larger than the shutters they had passed earlier. It was a deep, rusty orange color and stained with mold and algae. It was held shut with a screw wheel but was leaking in several places. Water seeped out from behind it and trickled into the sluice. There was a lot of building work in evidence here. The walls had been shored up with concrete and stone that was crumbling in these damp conditions.

Moving about was difficult, and James nearly slipped into the sluice. Moises grabbed him.

"Don' fall in there, Jaime," he said with a chuckle. "You slide all the way down to the sea."

In fact everywhere was slippery. The smell of damp and mold was very unpleasant, and it was mixed with a choking, fishy stink that James couldn't identify.

Their job was to replace the worst of the stone with new blocks they had painfully lugged behind them all the way from the entrance. James was in charge of mixing the cement for the mortar, while a couple of the men cut the new blocks to size.

There was nowhere to stand fully upright and James felt like his back was going to break. Today, though, the men worked quickly, anxious to be gone from this foul place. The old stones were eased out and the new ones fitted into place faster than James thought possible.

"What's on the other side of the door?" he asked Moises when he got the chance. He had noticed that the men were fearful of it and didn't like to go too close.

"Is a monster," said his friend. "Hun Came. He is in big pool of water."

James climbed carefully over the sluice and shuffled over to the door for a closer look.

"Can you open it from the other side?" he asked.

"No, only here."

The fishy smell was stronger here and was obviously coming from the tank. James looked up. There was a sort of chimney stretching about twenty feet to the sky. He stood up inside it and noticed a gap in the wall where a small stone had been removed. He tried to peer through into the tank, but it was too dark to see anything, and the fish smell was appalling.

"Don' stick your nose through there, Jaime," Moises shouted across to him. "He will bite it off." He then said something in his own language to the other men, and they all laughed.

James heard something move in the dark water, and he shuddered.

Precious had been right.

It would be an act of utter madness to go into the rat run.

But what choice did he have?

CHAPTER 27—MEXICAN HAT DANCE

Precious hated it in the laundry. Already her hands were red and raw from being constantly immersed in soapy water. She looked at the other women, leaning over the huge sinks, scrubbing dirty sheets with their big, powerful arms, and pictured herself like them in ten years' time: old and tired-looking.

She could see her life draining away down the plughole with all the filthy, gray water. She used to dream of what she was going to be when she was grown-up. Working in a laundry was not one of her dreams.

As well as washing she also had to do cleaning duties, usually in the guest rooms, but on the same morning that James was working in the tunnels beneath the rat run, she was sent up to El Huracán's residence. One of the girls who usually worked there had become sick, and just as the men were reluctant to go into El Huracán's tunnels, the women were scared to go into his house. Precious was given the job of filling in for the sick girl.

She crossed the plaza with three short, stout women, none of whom spoke any English and none of whom seemed to particularly like her. Halfway there she nearly bumped into one of the guests and recoiled in horror when she saw it was Mrs. Glass. She was wearing a dressing gown and had a towel wrapped around her head. She had evidently just been for a massage and beauty treatment at El Huracán's clinic. She looked Precious up and down with an expression of utter contempt.

"Well, well, well," she said coldly. "Look who it is. One of Huracán's little domestics." She tilted her head back and laughed. The sound was like shards of broken glass falling on a stone floor.

Precious bowed her head and hurried to catch up with the other cleaners. She saw them pause in El Huracán's doorway and cross themselves before going fearfully over the threshold, for all the world as if they were entering the gates of hell.

Once inside they steered Precious toward a toilet and gave her a mop and bucket, a cloth, and a stack of clean hand towels.

The toilet was the largest Precious had ever seen and was spotlessly clean. She nevertheless resented having to clean it.

So this was what she had come to: *a toilet cleaner.*

Well, she wouldn't do it. She was Precious Stone, Jack Stone's daughter.

She sat on the toilet, folded her arms stubbornly across her chest, and stared at the framed picture on the opposite wall.

After a while she realized with a jolt that she was looking at a drawing of La Avenida de la Muerte. She stood up and went across the tiled floor to look at it more closely. Yes. It appeared to be the original design for the rat run. It was hand drawn, possibly even by El Huracán himself, and showed all the passageways and chambers with notations for each one.

Her heart was thumping in her chest. She quickly looked at the other framed pictures in the room. They were all different drawings of the building works on the island, but none of them showed the rat run.

She locked the door, took the picture off the wall, and carefully removed the drawing from its frame. She folded it up inside a dirty towel and swapped the empty frame with another one that looked similar.

Then, quickly and diligently, she cleaned the room, changed the dirty towels for clean ones, and stacked the used ones into a neat pile.

The day seemed like it would never end, but at last she got away, the map now hidden under her clothes, and ran to meet James on the beach.

"You were right," she said breathlessly when she saw him. "I can't go on like this. I was miserable, that's all, but I won't give up. And I won't let that woman have the last laugh, James. I won't."

So saying, she pulled out the drawing and gave it to James.

He hugged her when he saw what it was.

"I tell you, it's fate," said Precious. "I was sitting there and there it was. This was meant to happen. We're going to do it. We're going to get off this island, and somehow we're going to get those stolen plans back."

"The plans . . ." In his obsession with escaping, James had forgotten all about the plans.

Well, for now they would have to wait. They would be locked safely away in El Huracán's bank. There was no way on earth James could ever get them out of there. The important thing right now was to plan their escape. They would have to come back for the plans later.

The drawing was not as detailed as it had first looked. Each chamber was referred to by the god it was named after, rather than by what it contained. But there were enough clues for the two of them to work out what a lot of it meant. There were even measurements and dimensions for each part.

"Look," said James, pointing to a spur that went off to the side at one end.

"This is where I was working today. It's a drainage sluice." He told her all about the *túneles*. "Whatever Hun Came is, whatever's in that big tank, must be the final challenge."

They started planning right there and then.

First they made a copy of the drawing, and in the morning Precious took it back into El Huracán's residence, hidden among some clean towels, and returned it to its frame. Then the following evening she and James met at some dilapidated ruins in the trees behind the beach that they had decided would be the perfect place to build a copy of the rat run.

They cleared away the vines and creepers and piled fallen stones on top of each other. They paced out measurements. They used fallen branches and small palms and lengths of pilfered rope and string. And when it was done they practiced running and jumping and climbing. They raced to see who could slither fastest on their belly. They dashed through the trees, trying to avoid branches and sharpening their reflexes. They looked at possible shortcuts and cheats. They worked on ways to get past each obstacle. They talked long into the night about what they might have to face, in the hope that talking would make it all seem familiar and not something to be terrified of. Because they knew that the hardest thing they would have to face would be their own fear. If they could only keep level heads and not panic, they would have a much better chance of making it through alive.

It was fun, the two of them working together. They could pretend that it was all just a game. The fire had come back into Precious. She was toughening up and getting stronger; the muscles were hardening in her arms and legs. Her eyes were bright, her hair glossy, and her skin clear. Each night they crawled into their beds, dog-tired but feeling that they had achieved a little more, and as their heads hit their pillows they fell instantly into a deep, refreshing sleep.

During the day, James worked as hard as he could with the repair gangs, swinging pickaxes and sledgehammers, hoisting sacks of sand and cement, digging, lifting, hammering, chopping. Building up his strength and his stamina. He would have to be perfectly fit, if he was to have any chance of surviving the run.

He had quickly created the impression that he was an energetic, reliable worker, the first to volunteer for the more unpleasant jobs and last to quit work in the evenings. Morales grew to trust him and gave him his own key to the big stone shed where all the equipment was kept. Every type of tool imaginable was stored in the shed. There was even a strong room at the back for explosives, which were occasionally used to break up big rocks.

Metal chests containing sticks of dynamite and neat coils of fuse wire sat on concrete shelves, ready to be used. James remembered Whatzat showing him how to use the stuff back at the abandoned oil field, and a plan started to form in his head.

After work, he would carefully clean all the tools his gang had used and return them to their proper places. He always left the shed immaculate. He wanted to be Morales's star laborer. He didn't want anyone to suspect what he was up to.

One evening after their training session, as they sat on the beach cutting shapes out of some pilfered steel sheeting, James was idly scratching his shoulder where the botfly maggot had made its home. It was still covered with the tape that the doctor had put on it.

"Does it hurt?" asked Precious.

"Not nearly as much as it did," said James, "but it itches like mad."

"Do you suppose it's dead yet?" said Precious.

"It must be," said James. "I can't feel it moving around anymore."

"Let's look," said Precious excitedly.

"It might be pretty horrible."

"So?" said Precious. "I like horrible things. Come on, I've been dying to see."

"All right."

James ripped off the bandage and carefully peeled back the strip of blackened bacon beneath it. There was the white head of the grub, nestling in a hole in his flesh. James was too disgusted to do anything more.

"Let me," said Precious, and with a look of mixed horror

and delight she pressed the edges of the wound together until the dead maggot was squeezed out. She flicked it into the sand where a crab quickly scuttled over, picked it up in its claws, and popped it into its mouth.

"Eurgh," said Precious. "That's revolting."

She paused a moment and then asked if she could do the one in James's back.

When she was done she suddenly leaned over and kissed him.

"What was that for?" said James.

"For luck," said Precious.

"Luck?"

"We can't put it off any longer," said Precious. "We're as ready as we're ever going to be. I'm beginning to think about it too much, and if I do that I'm liable to change my mind. What about you?"

"I'm ready," said James, jumping up and brushing the sand off his trousers. "We stick to our plan, yes?" he said.

"Yes," said Precious.

"All right," said James. "It must be about eight o'clock. There's one last thing I have to do. Get yourself ready and I'll meet you in the plaza in an hour."

James watched Precious go and then walked into the trees. About fifty yards back from the beach was a hollow under a tree covered with a pile of dead branches and palm fronds. He moved them aside and took his stuff out of hiding. He checked it all and double-checked it before setting off toward the entrance to the tunnels.

It was a Saturday night. The busiest night of the week. The

plaza was packed with people. A mariachi band was playing lively dance music. Trumpets blared, guitars strummed, strong voices sang out in unison. There was an air of fierce jollity among the guests. It was another night, another party, a party that would never end.

James turned up at nine, as arranged, and looked for Precious. As he was pushing through the crowd milling in the square, he bumped into Mrs. Glass. She was wearing a gaucho outfit, with loose trousers and a wide hat. The ring of golden hair that showed beneath the brim was immaculate as ever, but she looked older. She had put on a little weight. Her face was puffy. The soft life was not suiting her. She appeared to be drunk.

"Well, if it isn't James Bond," she said. "I didn't know Huracán allowed the help to mix with the guests."

"There's nothing you can say that will upset me," said James. "Because I'm getting away from here."

"Don't make me laugh," said Mrs. Glass. "There's no way off this stinking island."

"Not for you, maybe," said James. "You're condemned to rot here for the rest of your life, I'm afraid. But I'm off. Maybe I'll send you a postcard."

Mrs. Glass laughed. It was a shrill, bitter, grating sound, like an angry gull.

James stepped closer to her. "Take a good look around you," he said.

"What for?"

"Tell me if you see any old people," said James.

Mrs. Glass scowled at him, but did as he suggested. "What of it?" she said.

"Why do you think there are no old people here?" said James.

"Dunno." Mrs. Glass shrugged. "Don't much care. Never given it any thought."

"What do you think happens when you run out of money?" said James, and Mrs. Glass narrowed her eyes at him.

"What are you saying?"

"I've seen them," said James. "The old people. The ones who've been here too long and run out of money. El Huracán works them to death on his farm. Enjoy your stay."

Without warning, Mrs. Glass grabbed James by the throat.

"I should strangle you right here and now," she said. "You've been nothing but trouble for me."

James held her wrists and tried to pull her hands away, but she held on with an unbreakable grip. James couldn't speak. He could hardly breathe.

He realized it was useless trying to release her hands and decided that attack was the best form of defense.

He kicked her shin.

She snarled but still didn't let go. She was smiling now, and there was a wild gleam in her eyes.

James swung hard at her face, and she took a hefty backhanded slap across the cheek that whipped her head around and swept the hat off her head.

Mrs. Glass screamed and let go of James, as if he had suddenly grown red hot. She glanced desperately around for the hat, which had flown into the crowd.

James saw for the first time why she always kept her head covered. The ring of immaculate hair that always showed beneath her hat was all the hair she had on her head. Above it she was completely bald. And not only bald. The pale, hairless skin on the top of her skull was ridged like a ploughed field.

James remembered the story of how she had been strafed by machine-gun fire. It had obviously raked across her head and left it creased and naked.

He felt sorry for her. She was a pathetic figure as she scurried among the guests looking for her hat. And the guests were starting to laugh and point.

These were not people with any shred of kindness in their hearts. They liked nothing more than to see a fellow human being in distress. They were bored, too. Nothing ever happened on the island. This crazy, bald woman trying to find a lost hat was just about the funniest thing they had seen all year. A man snatched the hat up and held it out to her, and as she reached out to take it, he tossed it in the air. A second man caught it and played the same trick on her again. There now began a ghastly game of piggy in the middle, with Mrs. Glass running sobbing from one laughing man to the next as her hat was sent spinning in all directions. One man even patted her on her bald, lumpy dome, which sent up a great guffaw of merriment.

Someone had tipped the band off, and they started to play the jaunty "Mexican Hat Dance." Men took up the gag and sang along.

James couldn't stand it. He went over and joined the ring of men, and when he got the chance, he caught the hat and passed it to Mrs. Glass.

If she was grateful, she didn't show it. Too much damage

had been done. She tried to compose herself and regain her defiant look. James saw, though, that she was broken. She had always seemed like a woman with no weaknesses, but in the end everyone is vulnerable.

She put the hat on, turned away from him, and walked off without a word, followed by jeers and catcalls from the men who had gathered to mock her.

James found Precious sitting in the shadows near the band sipping a glass of iced soda water. He sat down next to her and gripped her hand.

"Have you got everything?" he asked, and she nodded, showing him the two letters she was holding. Both folded as small as they would go.

James knew what the letters said; he had written one of them, after all.

One was signed by Precious.

Please help me. My name is Precious Stone. I am being held prisoner here on Lagrimas Negras. Take this note to my father, Mr. Jack Stone of Tres Hermanas, Mexico. He is a rich man and will reward you for your help. With the same message written underneath in Spanish.

The other was signed by James and was nearly identical.

They waited patiently for the band to take a break. They played tirelessly for an hour longer, one lively tune after another, until two waiters brought over trays of food and drink for them and they stopped for a rest.

James studied the musicians. They were all blind, just as El Huracán had said. They stayed apart from the guests, and talked quietly among themselves. When James got a moment he drifted over and slipped his note into a trumpeter's pocket. Precious, meanwhile, was pretending to be a waitress. She moved among the band, picking up drinks, and James saw her slip the second note to the singer.

When she returned with the glasses, James said simply, "That's enough," and they moved off into the crowd. Finally they said "good night" to each other and went back to their separate dormitories.

The plan had been put into action. The ball had started rolling.

Now all they could do was wait and see if everything played out as expected.

CHAPTER 28—RUN, RAT, RUN

James was too tightly wound to sleep at first. He lay in his bunk and stared at the ceiling.

All the events of recent days were coming back to him. The flood in Puente Nuevo when JJ had nearly drowned. The grueling journey in the truck through the flooded lowlands. The battle with the soldiers. The time at the abandoned oil field and the deaths of Whatzat and Garcia. He remembered Sakata taking JJ to safety, and poor, crazy Manny with the hole in his head and their time in the jungle. He remembered the *chicleros*. He still had the gum, stuck to the underside of his bed. If he ever made it out of here it would be a good souvenir.

And he thought about Precious, how she had changed. He thought about how different people were when you got to know them properly.

Around him he could hear the other men snoring, mumbling, turning in their bunks. He longed for home, for the little cottage in Kent. He longed for the luxury of cool, crisp sheets and lying in his own bed on a calm, safe English night.

Slowly sleep crept up on him, or something like sleep. He fell into a half-waking, half-dreaming state that was interrupted in the dead of night when three armed guards came bustling into the dormitory. The other men woke and cursed, but the guards ignored them. They went straight to James's bed and hauled him out.

He just had time to put the gum in his mouth before they dragged him out of the dormitory.

It had begun.

"I told you! You know the rules. You cannot escape. It was a foolish and a childish thing to do. But then, I was forgetting that you are mere children."

James had never seen El Huracán show any emotion before, but now he seemed hurt and angry. Like a schoolteacher who had been let down by a favorite pupil, or a father let down by his son.

They were in El Huracán's dining room. Precious was there, looking as tired and glassy-eyed as James felt.

"Did you really think this would work?" said El Huracán, tossing the two notes down onto the table. "Did you really think that a hundred men have not tried something similar before?"

James kept quiet. The simple answer was *no*. He had not seriously thought for one moment that the musicians would take the notes to Mr. Stone. That wasn't the point.

"It was worth a try," said James.

El Huracán sighed. "You have disappointed me," he said. "I have been watching you, James. My men give me reports. You are a good worker, but you are clever also. I was thinking that you were wasted in the repair gang. But now this!"

He picked up the notes again and threw them into James's face. They fluttered harmlessly to the floor. He then turned to the window and looked out at the night. It was

317

cloudy and the sky was pitch black.

"What am I to do with you both?" he said.

"There's only one thing you can do," said James.

"What?"

"You'll have to put us into La Avenida de la Muerte."

El Huracán's eyes went wide, and then he frowned and shook his head.

"No," he said. "Not that."

"I thought you had a rule," said James, "that anyone caught trying to escape must be punished."

"Not this way."

"Rules are rules," said James. "Without rules what do you have?"

"I make the rules," said El Huracán angrily. "If I say you are not to be put into La Avenida, then you will not be put in there."

"Then we'll tell everyone," said James. "Tell them that the great El Huracán has gone soft, that he changes his rules to suit his mood."

"Silence," El Huracán barked, and then he caught himself and smiled. He sat down at the table and poured himself a glass of rum.

"Sit," he said.

James and Precious sat.

"My plans for you need not change," said the old man softly. "I will make you an offer," he said, looking straight at James. "You are brave and resourceful and clever, and I see you have a streak of iron in your soul, like me, James. I will not punish the two of you. And I will not ask you to stay here as servants."

"Slaves, you mean," said Precious, and El Huracán chuckled.

"I am a very busy man," he said. "I need good people around me. I need an assistant. Someone I can train. I will not be here forever, and it would be good to know that I could pass Lagrimas Negras on to a reliable pair of hands. Who knows, perhaps those hands might belong to you."

"Are you saying I could grow up to take your place?" said James.

"I have sons, James," said El Huracán, "but they are lost to me. Part of another life I have left behind. I was never good at keeping a family together. You are an outsider. You are not a criminal like these other men. You could one day rule here, and rule well. What do you say?"

"What do I say to becoming a jailer?" said James. "To becoming the nursemaid to a lot of thugs and murderers? I say 'no.' I am not what you think I am. You've lived here too long. You've forgotten how ordinary people think, how they behave. I won't be your apprentice, and I'll spend every minute of every day trying to escape from this hellish place. You have no choice, El Huracán. You have to put Precious and me into the rat run."

El Huracán looked sad. His brown eyes moistened. "You do not know what you are saying."

"I do," said James. "Trial by ordeal. We go in the run, and if we make it to the end, then you have to let us go."

"Nobody has ever got to the end," said El Huracán.

"There's a first time for everything," said James. "We demand the right to go through the run, and if we make it, we demand that you let us go free."

El Huracán's face hardened. "I was wrong about you," he spat. "I thought you were clever. You are not. You are stupid. And you will die stupid."

He called his guards back into the room.

"Take them to the cells in the ruins. Let them sleep. Then feed them well. I want them to give us a good show. At noon they will go into the run."

He paused and looked at each of them in turn.

"*Adios*," he said.

It was eight hours later when the metal door slid open and James and Precious squinted into the bright light that was flooding into the rat run. James squeezed Precious's hand.

"Ready?" he said, his mouth dry, the word sticking in his throat.

Precious nodded, too nervous to speak at all. Behind them two Indians stood waiting to prod them out into the run with their spears if they hesitated.

But they were not intending to linger. They had worked out that the best way to approach the run was to move through each obstacle as quickly as they could.

They walked out into the sunlight. There was a cheer from above, and a couple of gasps. There were about twenty men watching. They had obviously not been warned that today's victims were going to be two children. This would test their coldheartedness to its limits.

El Huracán had no doubt chosen these spectators carefully. The rat run was not just for their entertainment, it was also for their education. El Huracán wanted to show what would happen if any of them disobeyed his word. Maybe these men had been complaining, muttering rebellious thoughts, questioning El Huracán's authority.

Well, today they would see what would happen to them if they didn't settle down and toe the line. The lesson would be clear. If El Huracán could do this to mere children, what might he do to them?

Somewhere up there stood the man himself. He would be all smiles and politeness, behaving as if he were at a society horse race rather than a human sacrifice.

James tried not to think about the spectators. He had to focus on the challenges ahead one at a time and put all other thoughts out of his mind. He had to remember his training—all those long evenings on the beach with Precious—and keep a clear, level head.

There were animal droppings soiling the stone floor that began to slope downward into a pool of murky green water. They both knew that they would have to duck under a submerged arch and enter the chamber beyond.

And they both knew what had left the droppings.

The chamber contained a tank full of vicious, baby crocodiles.

The water stank, but James and Precious stank too. One of James's recent jobs had been to help place animal repellent around the edges of some of the buildings. It was a noxious paste made of mint oil, garlic oil, putrescent eggs, thyme oil, salt, and water.

It was designed to keep snakes and lizards away, and some of the men rubbed it onto their legs when they were working in the jungle. The paste was kept in soft leather bags in the store shed.

James had had no trouble taking two of the bags, and he and Precious had hidden them under their clothing the night before, strapped to their bodies. Before entering the rat run they had managed to smear their bodies all over with the foul-smelling stuff. They had no way of knowing if it would work on crocodiles, but it made them feel better thinking they had done something to prepare.

They waded down the slope into the water, which was blood temperature. James hoped that the repellent wouldn't all be washed off. At least the water would help to spread the evil smell and warn the nasty little snappers that perhaps this wasn't lunch swimming into their tank.

The water was up to their knees, their hips, their waists, their chests . . .

Their necks.

"Now," said James. "Let's go. Be quick."

They held their breaths and ducked under the stone arch into the chamber. Once they were on the other side, they stood up and surged across the tank like dervishes, thrashing at the water with their palms and yelling in order to frighten off the baby crocodiles.

At one point James thought he felt something nip at his heel, but he could have been imagining it. When they reached the other side, they dived under the second arch and splashed up the slope to dry land.

There was a cheer from the watching men, and a couple of encouraging shouts. James looked down at his body. There were no bite marks. A quick check of Precious showed that she, too, had come through unscathed.

James grinned. They had survived the first trial without

a scratch. They *did* stand a chance. But they couldn't hang about patting each other on the back. The pattern of tiny holes in the floor reminded them that, at any moment, sharp metal spikes would start stabbing up at them from below.

They faced one another, backed up until their heels were touching the outer walls, then leaned forward, and locked themselves together, holding on to each other's arms, as if they were opposing props in a rugby scrum. James's head was tucked under Precious's right shoulder, and her head was tucked under his. They had formed a human arch across the alleyway, braced by the walls, their faces about four feet off the ground.

This was the trickiest maneuver they had rehearsed, and James saw that the alley was very slightly wider than the one they built by the beach to practice on. No matter, they would just have to try their best.

Holding firmly on to Precious, he put one foot up so that it was flat against the wall. Precious did the same. They both now had to step up the wall in unison.

"On three," said James. "One, two, three . . ."

They both lifted their other feet off the ground and placed them higher up the wall so that they were now completely suspended over the floor, each held in place by the pressure from the other.

"Again," James grunted, and on the count of three they both took another step higher, and as they did so, they saw the first of the spikes shoot out and stab vainly at the air.

They started to move down the alleyway now, toward the next obstacle, sliding their feet sideways and keeping all their muscles tensed to stop their arch from collapsing. The effort required was immense, and already James could feel a fiery pain down his legs, but slowly, ever so slowly, they shuffled along, their bodies trembling and shaking.

Crushed against Precious like this, the smell of the repellent was strong, but James barely noticed it. All his concentration was spent on crabbing along the wall and keeping hold of Precious. Below them they could see the cruel spikes popping out of their lairs. James prayed that they wouldn't slip, because if either one of them lost their grip, the arch would collapse and they would both fall face downward onto the spikes.

At last, though, they reached the wall at the end of the alley. The next trial was scorpions. To get into their lair you were supposed to worm your way through a narrow gap at the base of the wall.

But James and Precious had no intention of crawling into the scorpions' lair. Instead, they were going to go over the top of it.

First, though, they would have to climb up to the top of the den.

"Are you okay?" said James.

"I think so," said Precious. "But I can't hold on much longer, my neck is killing me."

"Come on, then, let's go . . . one . . . two . . . three . . ."

On three they once more walked up the stonework together, lifting their human arch another few inches. They carried on like this until they were high enough to shift sideways and perch on the top of the wall that bridged the alley.

Now, all they had to do was drop down the other side onto the steel bars that spanned the scorpion pit and simply walk across them to the other side.

The spectators were clapping and laughing and whooping. James heard El Huracán's voice call out to them.

"That is cheating."

"Show me in the rules where it says we can't do this," James shouted back.

"Yeah," rang out another man's voice. "Hats off to 'em, I say. I like their style."

"Very well," said El Huracán. "Continue."

James and Precious took a moment to catch their breath. They were perfectly safe up there. They could see the scorpions through the bars, scurrying about harmlessly beneath their feet like an exhibit at the zoo.

At the far end they hopped up onto the low wall and looked down into the anaconda pit. There was the great thing, curled up, bigger than any snake James had ever seen before.

"So far so good," said James.

"Yes," said Precious. "That's three down, seven to go."

"Ready for the next bit?" James asked.

"As I'll ever be."

"Let's hope our luck holds out," said James. "I'll go first."

He closed his eyes for a moment, rolled his shoulders, and flexed his knees.

They were meant to have entered the snake pit from the scorpions' den, when they would have had no choice but to drop down onto the anaconda, but from up here it was possible to jump clean across the pit.

The gap was about twelve feet, and it was a standing jump, but they had the bonus of height.

It was one thing, though, to practice jumping on the beach, when to fall short meant nothing worse than a face full of sand. Making a mistake here would mean landing on top of an angry serpent.

James, though, was used to this sort of thing. He had learned the skill of taking dangerous jumps on the rooftops of Eton with his friends in the Danger Society.

He squatted down, steeled himself, then threw himself forward. He landed cleanly on the other side and rolled over to break his fall.

"Come on," he shouted, getting to his feet. "You can do it. It's just like we've practiced."

Precious took a deep breath and with a loud cry, sprang off the wall.

She made it easily and rolled forward just as James had done.

They had made it past Gucumatz, the serpent god, without even waking him.

James pulled Precious to her feet. They had to keep moving. They were in the part of the run watched over by Kinich Kakmo, the sun god.

They were on the hot plates.

They could already feel the heat rising from the fires beneath the run, and they could see the air shimmering above the metal sheets that made up the floor.

They moved quickly, but didn't run, knowing that if they slipped they would be badly scalded.

As part of their preparations they had laboriously cut out foot-shaped inserts for their shoes from the thin steel sheets used for repairing the water tower. The inserts would insulate their shoes, but once the red-hot floor burned through the soles, they would start to conduct heat, so they couldn't dawdle.

Their wet shoes hissed with each step, and there was a

strong burning smell. It was soon clear, however, that they had once again outfoxed El Huracán. In a minute they were plunging into the water-filled trench that divided this part of the run from the next.

They knew there were leeches in here, so they didn't wait around cooling their feet. Keeping their hands and arms above the surface of the water, they surged across the trench as quickly as they could.

After this it was going to get a lot more difficult. Chunks and Dum-Dum had painted a fairly vivid picture of the next trial, but after that they were entering largely unknown territory. The stolen drawing had helped. It had given them measurements and distances, but it didn't explain everything.

James tried to clear his mind. *One thing at a time.* He would need all his concentration to get past Balam-Agab, the night jaguar.

They walked slowly and carefully along the alley, watching out for the razor wires that were strung across it somewhere. A grating sound told them that the animal's door was opening behind them.

They had no tricks. There was no way of fighting the jaguar. They had thought of no ingenious way of surviving this trial. They just had to hope they could get to the razor wire before the big cat got to them.

James glanced back to see it trot out into the run, sniffing the air. It saw the children and curled its lip, then dropped into a crouch. It gave a long, low, rattling growl and took up the sinister pose James had seen so many times before when a domestic cat senses a mouse.

It was stalking them.

CHAPTER 29—SWEET TERROR

Possessed by the ancient instinct to hunt and kill, the jaguar crawled toward them, keeping low, its wide, staring, yellow eyes fixed on its prey. It was lean and sleek. El Huracán would have made sure that it was kept hungry.

James felt his heart thumping against his chest. His breathing was coming fast and shallow. For a moment he forgot about the danger ahead. He wasn't brave enough to take his eyes off the jaguar, and he turned away from the razor wire. He crept backward, tensing himself, repeating a string of words in his head, over and over again.

Please don't jump, please don't jump, please don't jump . . .

"James!"

James froze—just as Precious shouted—and he felt a pricking at his neck, then a tickle, as warm liquid flowed down his back.

He had reached the first wire. He stepped away from it toward the cat, and quickly glanced around. Precious was by his side, a terrified look on her face.

He put a hand to his neck. It came away wet with blood. It was his first injury in the rat run. If the jaguar pounced, it would not be his last.

Still the animal crept forward.

James had no choice now but to turn his back on the cat,

and face the wire. It took every ounce of bravery left in him to tear his eyes away from the stalking beast.

At first he was blind in his panic, but then he realized he was looking directly at a thin strand of razor wire, strung with tiny, ruby jewels of blood.

He crouched down. The shining strands of death stretched ahead of him for about fifteen feet, crisscrossing the alley like a giant spider's web.

There had to be a way through. This was not the last obstacle. *Yes*, the next wire was just below knee height, and there was room above it to fit through. He straddled the wire, desperately trying to keep his balance. Then, still keeping low, he shifted his weight and eased his body over. He couldn't straighten up, though, because he had spotted a third wire directly above him.

Precious was rooted to the spot. The jaguar had edged still closer and was only a few feet away from her.

"Move," said James harshly. "Do it."

Precious came to life and nodded.

"Keep down," said James, and he guided her past the first set of wires.

Now the jaguar stopped, waiting. *Did it know about the wires? Did it usually wait for its prey to get tangled and then make its move?*

It gave a frustrated yowl.

James and Precious had trained hard for this part. They had fixed string across their own alleyway, and by steadying each other they had practiced stepping over and ducking under it.

It was very different with the real thing. The wires were

hard to see, and they were placed ingeniously so as to be as difficult as possible to get past. With fear pumping around their bodies and the jaguar watching them hungrily, James and Precious felt clumsy and awkward. But they carried on, staring at the deadly wires, knowing that if they made any wrong moves, they would slip and the wires would cut through them like butter.

They crawled on their bellies, they high-stepped, they bent double, they contorted themselves in every way imaginable, but by helping each other, they made steady progress.

Soon the jaguar was forgotten. He dared not come after them into the deadly forest of wires. A furious snarl was the last they heard of him.

They crossed the final wire and for the first time realized that they had not come through unscathed. As well as the cut in his neck, James saw that his shirt was slashed at the front, and a thin red line showed across his chest. Precious had cuts to her arms and legs that were bleeding freely.

It could have been worse, though. Much worse.

They now became aware of a noise. The deep rumbling and grinding sound of huge stones moving against each other. They had studied the plans, and James had seen the workings below in the tunnel.

They knew a little of what to expect.

They climbed a flight of worn steps and looked out across the next trial.

Millstones, twenty feet wide. Laid flat and rotating fast. Three great circles set in a line. And rolling in place on top of them on the left-hand side, like huge steamrollers, were three immense grindstones, each one of which must have weighed at least a ton.

James and Precious would have to get across each spinning millstone in turn. The first and last ones were turning in a clockwise direction, but the one in the middle was spinning in the opposite direction, counterclockwise.

It would be very hard to stay upright. And if they fell, the consequences would be awful. If they spilled off the sides, they would be mangled in the workings below, and if they stayed on, they would be crushed to a pulp between the millstone and the grindstone.

The noise of the machinery and the crunching, booming sound of the grindstones were deafening. It sounded like huge rocks rolling and crashing down a mountainside.

Once again there was no clever way to beat the trap, and they had had no way of preparing for it. They would simply have to rely on skill and balance and timing. They would have to jump onto the first stone, which was turning toward them, outrun it, then jump over to the second stone and let it carry them around to the next jump, where they would have to repeat the process.

"Take off your shoes," said James. "You'll have better grip."

James pulled off his ruined shoes, and one of them fell onto the millstone. It spun around and went under the grindstone. A second later they saw it come out the other side, squashed flat like a bug on a windscreen.

"I can't do it," said Precious.

"Yes, you can," said James.

"It's impossible," said Precious. "We'll be crushed."

"We can make it," said James. "We've got this far, haven't we? We're nearly at the end. There are only three obstacles left after this."

"You go first," she said. "Show me how to do it."

"All right."

There was just room at the top of the steps to backtrack and take a short run up. James got ready, calculating that the safest bet would be to match the first wheel's speed until he got the feel of it and then accelerate for the second jump.

Well, there was no point in standing here worrying about it. He had to keep moving.

Don't think. Act.

He ran. He jumped. He carried on running.

He had calculated right. After a tiny stumble, he found himself running on the spot.

"See," he shouted, but as he did so, his pace dropped and he began to rotate around toward the grindstone.

He sped up and started to run faster than the wheel was turning, so that he moved around it toward the second wheel, which was separated by a two-foot-wide drop. Now it got more difficult. The second wheel was rotating in the opposite direction. If he got it wrong his feet would be taken out from under him. He jumped across. His landing was awkward, but he stayed upright and found himself being spun around at great speed.

There was no time to think. He had to make the next jump straight away or risk being carried on around and into the jaws of the grindstone. He used the momentum of the wheel to hurl him over onto the third millstone and was running in the air before he hit it.

As he landed he teetered and fell, rolling forward in a half-somersault. Somehow he scrambled to his feet and started running again, but he had slipped a long way back and was dangerously close to the grindstone. He could hear it behind him, roaring and tumbling, and he could feel it sucking in the air. He glanced back. He was right on top of it. If he clipped it with his heel, it would pull him down and under.

Move, dammit. Get away.

He forced himself forward, outrunning the wheel. And he moved steadily around it toward the ledge on the far side. He was nearly there, but knew he mustn't lose concentration. He wouldn't be safe until he was standing on solid ground. The distance shortened—six feet, five feet, four feet, three feet . . .

Now jump!

There. He had done it. The ground was no longer moving beneath his feet.

A great cheer went up from the spectators. They were enjoying the show. James knew that they would have placed bets on when he and Precious would be killed. He wondered how many of them had wagered that they would get this far.

Except, of course, Precious had yet to come across.

He looked back. She was still waiting.

"Easy!" he yelled, filled with a crazy elation. "Piece of cake. Come on. It's fun."

Precious was shaking her head.

"Come on!" James shouted.

The men above started up a rhythmic chant.

"Go, go, go, go, go, go, go . . ."

Precious suddenly yelled and ran.

She got onto the first stone.

She was very unsteady and was wobbling from side to side, but she was just managing to keep pace with it.

She struggled around it, at every moment threatening to trip and fall. There was a look of fierce determination on her face. Her eyes were narrowed and her teeth bared.

James felt proud of her. He would never forget how she looked at that moment. She was someone who would not be beaten by anyone or anything.

She made ready to jump across to the second stone.

With another yell, she flung herself through the air, hair flying, arms flailing.

As she landed, though, her ankle turned, and she was toppling forward onto her front.

Time seemed to stop.

James felt his heart turn to lead; a terrible sick feeling came into the pit of his stomach, which was flushed with acid. The blood hissed in his ears, drowning out all other sound.

And then he realized that he was in the air. As soon as he had seen Precious losing her balance he had started to move. In an instant he had leaped back onto the cold slab of stone, which was spinning toward Precious on the second wheel. He took one long step and was launched across. He slammed face first into Precious, even before she had hit the deck. James's momentum forced her back to the far side of the stone. Then, a fraction of a second before they reached the hungry, crunching teeth of the grindstone, he pulled her to her feet, and without letting go of her hand, ran, jumped, scrambled, flew back over the wheels, and tumbled onto the platform. It had all happened so fast, and in such a confused blur, that for a few seconds, neither of them could quite believe they were safe.

Then Precious looked at James and James looked at Precious, and they both burst out laughing.

James got to his feet and looked up at the spectators.

"Where are you?" he shouted. "Where are you, Huracán? Show yourself."

A group of men moved aside and El Huracán appeared. He walked to the edge of the parapet and smiled down at James and Precious. He was smoking a fat cigar. He took it out of his mouth and saluted them.

"You are doing well," he said. "But you are not finished yet."

"You don't scare us," James shouted back. "We're enjoying ourselves."

El Huracán looked at the boy, standing there so defiantly. He was quite something. A shame that he had not wanted to come and be his right-hand man. The American girl, too. She was tougher than she looked. He had thought she would fall at the first hurdle.

What a pity they would both soon be dead.

The two of them could have no way of knowing that the reason nobody had ever made it out of the final trap was because there *was* no way out. Once they were in there, they would stay in there until they were killed.

Ah well. He took a puff on his cigar, savoring the thick smoke. In his long life he had seen many people die. Some of them he had loved and had thought that he could never live without. He would gladly have died in their place. And now . . . now he could not even remember their faces. They were nothing more to him than characters in a long-forgotten book. It would be the same with James and the girl. People come and go in this world. Only the stones remain.

For now, though, they had made it past Ah Mun, the god of corn and farming. Let's see what the next god had in store for them: Ah Mucen Cab, the god of bees.

An amusing trial, a little different from the others, a little more subtle.

"Can you smell it?" said James.

"Yes," said Precious. "A sweet smell. What is it?"

The passage gave a sharp turn, and as they walked around the bend they were met by something unexpected. The plans had shown another sunken tank, and they had assumed that it would be full of water. Instead, four feet below them was a sunken alleyway filled with what looked like gold, its surface spattered with black dots. The sickly sweet smell was overpowering here and big wasps buzzed through the air.

The distance to the other end was about twenty feet, and there was no way of getting there without crossing the golden floor. From up here it looked quite solid, but it was very hard to tell.

"What do we do?" said Precious.

"What can we do?" said James, who was feeling light-headed and reckless. "We carry on."

Without another word, he jumped down, bracing

himself for a solid landing. Instead he hit the gold floor with a splat and sunk in up to his chest.

"It's honey!" he said, laughing. "A whole tank full of honey. I've often dreamed of swimming in honey."

As he tried to swim, however, he found that it required all his effort just to move one arm. His clothing, already clogged with honey, felt heavy as armor and was dragging him under. He pulled his shirt open and managed to peel it off.

"Take off any loose clothing you can," he shouted up to Precious, and she stripped off her outer layers.

Even without his shirt, it was nearly impossible to make any headway in the thick honey. It was like swimming in glue, and the harder he tried, the deeper James sank.

"Lower yourself in," he said. "Try to stay flat on the surface."

James pushed forward, struggling to keep his face above the sticky liquid. He could see now that the black spots covering the surface were dead insects. If he slipped below the surface he would end up the same way. He fought to keep his mouth and nose clear, but although the honey was more buoyant than water, to move took an immense effort, and if you stayed still you slowly sank.

He thought of Whatzat, drowning in the mud hole in the oil field. It would be horrible to drown in honey, feeling the sweet, sticky stuff seep down his throat into his lungs.

Precious had lowered herself in and was trying to crawl along the surface, clawing at the stuff with her hands. She soon found how difficult it was and how, as she kicked with her feet, they simply sank deeper.

They were creeping along, though, a few inches at a time, fighting the honey with every move, feeling it try to suck them down. It was incredibly tiring. They were using up all their reserves of strength. Precious's hair was matted and sticking to her face. She blinked her eyes, trying to keep the gummy liquid out of them. She couldn't wipe them, though, as her hands were covered in the stuff.

From above the men watched the weird spectacle in silent fascination. It was as if the children were swimming in slow motion, or through something solid. There were no ripples or waves, the only thing that told you it was a liquid were the football-sized bubbles that now and then burped and plopped to the surface. It was agonizing watching their slow progress. Most of the men had forgotten about their bets and were rooting for the kids to go all the way. They were fighters, they wouldn't give up. It would take more than this to stop them.

They were halfway, two-thirds, three-quarters. Going slower and slower. Then the boy slipped under and the girl fished him out, coughing, spitting, and choking. They didn't look human anymore; they were covered with gloop, like two flies trapped in a giant honey pot.

James and Precious were almost out of energy, completely exhausted and half-blind. Doggedly, James flung an arm out and felt it hit something solid. He groped with his fingers. It was a ladder, leading up out of the pit. They'd reached the end. He clung on and took hold of Precious's hand, dragging her through the honey.

They climbed the ladder, dripping great gelatinous gobbets of honey as they went, and flopped onto the paving stones.

It was almost worse being out of the pit. The honey had got everywhere, into every nook and cranny and fold. It was in their noses, their ears, between their toes, inside their clothing. They tried to scrape it off their bodies with their fingernails, but it stuck fast and was drying in the sun.

James would have given his right arm for a shower. Never had the thought of soap and warm water been so appealing. What would he give now for some Pinaud Elixir!

Precious groaned, trying to unstick her hair where it was plastered to her face. She swore, her voice cracking with misery.

James gripped her by her upper arms, blinking the honey from his eyes.

"It's not so bad," he said. "We've faced worse, and we're through it now. We've just got to press on. There are only two trials left."

"I'm so tired," said Precious. "I just want to lay down and sleep."

"There'll be plenty of time to sleep later," said James. "When this is all over, we can sleep for a hundred years."

"You're right," she said. "Let's go."

They waddled onward, leaving tacky yellow footprints on the stones. Wasps buzzed around them, and they tried to wave them away.

They had seen the plans for the next obstacle, and they had practiced hard for it. The drawing had shown a large log suspended over a pit and held in place by iron struts going off to the sides.

All they had to do was get across without falling into the pit.

What made it so frightening, and so deadly, was the fact that the pit was filled with sharpened wooden stakes. They could not risk walking along the log; they had decided they would crawl.

"We stick with our plan," said James when they spotted the log. "We crawl. Especially as we're covered in honey. And I don't know about you, but I can't see a thing."

"My eyes won't stop watering," said Precious. "I'm half-blind."

They peered down into the pit. It was a long drop, and the stakes looked even more lethal than they had in the drawing. If either of them slipped they would be impaled. They would have no second chance.

James now turned his attention to the log. To his surprise it appeared to be covered in some kind of furry, red material. But as he looked closer, he saw that it was moving.

"What is it?" said Precious, trying to make sense of it.

James's heart sank. This was the worst moment so far.

"Ants," he said. "Army ants."

"Oh no," said Precious. "Not that."

She had not seen Strabo lying in the ant column in the jungle. James had, though, and the memory of it would be with him forever. These ants were smaller, but their jaws were bigger. They swarmed all over the log, scurrying madly in all directions. There was a gentle shower of them falling off the bottom, and as James looked more closely into the stake-filled pit, he saw that it was teeming with even more of the little red devils.

What made it worse was the fact that James and Precious were covered with honey. El Huracán had designed these two trials carefully and cruelly.

"I'll go first," said James. "Maybe I can clear some of them out of the way."

"No," said Precious, hopelessly. "How can you? There are too many of them. Look, they're coming along the struts from the sides. They must have only just been released."

"I can try, can't I?" said James with a hint of anger. "We're not just going to give up here."

Once again El Huracán taunted them.

"You can make it quick," he shouted. "Throw yourselves on the spikes and it will all be over. You can offer yourselves up to the goddess who watches over this trial, Ixtab, the goddess of suicides. The Mayans believed that suicide was the quickest path to heaven!"

James swore at him.

The log was hanging just below head height. He reached out, took a deep breath and gripped it, feeling scores of ants being crushed beneath his hands. Immediately the others started biting. He jerked his hands away automatically. They were throbbing. He shook them hard, scattering honey and dead ants everywhere.

"I told you," said Precious. "It's no use."

"Shut up," said James, and without thinking, he took hold again and hauled himself up until his chest was on the log.

He wriggled farther on until he could get a grip with his elbows and knees. The pain was incredible. It was like being stabbed by a hundred red-hot pins, in his arms, his thighs, his chest, his crotch. Every moment there was a fresh little jolt of agony as one of them bit him and injected formic acid into his flesh.

His face was an inch away from the surface of the log, which was alive with angry, red ants. They were confused about where to go and lashed out at everything around them. The honey at least prevented them from swarming over him, but wherever they touched they got stuck. In no time at all he had a dozen of them glued to his face, their jaws slashing at him, their acid burning all down one cheek. He went to scrape them away without thinking. His hand was covered with a red fur of wounded ants and made things ten times worse.

He grunted and in his fury tried brushing his arms

across the log, but no matter how many ants were knocked into the stake pit, more surged in to fill the gap, and the more he brushed, the more of them got stuck to his arm.

The only thing he could do was slide along the log and try to get to the end as quickly as possible. He shunted forward, feeling ants beneath his belly, watching them pile up into undulating drifts as he swept his arms out in front of him.

"Don't think about it," he yelled back to Precious. "Just follow me, hold on tight, and ignore the pain. They won't kill you. Think of tomorrow. Think of next year. You won't remember the pain. As long as you stay on and keep moving."

The log moved and he heard Precious gasp and then shout as she climbed on behind him.

He started to move faster.

"Are you all right?" he called out.

"I'm right behind you," said Precious. "Don't stop."

"I don't intend to," said James hoarsely.

He could see a handful of ants hanging off his eyebrow. They were waving their legs and antennae right in front of his eye, and others were biting his eyelid. Still more had sunk their mandibles into his lower lip. He raked them off with his teeth and bit down on them. Feeling them crunch. He spat them out and cursed. He was angry now, his blood was hot, the pain was making him delirious.

He lashed out in front of him and lost his grip, lurching sideways off the log. He scrabbled at it with his fingernails and tried to cling on with his knees, but it was no use. The honey made it impossible to hold on.

He went down, and knew that this was the end. In a second he would be dead. Then he felt Precious's hand close about his ankle. She was holding so tightly it was like a metal vice around him.

He was dangling face-first over the sharpened stakes. If Precious let go he would be impaled. At least it would be quick. The ordeal would be over. He could offer himself up to Ixtab. Maybe she would get him into heaven by the back door.

No. That wasn't going to happen.

He looked up to see Precious's face, contorted in pain. Every muscle and sinew in her body was taut and strained; her teeth were bared in an animal grimace. He owed it to her not to give up.

"I'll get you to that strut," she said, and with a grunt she swung him through the air, first back, then forward. James arced his body and reached out and managed to grab hold of the metal strut.

Precious let go and he pulled himself up to safety.

It was extraordinary. He would never have thought that Precious would have had the strength to hold him like that. But under stress and in fear of its life the human body can do incredible things.

James got back onto the log and carried on, ploughing through the waves of red insects. If Precious could hold his weight with one hand, then he could put up with a few ant bites.

Screaming with every move, he forced himself on, praying that Precious was right behind him. To lose her now would be unbearable.

And then he had reached the end of the log. He slithered off and landed in an ungainly heap in a bed of chicken feathers.

A second later Precious dropped down beside him and sent up an explosion of dancing, white feathers.

James felt like he could never move again. He wanted to lie in the bed of feathers forever. His body was still covered in ants, wriggling in their death throes and biting him mechanically. He barely noticed them, though. His body was almost numb to the pain, and the relief of being alive was washing over him like a soothing ointment.

He closed his eyes and a small, quiet voice in the back of his mind told him to get up, to carry on, to keep fighting. Wearily he stood up and looked around.

There weren't just feathers here, there were chickens as well. They strutted about, pecking corn from the ground, squawking and squabbling with each other. This part of the rat run was filthy with their mess. James trudged along, not caring what he was treading in in his bare feet.

He stopped and waited for Precious to join him. She was a sorry sight, with the feathers and the ants and the honey stuck all over her. There were streaks of chicken droppings up her naked legs. In different circumstances it would have been funny. He remembered a time when he had first met her that he would have paid anything to see her like this. But this was too cruel.

He recalled the carvings that El Huracán had shown him: how specially honored Mayan sacrificial victims had been dressed in elaborate outfits, with beautiful capes made from brightly colored feathers. This was a ghastly pantomime version. A mockery. Not only was El Huracán going to kill them, he was going to humiliate them first.

James wiped some muck off Precious's face. She was crying, the tears mingling with the honey on her cheeks.

"This is it," he said. "Xibalba. We've come to the last challenge."

"It's going to be terrible," she said. "I know it is."

James saw the glyphs on the wall, but couldn't read them. They were a jumble of skeletons and monsters.

"Hun Came," he said, remembering the name that Moises had told him in the tunnels beneath the run.

"What does it mean?" said Precious.

"One Death," came a shout from above. It was El Huracán, standing with his hands on his hips. "The Mayans gave some of their gods numbers. Hun Came was the number one god of Xibalba, the place of fear, the Mayan underworld. The road to Xibalba was filled with many obstacles: vicious spiked thorns, a river of scorpions, a river of blood, even a river of pus. And once you were there you would have to face even more deadly challenges from the lords of the underworld. For you, however, there is only one more challenge. To meet One Death himself."

El Huracán laughed. "Look at you," he said. "You are not so cocky, now, eh, James Bond?"

One by one the other men joined in with the laughter, anxious to show that they were on his side.

"What's with the feathers?" said a beefy gangster at his side. "Is it just a gag?"

"No," said El Huracán. "One Death's favorite food is

chicken, but he also has a sweet tooth. He will smell the chickens and taste the honey, and he will attack. He has not been fed for weeks. He will be hungry. You will hear him make his kills and feed. You will hear their death screams, but you will not see them die. One Death deserves his privacy. He is a god after all."

"What is he really?" said the man.

"He is Hun Came," said El Huracán, and that was all he would say.

James and Precious walked on and came to Xibalba, the end of the rat run. La Avenida de la Muerte went no farther. The passageway opened out into a square, and in the center of the square stood a squat pyramid. It was a modern construction, based on a Mayan design, and they knew from the plans that it was hollow and built over a huge water tank.

There were steps up each of the pyramid's four sides, and at the top was a wide, stone platform.

"Let's go," said James, and he took hold of Precious's hand.

He knew exactly how the Mayan prisoners of war must have felt as they climbed the pyramid temples to their certain deaths. Ever since he had got up from the bed of feathers, he had felt weirdly detached and light, as if this were all happening to somebody else. It was unreal. The ants were biting somebody else, the tight suit of pain was being worn by somebody else, the smell of honey and chickens was coming from some other place.

When they reached the top of the pyramid, they discovered a circular opening cut into the floor. There was a long drop into water below, and a familiar, fishy stink.

"Listen to me," said James quietly and urgently, "I didn't want to tell you this before, because I knew you'd be too frightened to go through with it, but now there's no going back."

"What are you talking about?" said Precious.

"There's a way out," said James.

Precious smiled through her tears.

"Is there? How do you know?"

"Remember I told you about the iron door I saw in the tunnels," said James. "And the sluice they use to empty the tank."

"But you said we couldn't open the door from this side," said Precious.

"We can," said James. "I got the idea from Whatzat."

"What idea?" said Precious.

"With the right amount of explosives you can open any door you want."

"That would be fine if we only had some explosives," said Precious.

"Last night," said James, "before I met you in the plaza, I took some dynamite from the store shed and I went down into the tunnels. I rigged three sticks to the wheel that opens the door and threaded a fuse into a small hole above the tank. I left some matches too. We won't have long. Whatever's in there is going to come after us. But if I can get to the hole and light the fuse, we'll have about three seconds and then—boom!"

"We'll be blown to pieces," said Precious.

"It's always possible," said James. "But the water should

cushion the explosion. At least that's what I hope. Then we get out down the sluice."

"Are all English boys as crazy as you?" said Precious.

"Most of them," said James. "So what do you say? Do you trust me?"

"No," said Precious, "but I'd follow you to hell and back."

"Then, let's go," said James. "Satan's waiting for us."

The top of the pyramid was higher than where the spectators were standing. El Huracán was staring up and shielding his eyes from the glare of the sun with one hand.

"Will you keep your word?" James shouted down to him.

"Of course," El Huracán called back. "I do not break my own rules."

"If we make it out of the final chamber alive, we're free to leave the island?"

"Completely free," shouted El Huracán. "I will even give a feast in your honor before you go."

"There are no other rules?" James yelled.

"No."

"However we get out of there, it's fair?"

"You have my word, James. These men are witnesses to it. If you emerge alive from One Death's lair, you and the girl are free to leave."

Precious squeezed James's arm.

"I'll go first this time," she said.

"We'll go together," said James.

They sat down on the edge of the opening and held hands.

"Whatever it is in there," said James, "it won't attack straight away. It'll try to find out what we are first. But once it's made up its mind, it won't hesitate. Are you ready?"

"See you in hell," said Precious, and they pushed off the edge.

There was a moment of falling through darkness, and then they smashed into the water with a noise like a cannon going off. They sank to the bottom of the tank, which must have been about ten feet deep, and their feet touched slimy stonework. They kicked up and broke the surface, gasping for air.

At least the honey and the ants and feathers had been washed away, but there was no time to enjoy the sensation. James had to move fast.

There was just enough light from the opening above to show that they were in a large square chamber. There was a shelf along one side and on it lay the huge, dark shape of an animal.

James guessed that the wall with the door must be opposite the shelf. He quickly swam over and started searching for the hole.

He wished he could see better, and scanned the wall frantically, squinting in the gloom.

"Hurry, James," said Precious, and he heard the animal shift on its stone ledge and give a guttural grunt.

James felt all over the wall with his hand. *Why couldn't he find the hole?*

He heard the animal's body scraping roughly along the shelf.

Where was it? Where was the hole?

"There!" shouted Precious, her voice echoing and slapping off the walls. "You're looking on the wrong wall!"

James looked around to see her bobbing in the water and pointing to the left.

She was right. He could just make out a small, dark patch in the masonry.

He splashed over and reached up. It was the hole all right. He felt inside, treading water. There was the box of matches. He carefully closed his fingers around it.

If he dropped it in the tank they were done for.

"It's moving," said Precious. "Hurry. It's coming."

There was another grunt, and the animal shifted ominously again. It sniffed and snorted, and they could hear its claws rattling on the stones.

James gently pulled the end of the fuse until about six inches were showing. Then he carefully slid the matchbox open.

He glanced back to see the huge, dark shape sliding slowly off the ledge into the water. He thought he might be sick with fear. He wasn't going to make it in time.

He fumbled for a match, dropping several in his panic, but at last got one and struck it against the box. He had got it damp and it wouldn't light. He struck it again.

Still nothing.

He could feel the water moving as the beast swam toward them.

He dropped the damp match and took out another one.

He struck it. It sparked. It flared. It lit the whole chamber brightly for a second, and James caught a glimpse of a reptilian eye and huge snout drifting across the surface of the murky water.

He put the match to the fuse, and it lit first time. The

flame climbed up and disappeared into the hole. The chamber was plunged back into darkness.

"Move away from the wall," James yelled at Precious, thrashing the water to try to ward the animal off.

As they floundered across the pool, James felt a long, leathery body slide along his legs. He prepared himself for the awful bite, the jaws closing around his torso.

He could bear it no longer. He finally cracked.

He opened his mouth wide and started to scream.

The sound filled the chamber . . . and then there was silence.

It felt as if the whole building had been struck by a giant hand.

Time held its breath.

A tremendous shock wave passed through the water. James was stunned, unable to see or hear or feel anything. There was an awful pressure, crushing him from all sides. He felt as if his brain must be squeezed out of his ears.

Then the world erupted around him, and he was in a maelstrom of churning water and flying rocks.

His senses returned like a slap. He was being tugged through the water toward the wall.

The beast had got him, then?

No. It wasn't that. The water was being sucked out of the tank through a massive, gaping crack.

He lost sight of Precious as he was spun around and tossed about in the surging torrent. His head hit something. His ribs were pummeled, and then he realized he was in the sluice. It had worked. He was being flushed away like a spider being washed down a plughole. And there was Precious, sliding along just ahead of him, on the slick, stone slipway.

Had they really done it? Had they beaten El Huracán?

Not yet.

The Mayan gods were going to try for one last time to take James to Xibalba, the land of the dead.

One Death was not finished with them.

James heard a bellow and looked back to see a giant bull crocodile come barreling down the sluice after him, its soft belly glowing a sickly greenish white.

James hadn't thought of that.

He and Precious were escaping down the sluice, but so was One Death. And the crocodile was crazed with fear and anger. It snapped wildly with its ugly jaws and thrashed its head from side to side, roaring and screaming like a pig.

The sluice acted like a long slide. James could hear Precious shrieking as she was thrown about, bashing against the rocks and floundering in the rushing, filthy water. James didn't know if he was more scared of being dashed to pieces on the rocks or being savaged by the crocodile.

The sluice veered sharply to the right and James was hurled against the wall. The wind was knocked out of him, and he turned just in time to see the crocodile come slithering and slopping on top of him. He instinctively grabbed hold of it, and somehow managed to get his arms around its long snout. Then the two of them were sliding on together, and James was staring into the animal's mad, yellow eye.

Its whole body was twisting and jerking, its short legs scrabbling to get a purchase on the sides and carving big gouges out of the soft rock. They rolled over. For a moment James was on top; then, as they hit another bend, he was rolled back underneath the crocodile, and he was forced to let go. The animal was determined to get him, though, determined to kill the intruder who had blown its world apart. It arched its back and jackknifed, snapping at James.

The sluice suddenly split into two, and James was taken one way, the crocodile another.

There were a few brief seconds of peace and calm, as James slid on down the algae-coated rock, and then the paths reconverged.

Was One Death ahead of him or behind?

An enraged bellow told him that the crocodile was behind. There it came, all mouth and teeth. James's head struck the side, and he was momentarily stunned. He didn't know which way was up or down.

And then he was flying through the air. He opened his eyes to see, inches away from his face, the wide, gaping jaws of the crocodile. He could see its pink tongue and smell its awful breath. The two of them were falling together.

The crocodile lunged and James jerked away so that its teeth closed with a loud *CLACK* on nothing but air.

Then its massive tail whipped around and batted James away.

His unconscious body spun off into oblivion.

There was a small splash in the darkness.

CHAPTER 31—THE FIGURE IN THE TOWER

James awoke to find himself lying on a narrow, rocky ledge inside a sea cave. Precious was stroking his face.

"I'm getting used to fishing you out of the water," she said.

"What happened to the crocodile?" said James.

"I don't know," said Precious. "Maybe he swam off, maybe he's dead, but the main thing is, he's gone."

"So we made it, then?"

"Looks like it. It's been some day."

"And you're some girl."

"I know."

Precious bent over and kissed James lightly on the lips. They were numb and he felt nothing. It was like being kissed by an angel.

They waited there like that, saying nothing, James with his head in Precious's lap, until they heard the sound of a boat and voices calling out across the water.

Precious called back and presently a motor launch appeared, piloted by a crew of El Huracán's Indians.

James and Precious left their perch and climbed into the boat. The Indians looked at them as if they were creatures from another planet, and after giving them some blankets, they kept a wary distance.

The boat chugged out of the cave into the light. It was a glorious day. The sun glinted on the deep blue water. Seabirds swooped and dived after fish. Clouds scudded along on a light breeze. And for James and Precious it was made more glorious by the fact that they had cheated One Death, the chief lord of the underworld.

No day had ever looked so good. No air had ever tasted sweeter.

They motored around to the harbor where El Huracán was waiting for them.

He looked them up and down as they clambered stiffly off the boat, but it was impossible to read his face and tell what he was thinking.

"You're alive," was all he said.

"I'm afraid so," said James.

El Huracán shook his head, stamped out his cigar, turned, and walked away.

Two days later, patched up and rested, James and Precious were back at the harbor, waiting to board the steamer that was going to take them over to the mainland. El Huracán had been true to his word. He had laid on a feast in their honor in the plaza. And he had sat at the head of the table and toasted them. But his good humor had been forced, and James noticed that he drank a lot, but ate nothing.

A group of musicians was also waiting for the boat, and one of them was strumming a guitar and singing a sad song. James didn't know if it was the music, or the warm, sunny day, or the scent of flowers wafting across the island, but he felt almost sorry to be saying good-bye to the place.

Precious walked up the gangplank. James took one last look back and saw El Huracán walking toward the harbor, flanked by two of his guards.

He waited.

"I wanted to make sure you got safely away," said the wily old Mexican when he arrived.

"No tricks up your sleeve?" said James, and El Huracán held up his hands and drew back his cuffs to show that they were empty. His mood seemed to have lightened since the feast.

"No tricks," he said. "But I want to make a deal with you, James Bond."

"Go on."

"I want you to swear that you will not try and cause trouble for me. That you will not come back for Mrs. Glass."

"Why should I agree to that?" said James.

"I agreed to let you go," said El Huracán.

"You had no choice," said James. "You made the rules."

El Huracán shrugged and took a cigar from his pocket. "You cheated," he said, lighting it.

Now it was James's turn to shrug.

"Listen to me, James," said El Huracán. "If I wanted, I could kill you now, and that would be the end of it. Luckily for you, I am a sporting man, and I like you, despite all that you have done to me."

"I can't make any promises," said James.

El Huracán became serious. "I have friends in the Mexican government," he said. "I pay them enough money to leave me alone. And besides, once a dangerous criminal turns up at Lagrimas Negras, he never leaves. The island is still, in its own way, a prison. All these men and women will die here. Mrs. Glass with them. I have done the world a favor taking her in. Mrs. Glass has her punishment. You are free. You must leave it at that."

"I came here to get something," said James. "It's bigger and more important than me."

"The stolen plans," said El Huracán.

"Exactly," said James. "As long as you still have them, it's not over."

"What do you intend to do about it?" said El Huracán.

"As you say, you've got a perfect setup here," said James. "You are left alone. You are king of your own little empire. But how do you think the American government is going to react when it finds out, as it must do eventually, that you have the plans? And that you are going to sell their secrets to some foreign power? Do you think the Americans will leave you alone? The navy came here once before. They killed every man on the island."

"Except one," said El Huracán.

"Except one," said James. "Who knows, maybe you'll be lucky enough to get away like your father, but this place will cease to exist."

El Huracán was silent for a while. He took his cigar from his mouth and blew on the glowing tip, thinking. Finally he looked up at James and grinned.

"You have read my thoughts," he said, and clicked his fingers. One of his guards stepped forward and reached for something in a canvas shoulder bag.

James tensed. Was El Huracán going to kill him, after all?

Held in the man's hand, however, was not a gun, but the leather pouch.

El Huracán tapped his brown fingers on the familiar U.S. Navy insignia.

"The Mayans used to talk of a cursed treasure called hurricane gold," he said. "They believed that if you held on to hurricane gold it would, sooner or later, bring your house down around your ears and bring ruin to you and your family." He passed the pouch to James. "This is hurricane gold," he said. "It has caused nothing but death and destruction and misery wherever it has gone. I am rich enough. I am giving it back. This is yours, James. See that it is returned to its rightful owners."

James took the documents and shook the old man's hand. "You've got a deal," he said.

"Do you hear that?" said El Huracán, nodding to the musicians with a smile. "Do you know this song?"

"No," said James.

"It is very fitting. It is an old Cuban song called "Lagrimas Negras"—"Black Tears"—the same as my island. It is a song sung by a lover who has been abandoned. But after all that he has been through he still loves the one who has done him wrong. I will always remember you, James. Perhaps you will always remember my island, and me. The one you left behind."

"It would be hard to forget you," said James.

El Huracán walked him up the gangplank toward where Precious was waiting at the ship's rail. "Do you know how I bet on you?" he said.

"In your rat run?" said James, and shook his head.

"I bet on you to go all the way," said El Huracán. "To get to the last trial. To reach Xibalba. But I never expected you to get out alive. I said once that I would tell you the story of the Hero Twins. They were two boys who went down into the underworld to avenge the death of their father, who had been killed by the lords of Xibalba. They passed many tests on the way, and when they got there they had to survive several terrible ordeals before defeating One Death and Seven Death, the two most powerful of the rulers of the underworld. I shall always think of you and Precious as the reincarnation of the Hero Twins."

He clasped James by the shoulders.

"I will ask you one last time," he said. "All of this could be yours. You could be a king here."

"I don't want to be a king," said James. "I'm just a boy."

"*Adios*, then," said El Huracán with a wink, and he clattered back down the gangplank.

Presently the steam turbines fired up, and as the ropes were cast off, El Huracán called up to Precious from the quay. "I almost forgot to tell you, Precious," he shouted, waving his hand, "there is a surprise waiting for you on board. *Adios!* It has been interesting knowing you!"

They waved back at El Huracán as the ship steamed gently out of the harbor.

"A surprise?" said Precious. "Do you suppose it's a nasty one?"

"No. All debts are paid," said James, and he handed the leather pouch to Precious. For a moment she stared at it, not quite believing it was real. Then she burst into tears and threw her arms around James.

"Oh, James," she sobbed, but was too emotional to say anything more.

When she had calmed down, the two of them stood there in silence, watching the harbor grow smaller. At the last moment, just before they passed a rocky headland, they thought they saw the figure of a woman, wearing a wide-brimmed hat, watching them from the lookout tower near the harbor wall.

"Precious."

The two of them turned at the sound of a familiar voice, and there stood Jack Stone, looking older and somehow smaller than he had when James last saw him.

"Daddy?"

"Sweetheart . . ."

Precious ran to him, leaving James alone at the rail.

Precious and her father were sitting on a bunk in a small cabin below deck. They had both been crying. The leather pouch sat on the blanket between them.

"And JJ?" said Precious. "Is he all right? Did they save his leg?"

"They did," said Jack Stone. "He's fine. A little weak, but he's walking around, and talking. Boy, that kid sure can talk. All day long. And all he ever talks about is his big sister and that boy, James Bond."

"What happened to Sakata?"

"He took JJ to the hospital and disappeared before anyone could ask him any questions. JJ owes him his life." Stone hugged Precious. "We'll be together again, sugar, the three of us. I'm gonna change, just you see. . . ."

Precious glanced down at the pouch.

"First, you have to give this back," she said.

"Sure," said Stone. "I was gonna, all along."

Precious shook her head and turned away from him. "No more lies, Daddy. Not to me."

Stone hung his head, rubbed his face, and sighed.

"I've been a fool," he said.

"You will need to tell one last story, though," said Precious. "You're good at that. You should find it easy. You're going to take those papers to the government, or the navy, or whoever they belong to, and you're going to tell them how an American woman called Mrs. Theda Glass came to you and asked you to fly her to Argentina. They'll know all about her. They'll believe anything you tell them."

"Sure, honey," said Stone.

"You never made it to Argentina, though, because you found out that she was a gangster and a spy and that she had some stolen documents she'd taken from an American naval officer. You landed in the jungle, there was a fight, you won. And then you set off back to the States to return the stolen plans. You'll be a hero all over again. We'll start a new life, just like you said."

"You sure have grown up quick, princess. I'm proud of you."

"I used to be proud of *you*, Daddy."

"I was only trying to make a good life for you and JJ."

"But don't you see, Daddy? If you do bad things, even for a good reason, in the end they will always catch up with you."

James was still at the rail. He could just see the dark top of the island. He was thinking about Precious and her father. He would never have a father to go home to after an adventure like this, or a mother. He wondered if he would spend his life traveling, seeking out one new experience after another, knowing that there would be nothing and nobody for him at home.

He felt a hand on his shoulder and turned to see Precious. She had an expression on her face that he couldn't read. There was the hint of a smile on her lips, but a deep sadness in her eyes.

"Your Aunt Charmian is waiting for you in Veracruz," she said. "She stayed to look after JJ."

"He's all right?"

"Yes. Thanks to you."

"In the end," said James, "it was a team effort."

"In the end," said Precious.

"I wonder how different things would have been if I'd never turned up at your house that night in the storm," said James.

"I think I'd probably be lying dead in a swamp somewhere," said Precious. "I'll always love you for what you've done for me."

"And here I was, thinking you hated me," said James.

"I never hated you."

"You certainly acted like you did."

"Oh, boys can be so stupid sometimes," said Precious. "I think I've loved you ever since I first set eyes on you."

"What?" said James. "You're joking."

"I wouldn't show it, of course," said Precious.

"Girls can be pretty stupid sometimes, too," said James.

"The thing is, James . . ." Precious was staring out to sea. "I've learned not to give in to love. I've learned to keep my distance from something I really wanted with all my heart, because, as far as I can see, everything you love gets taken away from you."

"I know how that feels," said James.

"I'll lose you as well," said Precious quietly. "Once we get back to Mexico, who knows what lies ahead? I don't know how things will be with my father. But it will be different, I'm sure of that. And you? You'll go back to England, and maybe you'll write for a while, but you'll soon forget me."

"I'll never forget you," said James.

"Maybe not soon," said Precious. "There's one thing I've found out lately: you never know what's going to happen tomorrow."

"Don't worry about tomorrow," said James, and he gave a little laugh. "Tomorrow can take care of itself."

He put his arm around her, and together they watched the island as it slowly disappeared over the horizon.